MORGUE DRAWER FOR RENT

Previously by Jutta Profijt:
Morgue Drawer Four
Morgue Drawer Next Door

Forthcoming by Jutta Profijt:
Dust Angel

MORGUE DRAWER FOR RENT

Jutta Profijt

TRANSLATED BY Erik J. Macki

amazon crossing

Morgue Drawer for Rent by Jutta Profijt was first published in 2010 by
Deutscher Taschenbuch Verlag GmbH & Co. KG in Munich, Germany,
as *Kühlfach zu vermieten.*

Translated from the German by Erik J. Macki.
First published in English in 2012 by AmazonCrossing.

Published by AmazonCrossing
P.O. Box 400818
Las Vegas, NV 89140

ISBN-13: 9781611090420
ISBN-10: 1611090423
Library of Congress Control Number: 2012911052

ONE

So if I were going to put a date on when the series of crises at the Institute for Forensic Medicine in Cologne began, it would have to be July twelfth. I remember this clearly, because July twelfth is my birthday. Or, should I say it *was* my birthday? I have no idea. I still cling to the tradition of celebrating my birthday, although my deathday has also become an occasion for an awesome party. It's really just the same as with other dead guys, actually. I mean, the various commemorative celebrations for Goethe, Schiller, Bach, etc., basically don't have anything to do with those guys' births, only their deaths. Kind of fucked up, isn't it, people celebrating the last breaths of the cultural elites? By contrast, *I* think that we artists should be celebrated exclusively on our birthdays. Oh—did I say "we artists"? Yes, that's right—consider me now among their ranks. As a writer. But more on that later.

So, getting back to the crises. This past spring we actually had a couple of little "pre-crises," so to speak, just to break ourselves in. First, there was the thing with the boss at the Institute for Forensic Medicine. One morning, the boss appeared gray-faced before his secretary and announced he was going to take the rest of the day off because he wasn't feeling that great. By the time he got home his appearance so worried his wife that she had the doctor come over right away. First finding: hypotensive syncope. That means "fainting," if you didn't know. A couple of days later they were thinking it was the flu, and a week later the diagnosis became myocardial infarction. Which means "heart attack," if you didn't know.

Now, this all happened at the end of May, right before the next little pre-crisis: the institute was scheduled to move into a temporary new office space during its renovation, and everybody at the institute realized that they would now have to make the final preparations and go ahead with the move without the boss's guiding hand.

But then came the full-on Crisis No. 1: Just two weeks after the boss's medical leave began, the entire staff was called together to meet the institute's new director. At nine o'clock sharp the whole staff was fidgeting in the conference room. Martin, Jochen, Katrin, and four other coroners had taken seats at the conference table, and the pathologists, toxicologists, biologists, chemists, lab rats, assistants, secretaries, admin assistants, and janitors who'd all arrived a minute or two later were standing in the back of the room, chatting quietly among themselves. The million-euro question the cadaver divers were all asking each other was: Who's the new guy going to be?

And then he appeared: tall, midforties, golf-course tan, in shape, the suit and arrogance quotient of a male model, loafers with little tassels on top, gold watch on his wrist, and a signet ring on his pinky. Exactly the type of retinal assault you get from one of those billboard ads for menswear or luxury brand watches, the type of guy you never believed *really* existed. In one fluid motion he unbuttoned his jacket, took a seat at the head of the conference table, tugged each shirt cuff just low enough to show a centimeter of white below his

sleeves, and folded his hands on the table in front of him—
he was even wearing cuff links, total poser! (Note to editor:
only posers spell it *poseur.* Geez.) With a triumphant gleam
in his eyes, he looked around the room pompously.

"Ladies and gentlemen, let me put it this way: it was a
happy coincidence that I happened to be available on short
notice, as Dr. Schweitzer will not be returning as director of
the institute anytime soon. If he ever returns at all."

The staff stared at each other, horrified.

"First, allow me introduce myself: Philip G. Forch, age
forty-eight. Undergraduate and MBA from Cologne, master
of public administration from St. Gallen, and master of eco-
nomics from Harvard. Both my academic and professional
backgrounds have focused on increasing productivity and
cost effectiveness in the public sector, specifically in the
medical sector. I was just finishing off a review of operations at University Medical Center here at the University of
Cologne when it came to light that the directorship of this
facility was going to be vacant for some time. I have now
been tasked with this assignment with the goal of imple-
menting a few optimizations under the rubric of cost effectiveness, and so—*voilà*—here I am."

He blathered to the end of his spiel, then gently rolled
his hands out, palms up. Like he was waiting for applause.
But there was none. In the ensuing silence you could have
heard a flea fart. It wasn't a silence of rapt, professional
esteem; it was a stunned, disbelieving, appalled silence.
Incidentally, my editor insisted on all those adjectives. If I'd
had my way, I'd have said that the people looked like they
were hunkered down inside the toilet bowl while fate was
having a serious case of the runs.

Martin took a moment to clear the horrified fog shadowing his thoughts, but he was still the first to regain his linguistic faculties. "Well, this is unexpected," he said thoughtfully. "Does that mean you will be taking on technical forensic oversight as well? Certainly someone would need to assume responsibility for the content of—"

"Are you not confident in the content of your work?"

"Certainly, of course," Martin replied. In professional settings Martin is a much, much different guy from the one he is in private. More confident, more resolute. "However . . ."

"Then we have indeed addressed everything. Thank you all for your trust, and I know that our collaboration will be successful. So, back to work."

With his final words he clapped twice, jumped up, and loafered out of the conference room, the tassels on his shoes wagging back and forth.

After that debut, the snooty mannequin entrenched himself in his office for several days, where, as I periodically reported to Martin, he pored over files while overheating his pocket calculator. Then, as a finale, he canceled the contract with the moving company just ten days before the temporary office relocation and hired a new company charging thirty percent less. However, this also meant that the staff would have to schlep their own boxes downstairs from their offices to the surrounding streets where they would stack them on a bunch of pallets, following a precisely keyed system. And then the whole procedure would run in reverse at the new offices.

This big move had been looming on the horizon for months, like the annual emissions check that you just *know* your 1970 VW camper will never pass. By the end of June things were getting serious—the moving process had finally begun.

"I think this whole thing is infernally, ginormously, idiotically stupid," I complained for the thousandth time.

Martin nodded absentmindedly as he emptied the last of his desk drawers, neatly packing its contents into a box labeled with his name.

"You can't just leave us here alone in this ramshackle old bunker," I continued.

By "us" I meant the other corpses and myself, since of course I'm dead, too. Well, my body has been interred for a while now, but my soul is in fine fettle. So I've been stuck romping around the no-man's-land between the world of the living and the realm of the dead while other dying people's souls make only a short layover in my zone before vanishing "into the light." I have yet to learn any more about that particular destination. Not even from Marlene, the dead nun who kept me company last spring for a few weeks. She hasn't reported in again since. That was pretty much expected, of course, so I wouldn't really say it surprised me, but, yeah, it still hurts.

Following Marlene's disappearance, I felt lonelier than ever, so I clung like a leech to Martin, the only person in the whole world I can communicate with. Dr. Martin Gänsewein has been anything but thrilled about my inability to "move on" the way Marlene did: he and I are not always of one spirit. Well, that's worded kind of euphemistically. You might also say we're more opposite than black and white, Bruce Willis and Édith Piaf, a dinosaur and the Easter bunny—well, I'm supposed to start making some use of civilized language here and not constantly "resort to dichotomy and exaggeration," so I'll leave it at that. These rules stem once again from my editor, but we'll return to this business of *Writing* later.

In any case, Martin and his colleagues were about to head out to the "Cologne Carpathians," their lame nickname for their new temporary offices in the hills just outside of town—offices that were free of asbestos, or at least not at a life-threatening level, unlike in this grim old building squatting here like a sarcophagus, surrounded by the old Melaten Cemetery. Asbestos was the reason for the big move, and soon the contractor would remove it and install new insulation, wallpaper, and carpets. Then the staff could move back in again. Meanwhile, the only people who would be staying behind during construction were the corpses. Asbestos doesn't bother them a bit.

Of course, the physical distance between the new office space and the corpses was a logistical nightmare. After all, a coroner's job doesn't start and stop at slicing into random dead bodies; he also has to write unending reports about what he found inside any given dead person. That might include bullets, broken-off knife tips, poison, or any number of other things. This meant that the slicers were going to have to drive out to the temporary offices every morning, flip through their mail, then get back into their cars, drive over to the autopsy section here at the institute, fillet a corpse into all its little parts, drive back to the office, and then write up their reports. And of course it would be kind of a hassle if he realized only after he was back at the office that he'd accidentally stuck someone's eyeball into his pocket, because then he'd have to get back into his car or take the train over and return the eyeball to its rightful socket.

OK, granted, I have not yet seen a coroner stuff an eyeball into his pocket, but if he did, it would be a pretty big pain to have to go put it back where it goes. That's all I'm saying.

Therefore, no one, including me, was exactly thrilled about the move. I'd been clinging pretty close to Martin due to my aforementioned loneliness, and I was not a fan of his 2CV. I could *not* imagine spending the next few months swaying through half of Cologne inside that little trash can on wheels, meandering several times a day from his temporary office to the autopsy section and back again. But hanging out with dead bodies all day wasn't going to do it either. I sighed.

"Oh, pull yourself together, Pascha," Martin thought in my direction. "You can easily fly from office to office, after all. The commute will be least inconvenient for you, out of all of us."

You just can't discuss things like this with a scientist, I've learned, so I kept my trap shut and made for the refrigerated morgue drawers in the basement of the institute. The drawer labeled No. 4 used to be mine, actually, but at the moment it was host to a man who had dropped dead on the street the day before yesterday. Just like that. And he wasn't the only one. People were literally dropping dead because of the weather . . . which brings us to Crisis No. 2.

The mercury hadn't dipped below sweltering for two weeks now. Not even at night. So the refrigerated drawers were slowly but surely filling up with heat-related deaths, and Martin and his colleagues had fallen behind on the autopsies, what with all the stress of the move. So the guy in morgue drawer No. 4 hadn't been autopsied yet, nor had the four additional bodies that had been carted in since he'd arrived. I was curious to see how the slicers were going to catch up on their backlog.

For the moment no one was making any headway; instead, they were all lugging their boxes to the designated neighborhood collection points, where the moving company was supposed to pick everything up and haul it to the new building overnight. Naturally all of the employees were wearing long faces because they had to carry their boxes to the collection points themselves. The lab techs were having the hardest time of it because they had to haul not only their files and paperwork but also their microscopes and other instruments, all by themselves. And that stuff is as heavy as a mafioso's trousers and as sensitive as a chick with PMS, so they were dripping with sweat not just from the heat and physical exertion, but also from worrying about their delicate equipment. I mean, if a box filled with stuff like that tips over, you've just sent umpteen thousand euros down the drain—and it's not like they can do their work without those instruments. So everyone was pissed off at the new director, who was risking the very ability of the institute to function just to save a couple thousand euros on the move. Money that had already been set aside in the budget a long time ago.

"We obviously have a boss who can count," I overheard one lab rat say as he wrapped some kind of gore-oscope inside a cuddly quilt he'd brought from home, before he started dragging it in a sustained panic to within sight of the collection point. "If only we had one who could *think*, too."

"Yeah, and he needs his calculator to do the counting," a colleague replied. "The Turkish guy who runs the grocery stand around the corner can do numbers faster in his head."

God, I can't stand whining academics, so I left the institute and roamed through the city. It was Thursday, the day the new releases come out. At the movies I felt almost like I used to, when I could stroll through the neighborhood inside my own physical body. Of course I couldn't drink a Coke anymore, throw popcorn around, or make out with some hot babe—but movies were one of my rare opportunities to forget the loss of my corporeality for a couple of hours. Assuming the movie was good, that is. But then again, it wasn't like I needed to buy a ticket, so I could take my chances and give practically any movie a try. Only *real* movies, of course. Action blockbusters. Tearjerkers and fairy tales were out, and definitely dramedies, too. To me, if the writer can't make up his mind if he's doing drama or comedy, then he should switch to making paper airplanes until he knows what he wants.

So I was hanging out in my favorite movie theater, floating at about the altitude of the VIP box, centered in front of the screen above the heads of the rest of the audience, and I'd already taken in the first third of a proper spy thriller chock-full of great-looking broads in supporting roles as tiny as their string thongs, when some kind of disturbance cropped up in the third row in front of me. Someone was moaning; a female voice was whispering at the acoustic level of a VW Golf 2—with the original tailpipe—starting up; and someone else was rustling and jingling keys.

"Hey, be quiet up there," the guy right underneath me bellowed.

The rustling and whispering continued.

"This isn't a playground," the guy continued. "Shut up or get out!"

I did a quick flyby to see the reason for the disruption when a soul zipped right past me, missing me by only the width of a ball-sack hair. And as usual the little soul was in a terrible rush and didn't stop to exchange even the scantest of pleasantries with me. Instead it just rocketed past me at an angel's gallop. Finally, the chick in the seat next to the now-soulless husk noticed that something was pretty seriously off with the guy, and in a panic she screamed for help.

I immediately decided to catch the rest of the movie tomorrow—I was not in the mood for this kind of drama. I'd seen what would come next a hundred times before: multiple resuscitation attempts, sedative shots for the dead man's hysterical companion, more resuscitation, paramedics, ambulance, electroshocks. And at some point they'd realize what I already knew, since the guy's inner spirit had almost run me over: the bastard was dead. I fully expected to see him again at the institute later, another carefully managed statistic at the Office of Public Health under the category of "heat-related deaths." This heat wave was quickly turning into an epidemic.

———

The institute had set aside Friday and the whole weekend to move and set up the new offices, so for three days there had been sweaty, whiny medical types from various departments scurrying around the new rooms, hauling boxes, plugging in cords, adjusting instruments, organizing files, and complaining more or less vociferously about their awful lot. They were able to do so with impunity since the new boss wasn't in the building. The man had been in his job for just four weeks, but already the entire staff ranked his popularity below silverfish, having your driver's license suspended, and genital herpes. This was also the weekend that his official nickname was invented, and it spread faster than Schumacher's rain-slicked lap record in Monaco: "Piggy Bank" was born.

The mood in the autopsy section after the offices upstairs had been cleared out was so low it was subterranean. Plus, you need to know that the autopsy section was in the basement of the now-empty building, right underneath all the construction. By day jackhammers rumbled and vibrated through the floors, making any regular work impossible. Regular work would have meant one slicer hacked up a body while another blabbered every finding into a voice recorder. But dictation wasn't feasible with all the noise, so now the blabbering colleague had to stand silently next to the body, holding a small notepad and a pen and constantly muttering: "Wait, not so fast. What was that last part again?"

But by night it was quiet. Too quiet, in the opinion of the weaker sex. With the offices abandoned, reception desk unstaffed, and power tools off for the night, the institute sat lonely and forsaken by all living souls. To top it all off, three sides of the building abutted the vast Melaten Cemetery, which is not exactly a carefree place of *joie de vivre*. Now that the building had been largely abandoned, in fact, it had started attracting all kinds of creepy characters by night from

Cologne's largest complex for the croaked and buried. The construction fence wasn't keeping these goth freaks out, and it had happened more than once that an institute employee on the way down to, or up out of, the autopsy section at night would notice a candle or small fire flickering up in one of the windows of the now-vacant offices above. Coroners in for an urgent night autopsy had twice reported feeling watched as they descended the exterior ramp to the basement lobby outside the autopsy section and morgue. You knew it was bad if the building was giving coroners—who'd spent years rummaging around inside half-dissected bodies—the creepy-crawlies.

Katrin Zange, whom the Good Lord had bestowed not only with stunning femininity but also with the ability to give some serious lip, had been volunteered by the other coroners to go see Piggy Bank and voice their complaints. Since I was bored, I went along with her, hoping that the result would put everyone back in a good mood.

"Mr. Forch, I'd like to speak with you about the nighttime situation in the autopsy section."

Forch was sitting, wearing a suit and tie in his air-conditioned Supercomputing Center, as the colleagues had started calling his office. He was the only one in the building—if not the entire city of Cologne—with a portable air conditioner on wheels gurgling away next to his desk with a tube to the window. Katrin was wearing a sleeveless blouse, a pair of linen slacks, and sandals consisting only of a sole and two thin leather straps. She had put up her long, wavy hair, and the fine hairs on the back of her neck were damp and curly. The thin sheen of sweat over her tan skin glistened alluringly. She was still by far the hottest bunny in the whole Forensic Medicine Department, and she looked good enough to eat.

Forch could not manage to keep his eyes focused on her face after she walked in; his gaze kept sliding lower. Then he pushed a few papers to the side, pulled out a drawer, slid the papers in, and then his manicured mitts reached a little farther to the right in a conspicuously inconspicuous motion. I zoomed over to see what was over there to fumble with, and I had to grin. He had adjusted his air conditioner colder by five degrees. The result of his cooling plan became clearly visible two and a half minutes later through Katrin's thin blouse. Piggy Bank was a piggy in more ways than one! *Finally.* A real man in the house! I instantly liked the guy.

"Mr. Forch, our colleagues have a request that I would like to present to you. I wanted to say that, when we're working in the autopsy section, especially at night, we are feeling very uneasy or, uh, unsafe. We'd like to ask you to tighten our security measures."

"But the autopsy section is every bit as safe as it was before," Forch objected. "The construction work doesn't affect it at all."

"Yes, but a fair number of suspicious figures have been prowling around at night. Both in the parking lot and on the access ramp down to the basement lobby to the autopsy section. People would prefer not to have to go down there alone in the dark anymore."

While Katrin shivered, Piggy Bank leaned back, relishing the view, and took his time to reply. "What do you have in mind?"

Katrin folded her arms in front of her body. "Well, video surveillance perhaps? Or some kind of security service that regularly . . ."

"Video surveillance is not necessary, given what we do, and thus hardly appropriate as a capital investment," Piggy Bank explained in a firm voice.

"Capital investment . . . ?"

"Yes. Business assets. Assets on the balance sheet. For a medical services institution like this, there is no budget to pay for cameras, cable linkups, recording devices, or even transmission to a monitoring service. Which budget column do you suggest I make such an investment from?"

Katrin had since pulled her feet tightly together, trying to warm them up against each other. "How about a security service to check that everything's in order? Maybe twice an hour?"

"For heaven's sake," Piggy Bank retorted. "To cover these additional costs you would have to increase your productivity by twenty percent. Can you do that?"

Katrin looked at him, stunned. "Productivity? Listen, we all do our jobs very well, and we all put in overtime. Nothing has ever been left undone. I'm not sure what you mean by productivity, but I know that we feel unsafe in the autopsy section. And that is all of the colleagues, not just the women."

The fact that Martin had been the first to claim to be scared shitless didn't surprise me in the least.

"You know, feeling unsafe is much more an individual— and generally also a nonspecific—feeling that does not first and foremost have to do with one's work environment. Perhaps you should give some consideration to taking a self-defense class. That wouldn't be the worst thing for safety outside of work, as well, wouldn't you agree?"

I imagined what Katrin would look like in a judo uniform, spinning into a Major Wheel throw to drop her training partner to the mat and then jumping on top of him . . . Frankly, I'd be the first to volunteer as her training partner, no matter how many bruises it cost me.

Forch stood and offered his hand to Katrin over the desk and shook it long enough to feast his eyes on the cold-induced scenery. Katrin broke free of his grip, said a hasty good-bye, and ran out of the icebox. Storming down the hallway, she stuck her head into the doorway of the large office everyone was sharing and said: "Meeting in the break room." Then she rushed on, shivering, and pushed open the door to the break room, grabbed the first cup she saw, positioned it under the hot-beverage faucet, and pressed the button for some injection-brewed belly wash with some pleasant Italian name.

I had been there when the dwarf of a coffee machine serviceman refilled the containers last week, so I'd read the ingredients listed on the bags whose powdered contents formed the base of the various "beverage specialties brewed fresh for you": powdered milk; artificial flavor; EU food additives E473 and E322 (emulsifiers) and E407, E460, and E466 (stabilizers); sugar; carrageenan (thickening agent); modified food starch; E500 and E332 (pH control agents); and salt. For actual *coffee* drinks there was another bag with coffee extract, and for chocolate drinks there was in fact—drum roll!—cocoa. Mercifully the machine didn't spit out the package insert along with the drink.

Not that that would have mattered to me; I used to down liters of stuff like that, and I would gladly do so again today. Here, however, there were several colleagues who chowed down exclusively on organic, vegan, acrylamide-free, and nongenetically modified foodstuffs but also downed this automatic bilge like there was no tomorrow.

The dark dishwater finally filled Katrin's cup, with an airy industrial foam on top, and she impatiently slurped on the slop much too loudly. But slowly the goose bumps on her arms relaxed. But not the other bumps. I was liking this.

Martin and Jochen came in, wondering what was up.

"Extra security is available to us only in exchange for a twenty-percent increase in our productivity," Katrin grumbled.

"That horndog turned the temperature on his air conditioner way down so Katrin's nipples would perk up," I explained to Martin, smirking.

He turned red. "No!"

"Yes," Katrin said.

Martin turned even redder.

"And how are we supposed to increase our productivity?" Jochen asked. "Should we beat a few people to death on the street to bring in a couple more bodies a week?"

Sure, just like volunteer firefighters who keep dropping matches to prove how critical they are to putting out fires.

"If there's no improvement to the security situation in the building, pretty soon we're going to be able to cherry-pick our bodies from right outside our door," Katrin hissed. "Or maybe even inside the autopsy section itself."

"Well," Martin said, "the door to the actual autopsy section is pretty secure with the electronic access control system."

"It still creeps me out down there," Katrin said.

"Yes, me too," Martin admitted sheepishly.

God, how embarrassing for a full-grown man to admit he's a whiny coward—and in front of a chick, to boot!

———•———

A week later, my birthday came, and it so happened that Martin had an autopsy scheduled first thing in the morning, so he drove the now-familiar route to the Melaten Beltway, parked the trash can in the almost-empty parking lot, and carefully locked the ridiculous thing up. As if anyone would want to pinch a purported means of transportation like that. I've told him so at least a thousand times, and I should know since I used to make my living stealing motor vehicles. But I'm not someone he listens to.

All morning I'd been yakking at Martin about my big day. My birthday is very important to me, especially given the situation I now find myself in. It might be hard to understand, since it's so different for you: you wake up to some morning wood and then you realize you've got a hangover or heartburn or something—all clear signs that you're chipper and alive. For me this no longer happens. First, I don't wake up, because dead guys don't sleep. Second, I don't have any erectile tissue, so no morning wood either. Nor can I suffer from a hangover, heartburn, or scabies for that matter, disembodied as I am. No one can see me, and only Martin can hear me. My birthday is a damn important opportunity to reassure myself that I exist.

"So what are we going to do to celebrate?" I asked Martin.

I had already spent the past half hour providing him with extensive descriptions of my previous parties, but he just kept wincing every time I mentioned alcoholic beverages or lascivious women. Martin probably still gets a homemade cake for his birthday, decorated with M&Ms and those stupid trick candles that reignite after you blow them out.

"We could see a film," he suggested while walking down the ramp to the institute's basement.

"I hang out at the movies almost every night," I grumbled. "That's not anything special."

"Well, food is obviously out . . ."

Har har.

Martin held his ID badge up in front of the electronic lock and pushed the door open. He managed to take one more step before plunging into a sudden paralysis: he had stopped midmotion, looking completely inane and rather unstable on only one foot.

The basement lobby where they handle body admissions was completely trashed. In the refrigerated part of the morgue, two morgue drawers were ajar and the irritating temperature alarm was beeping away relentlessly. Something was hanging out of the drawer on the left, and it did *not* smell good. OK, let's just say it like it is: the room reeked with the putrid odor from all the stuff that's normally inside people—blood, bile, contents of the stomach and intestines. Sure, that's all nasty enough, but add to that the distinct stench of decay. Anyone who's ever seen rotting ground beef push open a freezer door from the inside during an extended power outage knows what I mean.

There was also a long trail of blood on the floor, leading from the now-empty drawer on the right to just in front of the door. Martin was standing with one foot right in the middle of it. He still hadn't moved.

"Martin," I roared. "Pull yourself together. In or out, but do something!"

He was still holding the door open, which pleased the flies, of which quite a few were already buzzing into the other open drawer.

He finally moved again, untaking the step he had taken to enter the autopsy section. Then he leaned against the outside of the door and called the cops on his cell.

———•———

Since I've been dead, I've developed a much better opinion of the cops than I had before. This may have something to do with my life story. As a car thief, I naturally regarded the cops as predators whose sole reason for existing was to make my life difficult. By contrast, as a mostly dead guy interested in solving crimes, the cops are sort of like my colleagues now.

Two officers arrived in their bucket-mobile with the flashing blue lights and tried get a couple of coherent sentences out of Martin.

"When did you arrive here?"

"Um . . ."

"At seven fifty-eight," I prompted.

He parroted.

"How do you know the exact time?"

"Um . . ."

"Because the ads had just started on the radio. It may have been two seconds sooner or later, but you can find that out from the station."

Martin repeated my words.

"And then?" the uniform asked, his forehead dripping with sweat under his cap. It was this hot at only eight in the morning? I was starting to worry how long the city could keep functioning in this kind of heat.

Martin haltingly recounted how he had opened the door and seen the mess.

"Was the entrance locked when you got here?"

"Um . . ."

Martin listened in my direction, but I couldn't help him on this one either. He had held his magnetic employee ID up to the electronic door lock and then pulled the door open, assuming that his pass had unlocked it. But neither of us knew if it had been locked before or not.

"Who normally has night access to this area?" the cop asked.

Martin said nothing.

"Your colleagues, the fire department, the funeral homes that deliver the bodies . . . ?"

At first the cop had trouble forming a more or less coherent picture of what had happened from Martin's stammering, but with the help of his plainclothes colleagues and the crime scene investigators who soon arrived, a likely scenario emerged. Apparently a power line had been cut during the work in the office section upstairs, so the electronic door locking system downstairs had been inactivated, allowing free access to the morgue drawers. Overnight the buzzards who bring the bodies to the morgue for admissions had hauled in two specimens: a guy from a pub who'd keeled over dead off his stool, and a second man who, according to the information the detectives had, had been the victim of a knife fight.

That was the guy who was missing now.

Martin immediately drove back out to his temporary office to apprise his new boss of the situation.

"A body is missing, you say?" Forch asked, visibly irritated.

Martin nodded. He had pulled his jacket on as a security precaution before going to see Piggy Bank, although I had discreetly pointed out that the man was probably not all that interested in seeing Martin's nipples.

"Who?"

"A knife fight victim, according to his admission form. Apparently no one had called a coroner out to the body discovery site."

Piggy Bank looked questioningly at Martin.

"Normally, the police ask the coroner on call to examine a body at the scene when the cause of death is questionable or when a blood-spatter analysis is necessary," Martin explained. "But apparently our colleagues in Criminal Investigations did not make that request this time."

"Is the institute paid for such off-hour services?" Piggy Bank asked.

Martin looked at him blankly.

Piggy Bank dismissed the question with a wave of his hand. "Fine, I'll clear it up myself. Next question: Are we insured for this type of event?"

Bold question marks started emerging from the soup of thoughts in Martin's brain. "Insured?"

"There was a theft, correct?"

"Uh, I'm not quite sure what the legal ramifications are in a situation like this," Martin mumbled. "On the issue of our liability for the whereabouts of the corpse, however . . ."

"Well, then let's find out. About the insurance, I mean. Would you happen to have any idea what value we should place on a body? Perhaps . . ." Piggy Bank briefly closed his eyes. "Including the cost of the autopsy, as well as all incidental expenses and overhead." He looked questioningly at

Martin. When Martin didn't move, Piggy Bank waved his right hand to shoo him out. "Thanks for letting me know."

Martin left his boss's office in a mental muddle and reported what had happened to Katrin and Jochen.

"Damn it, I warned him," Katrin said. "Now even the dead aren't safe anymore? From now on I'm not going down there without some pepper spray."

"Me either," Jochen said.

Hmm. Jochen was already on the older side, at least fifty, so he didn't have much more to expect from life anyway. So what was he shitting his pants for?

"And what the hell would someone want with that body of ours?" Katrin asked.

"I'd rather not imagine, frankly," Jochen said with a frown.

"Let's think about what we should do now," Martin said.

"What's there to think about?" Katrin asked, irritated. "What is our well-paid boss for, right?"

No idea flashed briefly in Martin's brain, and that was pretty much the most heretical thought he would ever allow himself on the topic. Of course he didn't utter it aloud. "We should take an inventory of the other bodies and see if another one is missing or if something has been tampered with on the others."

Together, Martin, Jochen, and Katrin spent two hours on the external examination of each individual body in each individual drawer. They used each body's documentation to check whether it had been tampered with. As Katrin checked the second-to-last one, she let out a soft scream. Martin and Jochen dropped everything and ran to her. Together the three of them stared into the drawer.

It was a woman. Age is always difficult to determine from looking at a corpse, but I estimated her to have had one foot in the grave already, so around forty. She had already been autopsied, which you could clearly tell from the long incision from her chin to below her belly button. Based on the coarse suturing, I knew it was Martin's work.

"Ruptured appendix," Martin said, recognizing the woman instantly.

Bingo. I'd been able to tell his suturing ever since he'd crocheted my sorry innards back into me in similar fashion.

Jochen recoiled. "My God, that's twisted!"

Martin's suturing was ugly, but it wasn't *that* bad. I took another look at the corpse in the drawer.

Oh. Someone had peeled off wide strips of her skin, too.

"What was the name of that movie . . . ?" Jochen asked. I think he was trying to sound casual. But he didn't. His voice trembled and squeaked like a pubescent troublemaker trying to belt out "Swing Low, Sweet Chariot."

"Maybe the guy was afraid someone was going to discover him, so stopped doing this and took the other body with him instead," Katrin said. "That way he could continue in some dark corner without being interrupted."

"Then why not take this woman?" Martin asked. He had switched into professional mode, so his mind was working in its usual analytical form.

"Maybe he didn't like your sewing job," I suggested.

Martin winced.

"Maybe he didn't—" Jochen started.

"Like my sewing job," Martin said, finishing his thought. "Yes, thank you, I know."

"We should call and have someone from Criminal Investigations come," Katrin said. "And as soon as the police have taken their pictures and written their reports, we're going to have to thoroughly examine the body one more time as well. Take DNA evidence, just the usual."

It took ten minutes for the cops to make it back on-site and another whole hour for the three forensic doofuses here to go over every millimeter of the skinned bunny for genetic or other evidence of the skin fetishist.

Katrin drove back to the office, and Martin and Jochen performed the originally scheduled autopsy. This time Martin had to do the writing. I hung around the two of them, flying outside at regular intervals to make sure the grounds were secure, but since the construction work was in progress, at that moment there were no cemetery freaks to be seen. Presumably it was too loud for them as well.

Gregor came into Martin's office around four. Gregor is Martin's best friend on earth and Katrin's boyfriend. Of course, I am Martin's *closest* friend, even though Martin likes to repress that fact. But back to Gregor. Gregor is also a detective sergeant in Criminal Investigations with the Cologne Police Department, and as such he was responsible for the investigation into the missing body of the knife fight victim. Gregor gave Katrin a long kiss and then with a silly grin bent over to kiss Martin, too, who frantically fended him off. I belly laughed. I liked Gregor's sense of humor.

"So, the digest version?" Gregor said, plopping onto the visitor's chair.

Martin recounted everything he knew. Methodically, precisely, dispassionately. Typical forensic-pathologist

Martin, in other words. Totally different from private Martin.

"We've never had a case like this before," Gregor finally said. "And I've got to say the department is not thrilled that a body has gone astray."

"Nor am I," Martin said.

"The man didn't have any ID on him, so we have no clue at all to his identity. No photo, not even a scrap of paper that might tell us what language the guy even spoke."

"Why . . ." Martin began.

"The CSI who physically picked the body up off the street said the guy looked like a redshirt from some kung fu movie."

One of the reasons I like Gregor is because he's politically incorrect like that. Of course, only when he's among friends. And since only Katrin and Martin were there, this qualified as such an occasion. Of course, I was there too, but Gregor didn't know anything about that. Still, I considered us friends as well, as kindred spirits.

"Why didn't the CSI call a coroner out to the discovery site?" Martin asked.

Naturally, Martin is too polite to ask the name of the cerebrally amputated Neanderthal of an investigator who would pick a knife fight victim up off the street without forensic assistance.

Gregor shrugged and collegially kept his trap shut, but he did make an angry face.

In principle it's at the discretion of the lead CSI on-site whether to call out a coroner. They always do so if there are specific forensic issues, such as the need for an official estimate of how long the body had been lying there. In officialese this is called "time since death." Or if they need a blood-spatter analysis to determine what direction the attacker came from, where the victim was standing, whether the attacker was taller or shorter or right- or left-handed, or anything else one might be able to discern about the relationship between perp and vic.

But if a cop was sure on his own that there had been foul play and didn't need any additional expertise from a forensic pathologist, then he didn't need to call the coroner on duty.

In this case, of course, it was a bummer that the CSI ditz hadn't done so, because the evidence on the body itself—unlike that at the discovery site—had not been secured yet. And the now-stolen Asian stiff had not been subjected to even a fast-track exam by anyone with any medical training whatsoever. Shit happens, I guess.

"I assume there's no missing-person report that he matches either?" Martin said.

"Correct." Gregor didn't say anything for a moment and thought. "Why do you think someone would swipe *him*?"

Martin thought briefly back to the conversation between Katrin and Jochen by the morgue drawers and was about to open his mouth when Katrin butted in.

"Because Asians have cleaner, brighter skin than do middle-aged German women with all their conspicuous moles and birthmarks."

The two men were stunned.

"Well, I've envied many an Asian for her small pores and smooth skin," Katrin said. "Men and women both. So if I were the kind of psycho who steals other people's skin to wear myself, I'd opt for beautiful skin, wouldn't I?"

"I feel like we're finding out a lot of new things about you . . ." Gregor joked. He turned to Martin and said, "Once you get the results of the blood tests, or if anything else occurs to you that might help me make some headway in this case in which we're now lacking a body, call me. Because I'm completely at a dead end."

Martin didn't answer, but I could see the resolve surging inside his skull. Martin would do everything he could to help Gregor with this case as a matter of personal responsibility. It was the institute's fault, after all.

People who create their own drama deserve their own karma . . .

"So what are we going to do tonight?" I asked later.

"Huh?"

"It's my birthday, or did you forget already?"

Martin groaned. "Birgit is coming over tonight; we were going to . . ."

He switched off his mind at the last moment. He's gotten pretty good at that. It works with me, too. Over the past six months, as we've gotten to know each other we've learned how to block each other out of our thoughts whenever we want. I can be with Martin without him noticing, which can be quite interesting at times. Martin can block me out of his braincase as well, which I of course find infernally cruel. After all, he's the one and only person I have any contact with, and when he switches off, I'm all alone.

So today he had plans with Birgit that I knew nothing about. Screwing was probably out: those two had been doing it regularly for a while now, and it wasn't anything special for them or for me anymore. Besides, spectating is not as spectacular as people generally suspect. Especially not when you're always watching the *same* two people. And especially not when the guy is a fabric-softener-soft stuffed animal like Martin. Personally, I would . . .

Anyway, watching doesn't do it for me anymore.

See, Martin has strung up an antielectrosmog net in his bedroom, which looks like metallic mosquito netting and creates an impenetrable barrier for me. He explained the gizmo to Birgit by saying he occasionally hears voices from the beyond and can protect himself from them using the netting as a shield. The coward hasn't managed to tell Birgit that I, Pascha, am not only an occasional voice from the realm of the dead but also a totally *real* guy who merely and unfortunately has been dispossessed of a body. Now, Birgit does know that Martin talks to dead people, but she still doesn't know anything about me specifically. I think this is basically megawhacked, and we've debated it about a thousand times, but on this issue Martin is unfailingly pigheaded. He is still keeping his closest friend a secret from his girlfriend.

"Why don't you go do a little sniffing around into our secret case about the absconded corpse?" he suggested, tired.

Well, sure, I *did* solve the case of my own murder as well as the case with the nun's, but that *so way* did not mean I wanted to start doing the cops' work for them every time they had a suspicious death on their hands. Especially not with a completely opaque story like this one, where they hadn't even IDed the body yet. I mean, where was I even supposed to start?

"Why don't you go to a concert?" Martin suggested.

"Do you know what's special about someone's birthday?" I asked him in response. "Not having to spend it by yourself!"

Martin groaned again.

"I can go to a concert any day. I can also go the movies or the nail salon, for that matter, any day of the week. But today, we can do anything you want as long as you come along. I don't want to be alone on my birthday."

As he imagined accompanying me to a business specializing in the purveyance of sexual services (even mentally, Martin always uses politically correct terminology), he started getting a little worked up. Not from anticipation but from horror.

"But what about Birgit . . . ?"

"Just tell Birgit about me already and you won't have this problem anymore," I suggested. Salt in his wounds. At some point I would eventually wear him down.

"You will not wear me down," he shot back.

"Whatever you have planned with Birgit, I'll be happy to come along," I said.

Martin winced. Then he tried to put on a poker face and act all deliberately cool-like. "OK, then, let's see a film."

"Fine, but I'll pick the flick."

I should have known that nothing would come of our plan.

I still wanted to take one more spin around town and check out scantily clad chicks in our summer heat wave before the movie. After all, checking people out is one thing I can still do, and at current temperatures it was worth it. So Martin and I arranged to meet at eight. When I caught up with the two of them again, Martin had already bought the movie tickets.

At first I thought they'd both picked the movie in honor of my birthday, since it was a vampire flick. Horror movies are fine by me, at least sometimes. Of course I prefer action movies with tons of hot rides, insane stunts, gigantic explosions, and a superhero who saves the world in a tattered shirt. *But fine,* I thought, *we'll do vampires tonight.* But then what followed was simply unbelievable. A teeny-bopper movie without sex, horror, or even a plot—most of which deficiencies I don't really mind so much as long as the explosion rate is right. But this was a movie without *anything*—except that one of the guys is a vampire. And an aristocrat, to boot. And a real gentleman. Who doesn't bite and doesn't screw because he doesn't want to hurt the chick. I mean, how lame can you get?

Purely for revenge, because Martin was apparently completely ignoring my birthday and all of my wishes related to it, I spent the whole movie from the first second to the last commenting on every frame to him, using the rudest expressions I could. I was going to include a few examples here, but my editor deleted them all. So you'll just have to imagine them for yourself. Thanks to my mental interference, Martin was unable to follow the brain-shriveling plot, so when he and Birgit went out for gelato afterward Birgit quickly lost interest in talking about the movie with him.

"Are you having some kind of trouble at work that kept you from concentrating on the movie?" she asked Martin sympathetically.

Birgit's blonde hair had grown even blonder from the sun. It looked perfect with her tan skin and blue eyes, but the rest of her doesn't leave anything to be desired, either. Ah, if only it were always summer—with women in loose-fitting, thin togs that I can easily fly in and underneath, taking a little spin around their belly buttons.

"Well, we did have an incident today," Martin began, and then he jabbered Birgit an earful about the missing corpse.

Birgit works at a bank, and she's not only a major babe but megasmart to boot. Which is why I've never really gotten what she's doing with Martin the Meticulologist. But who really understands women anyway? And yet somehow she listens to his forensic medicine stories with the patience of an angel.

"Birgit's cold," I interrupted him at some point. He stopped midsentence. Blushed. Took off his sweater and handed it to Birgit, who stared at him in astonishment.

"What's that for?"

"You're cold."

"No, I'm not . . ."

"I can see that you are." Martin glanced meaningfully down at her tits.

Birgit grinned at him. "And what if that's not because of the temperature?"

Martin turned even redder.

Birgit tossed fifteen euros onto the table, stood up, grabbed Martin's hand, and pulled him along after her. I sighed and stayed behind. In a gelato joint where half the city seemed to be having fun. On my birthday. Without me.

Martin has to go for falling asleep. He thinks that's normal. Maybe it is, too, if you inhale a liter of relaxing tea before you hit the hay. Since I couldn't wake him up from under his antielectrosmog netting anyway, I just waited for him in the bathroom to unload my concerns.

"All right," I said. "Now let's go out just the two of us and celebrate my birthday—boys' night out!"

Martin winced. This didn't cause any trajectory-related mishap, however, since he pees while sitting down at night.

"I'm sleeping," he said.

"Wrong," I said. "You're talking to me. And now you're going out to toss a couple back with me."

"It's the middle of the night," Martin said.

"You didn't want to before."

"Well, Birgit . . ."

"Let her sleep."

"But I've got to get up quite early tomorrow and . . ."

"You could have spent the evening with me, and *then* you could have been snoozing now."

For a brief moment Martin thought that all he'd have to do was hurry back under his protective netting and then I couldn't start anything with him. But even he knew that he'd be way too slow. I'd flash under his magnetic wave curtain like lightning, and then I wouldn't be able to get back out and he'd be stuck with me in his ear the whole night long.

"Exactly," I said.

Martin sighed, went into the bedroom, got dressed, and whispered to Birgit that he had to go out. She whispered that she hadn't even heard his phone; he whispered that she must have been sound asleep and she should go back to sleep. And then the two of us went around the corner to the pub. The streets were still busy; it was way too hot to sleep, and people were just staying outside because they couldn't stand it in their apartments. Martin was one of the few who didn't want to take his drink outside to the tables on the sidewalk. He sat at the bar and ordered a sparkling mineral water.

"A beer," I insisted.

"I don't like . . ."

"I'm not here to water flowers or wash socks. I want to celebrate my birthday. Kindly order a beer."

Martin obeyed. Then he ordered a candle.

"A what?" the bartender asked. She was wearing a top that revealed all the tattoos around her belly button. A sun centered on the belly button, and a couple of stars around it. Martin took pains not to look. Not me. Instead he had to focus on the lead zits all over her face. I've never been into those idiotic piercings.

"A candle. It's a friend's birthday."

She nodded. "Of course. And where is your friend?" She put out a tea light in a colorful glass in front of Martin on the bar.

"He's in my thoughts, and I'm in his," Martin said funereally.

"Hey, Mr. Poet, the candle is a great idea," I said and tried to blow it out. Didn't work, of course.

Martin's face contorted in disgust at the beer, but then he summoned a look of defiance as though he were facing death and emptied his glass. And then chased it down with another, and then a third. I was enjoying sitting around with my only friend in a pub, watching the people all around us. And I went to the trouble of acting as though I were still one of them.

"Send a little beer over to that buxom blonde over by the window," I asked Martin.

He scanned for the chick I meant, figured out who it was with my help, and then balked. He goes more for the natural type. That is, less makeup on her mug, less peroxide in her perm, and fewer beanbags in her bra.

"Is she your type?" he asked.

"Well, Lara Croft isn't here right now," I retorted. You had to focus on the available selection, but Martin didn't grasp that.

He told Sunshine behind the bar to bring the bird of paradise the drink of her choice.

She came over to Martin right away.

"That is so sweet of you," she cooed at him. Her breath was no longer quite fresh. Some kind of sweet cocktail was wafting into Martin's face. He had to make an effort not to turn his head away.

"I'm celebrating the birthday of a friend, who is, uh, unfortunately not in town today," Martin explained.

"Ask her where she lives," I told him.

"That's not appropriate," Martin thought.

"Ask her."

"Say, do you live anywhere near this, uh . . ." he stammered, looking down into his beer glass.

"Wow, you get right to the point," the buxom bombshell said, laughing and setting her hand on his upper thigh—which sent Martin's muscles into early rigor mortis. "Three buildings away, way up on the top floor. It is ca-raaazy hot up there. I've hardly been able to sleep for weeks now, and when I do it's only completely nude and without any covers."

She batted her eyes at him promisingly, her lips slightly parted at the rim of her glass.

Martin's head was in a dead heat with the tea light to see which could glow hotter.

"Well, it's been the same everywhere," Martin mumbled noncommittally.

That was a lie, because he'd bought himself some special super-lightweight pajamas just so he wouldn't have to go to bed naked.

"I've got to go to bed," Martin whined as soon as she took her hand back off his leg and he could breathe again. Meanwhile the cookie had ordered a corn whiskey on Martin's tab.

"All right, fine," I mumbled. "Party pooper."

Martin threw a twenty-euro bill on the bar, slid awkwardly off his barstool, and bowed slightly to the blonde, who was staring at him blearily.

"You're going already?" she asked. "You'll stop by my place, right? Number twenty, the top button. It's under my stage name. I'm Saskia. From TV."

Martin sort of fidgeted noncommittally. I, however, made firm plans to pop in and visit Saskia from TV. Unfortunately she wouldn't be aware of any of it.

Martin snuck out the door. "Good night, Pascha," he said outside. "And happy birthday."

Today I would have turned twenty-five.

TWO

Four and a half hours later, Birgit sniffed Martin's clothes, wrinkled her nose, and furrowed her brow. "You totally reek. Like a bar. Did you go out drinking last night after work?"

Both the tone in her voice and the expression on her face clearly let on she thought that notion about as likely as Martin being abducted by aliens overnight and whisked away to some celestial pleasure palace.

Martin turned pale. "Uh . . ." He cleared his throat. One of the difficulties Martin had with his little homemade problems was the issue of white lies. Martin could not lie at all. If he would just finally tell Birgit the truth about me, then he wouldn't need to keep making up whatever bullshit he came up with. But, because he preferred to keep me a secret, he kept landing in situations like this, fidgeting around like an earthworm between the open blades of a pair of scissors.

"Or were your colleagues all standing together outside smoking after your shift?" Birgit asked.

Martin nodded in a both relieved and maximally waffly way.

They left the building at the same time, Birgit climbing into her frigging awesome BMW drop-top with red leather seats and Martin climbing into his trash can on wheels. You will undoubtedly guess correctly which vehicle I preferred.

I accompanied Birgit to the bank in her hot ride, then peeled off in front of her branch's swanky glass façade and rocketed over to Martin's office.

The Institute for Forensic Medicine in Cologne can routinely accommodate ninety bodies. That's assuming one body per morgue drawer. Everyone gets his or her own little studio apartment, no matter how big he or she is. Even if the body consists only of a pile of ashes.

In the case of a major disaster like, say, a chemical spill, epidemic, or a Christmas Eve bomb attack on Cologne Cathedral, the institute could house a couple hundred bodies. For this, the entire basement area, where the morgue is located, would be cooled to the requisite four to six degrees Celsius. In that situation the bodies would be stacked everywhere. Including the spot where Martin and Katrin now stood in shock in front of a shattered coffin.

"Goddamn it, not again . . . I have now officially had my fill of this nonsense!" Katrin was just yelling as I joined them. Her face was crimson, and bolts of lightning were shooting out of her eyes at the coffin, which was blocking three morgue drawers. I could understand why she was upset. Where would they put us all if each body insisted on its own coffin-parking spot?

"This institute has been a total madhouse since the boss went on leave," she said.

"But we do have a new one . . ." Martin said cautiously.

"Piggy Bank is an idiot, not a boss," Katrin said. "He doesn't have the least idea what forensic medicine is, and he isn't even remotely interested in it, either. The only thing he knows how to do is save money."

Meanwhile, Katrin's shouting had drawn over the dissectors who were working in their separate chamber off the back of the autopsy room itself. Their eyes darted back and forth in disbelief between Katrin and the busted coffin.

"In case you didn't know," she told the assembled crowd, "starting today we have to pay for the power to operate the coffee machines and electric kettles in the break rooms ourselves. There are meters mounted everywhere now, and at the end of the month the costs will be divided among the employees."

"Well, maybe that's fair, but still . . ." Martin began, but a fiery look from Katrin's eyes brought him to silence.

"They aren't paying overtime anymore, either."

And now even Martin and the assistants turned pale.

"We have to take time off in lieu instead."

"That's never worked in the past," one assistant said. "And if people keep dying in this heat like brain cells during a drunken bender, the next few months are starting to look really ugly."

Katrin just shrugged and pressed her lips together, her rage of a moment ago replaced by a grim, apocalyptic mood.

"All right, back to the topic at hand," Martin said after a bit of communal silence. "What kind of coffin is that, where did it come from, and how can we get rid of it?"

All that was left of the coffin was basically a heap of kindling. One whole side had been pushed in, splintering the wood, so that the lid wouldn't close neatly anymore. It didn't look exactly like fine German oak . . .

"Who has the overnight admit log—" Martin began, but Katrin exploded into yet another firecracker-on-a-short-fuse tirade.

"I do, damn it! Nowhere in the log does it say anything about a coffin," she shouted at him.

Martin didn't dare speak.

"Sorry," Katrin said. "God, my nerves are really at the end. I haven't had a good night's sleep in weeks now because of the heat, and then there's all the chaos at the institute . . . apart from just not having time for all this red tape. It's really Piggy Bank's job."

Martin is a conciliatory man, so he immediately put his hand on Katrin's arm. "It's OK. I'm sorry for asking a stupid question. I think the chaos around here is getting on all our nerves."

Katrin nodded. Gratefully, it seemed to me. All of this honey-I-understand-you drivel was lovely, but I actually had concrete information to offer.

"I know where the coffin . . ." I began, but Martin mentally pushed my intrusion aside.

"Piggy Bank is probably not responsible for an undocumented coffin turning up overnight."

Martin's attempt to placate Katrin with this statement completely backfired, of course.

"Right," she said in acid tones. "We have on-call duty, we put in overtime, and we're constantly at work while that popinjay darts in and out as he pleases, and you can never get hold of him."

"Martin," I yelled. "Last night the coffin was . . ."

"I'm sure the police must know something about the coffin," Martin suggested. "Why don't I . . ."

"That would be great," Katrin replied. "I would be so grateful if you could take that on."

Martin took his cell phone out of his pocket, walked a few steps to the side, pushed on the keys a bit and thought, "All right. What's with the coffin?"

It took me a moment to get that he had merely staged the cell phone performance to create a credible justification for the giant leap in knowledge he was about to make. I would never have ascribed that level of acting talent to him.

"Yes, Gänsewein here," he mumbled into his cell phone, on which the menu functions were blinking. "I've got a question for you."

At that moment his cell phone rang.

Martin almost dropped the thing, staring in dismay at the display and hectically turning around to look at Katrin, who actually had not noticed anything because of the jackhammering that had just started again. Martin silenced the ring and stormed out the door.

"All right, so what's up with the coffin?" he asked.

"After our birthday outing last night, I hung out in a squad car and listened to the police radio for a while. There was a call that came in: 'Accident with fatalities.' "

Martin nodded. He knew I always liked to be on-site when people were dying, in the hope of finding another soul to keep me company.

"The cops responded to the call, and I went with them."

"I don't need a blow-by-blow," Martin said. "Just tell me what's going on with the coffin."

"Truck rammed into hearse; coffin in smithereens; corpse learning how to fly; truck and hearse drivers in shock."

"And then?" Martin asked impatiently.

Boy, someone was in a rush today. Ever since the move people had been running around like headless chickens at the institute. Annoying as hell.

"The cops couldn't get through to the funeral home. The hearse driver was out of it, trembling and brainlessly drooling his bib full, so the medics hauled him away. Then the cops were left standing there with a shredded coffin and a dead body in a well-tailored suit at some intersection in the middle of the night, and they didn't know where they should take everything. Until one of the cops came up with the idea of unloading the whole shebang here."

Martin closed his eyes and shook his head. Then he went back in and told Katrin and the assistant what he'd learned.

The two cookies looked at each other flabbergasted. "Now what?" Katrin asked.

"No idea."

Of course, they did finally do the autopsy that Martin had originally come to the institute for, because as far as work goes Martin is meticulous and astonishingly single-minded. Next up was yet another of what they were calling "heat deaths," this one from an old folks' home who had apparently died of thirst. But after that autopsy was done, Martin and Katrin had to forsake the pleasant basement chill of the autopsy section for the pizza-oven heat back out at the temporary offices. At least it was quiet there.

"Say, Pascha," Martin thought later when he was babbling reports with his dictation software into his computer at his desk. When he uses that tone I know from experience that the utmost caution is in order. "Would you maybe like to do a favor for Katrin?"

Aha, so I'm supposed to do a favor for *Katrin*. Now, Martin isn't actually stupid. He may be completely unfit for survival, embarrassing to the max in terms of hair, duds, fodder preferences, and drug use, not to mention his car, but stupid he is not. Not in terms of intellect, anyway.

"What kind of favor?"

"Maybe keep watch a little overnight?"

Hey, now. I always pay attention overnight. I pay attention where the next action flick is playing, I pay attention to the hottest babe, I pay attention to the wildest sex. And I pay attention anyplace someone happens to be kicking it so I can catch his soul . . .

"In the autopsy section, I mean."

"Then you shouldn't have stuck someone else in my morgue drawer," I replied.

Martin rolled his eyes—physically that is, not just mentally. Katrin, who had just been looking in Martin's direction, quickly looked away.

"Why don't you do it?" I asked.

"Well, it could be dangerous for a—"

"Scared, eh?"

Martin blushed. Katrin noticed that, too.

At that moment Piggy Bank loafered into the room. "What did I just hear?" he asked into the room, at no one in particular. "There's a funeral director using Forensic Medicine for storage?"

Forensic Medicine was the proper term for the entire department where the coroners did their work—from dead body admissions and the refrigerated morgue drawers to the autopsy room itself. Piggy Bank had apparently learned a thing or two, after all. A bit late, though, since the staff was still a full step ahead of him: the *real* slicers had started calling the area simply the Basement.

"Well, there was an accident involving a hearse . . ." Martin began, since Katrin and Jochen had immediately lowered their eyes to their keyboards. In terms of vitally important avoidance strategies like that, Martin's simply not fast enough.

"In the meantime I have been studying the market situation," Piggy Bank said, flashing teeth white as a limousine rented for prom night. "There are over a hundred funeral homes in Cologne alone. Of these, approximately half do not have their own refrigeration systems. The heat wave is resulting in an acute backlog, and capacity is insufficient. We are thus seeing stronger demand in the face of stagnant supply."

Katrin and Jochen stole looks at each other with their heads still down.

"Uh, yes, well, the police apparently didn't know . . ." Martin said.

"Determine the name of the funeral home that the coffin is from. We will charge one hundred euros per day for the morgue drawer rental, plus VAT. Billing will be in twenty-four-hour units. Convey the necessary information to my secretary."

Piggy Bank was already turning around again. Katrin was the first to formulate and articulate a coherent thought again.

"Rent?" she asked, stunned.

"Naturally," Forch replied. "Surely you don't think we can allow the utilization of our business assets—such as our morgue drawers—by a private, for-profit enterprise free of charge? That would constitute a government subsidy and thereby an inexcusable waste of the public monies with which we operate."

"But it *was* an emergency . . ."

"Exceptions render any business model unnecessarily complicated. Anyone who wishes to utilize our morgue drawers must pay, emergency or not. After all, we certainly don't have time to be assessing and evaluating all these cases individually, either."

"All these cases?" Martin mumbled, irritated. "Do the police have another . . . ?"

"Once the mailing that I have prepared for local funeral home operators goes out, we will certainly see an increase in demand. We will remain in a comfortable market situation at least for the duration of this heat wave. In such crises, the provider of a scarce commodity can dictate pricing and terms."

With that, Piggy Bank left.

"Business model?" Jochen asked.

"Does he want to . . . ?"

"Apparently that's exactly what he wants," Katrin whispered in shock. "He is renting out our morgue drawers."

"That is an interesting idea," Birgit said that night when Martin told her about Piggy Bank's latest idea. They were sitting with Katrin and Gregor at an Italian place. "Rental income is a reasonable approach to seeing a return on the investment costs for the morgue drawers."

Now, I think Birgit is really great, but when she starts jabbering bankerese she becomes completely alien to me.

To make matters worse, now she was spouting the same garbage as Piggy Bank.

Katrin puckered her face in response.

"If you rent out number four, I want a say," I told Martin.

He winced. Apparently he hadn't noticed me until now.

"Return, investment costs, all of that may be appealing to a for-profit business, but the institute is a part of University Medical Center and attached to the DA's office and publicly funded," Martin told Birgit.

Go, Martin!

"But even public institutions would do well to leverage a financing option if one presents itself. The morgue drawers are there anyway, and if they sit empty they don't bring in any revenue for the institute," Birgit said.

"Or better yet: I'm going to permanently rent my drawer, for me," I suggested. "Then it won't be occupied all the time and I won't be homeless anymore."

"And how do you expect to pay the hundred euros a day?" Martin thought derisively.

"You'll pay it," I countered.

"Rental income or not, Martin's right," Gregor said. "The Institute for Forensic Medicine is a part of law enforcement. The bodies that end up at the institute are subject to the same rules as items kept in the evidence room at police headquarters, so the institute has to make sure no one has unauthorized access to the bodies. I doubt that part of its mission is compatible with renting out the morgue drawers."

Martin's guilty conscience about the absconded body reared its head again. And again he sent a pulse in my direction to see if I wouldn't mind performing pro bono guard duty for the institute.

I pretended not to hear anything.

"The whole thing is a big mess now," Katrin said. "And Piggy Bank isn't the least bit aware of these problems because he has no idea what forensic medicine entails." She took a big gulp of white wine and a droplet fell off her breath-fogged glass and landed on her big—

"Pull yourself together," Martin mentally shouted at me. "Your sexist thoughts really get on my nerves."

Spoilsport.

"Now don't get all upset about that guy again," Gregor said, kissing Katrin on the ear. "Let's forget all of today's crap and enjoy our evening. It's rare enough that all four of us are free at the same time. So let's switch to talking about something more pleasant." He turned to Martin and Birgit. "How are things going with your—"

Martin's foot slammed into Gregor's shin. Gregor stared at him uncomprehendingly. Katrin and Birgit hadn't noticed the kick and were staring at Gregor.

Martin blushed. "Uh, let's not talk about ourselves for the moment. Instead let's talk about—"

"The British royal family?" Gregor said. "What's up with you, man?"

I'd been wondering that myself. Something *was* up with Birgit and Martin that I wasn't supposed to know about.

"Just you wait," I thought in Martin's direction. "I'll get to the bottom of whatever you're up to soon enough."

———————

As it happened, I lost all interest in this mystery a short time later when I encountered *her*. The woman of my eternal limbo-life: *Irina*.

Irina was the granddaughter of Viktor Kvasterov, the new night watchman at the institute. It happened quite suddenly, because Gregor had asked the DA's office for an official response to renting out the morgue drawers. The DA, of course, initially thought Gregor was trying to bullshit him. Can't blame him. The DA's laughter quickly subsided, however, when Gregor pointed out that this was in fact the serious intention of the new director at the institute.

"How do you know this?" the DA had asked.

"Confidential source."

"But verified?"

"Hundred percent."

"Section something or other of the German Federal Code of Criminal Procedure blah blah blah"—you can't really expect me to remember details like that—"states that 'bodies of decedents taken into possession by a public prosecutor must be stored in a secure environment and free from exogenous influences. In addition, bodies of decedents involved in a criminal investigation must be kept strictly separate from bodies of decedents that are part of inquiries regarding contracts, torts, insurance, probate, or other matters of private law.' "

Gregor thanked him for the information. Only ten minutes later the DA was on the phone with Piggy Bank.

They agreed that an employee of the institute must oversee the admission of bodies and the assignment of morgue drawers at all times. During the day the coroner or dissectors on-site would do this; at night, Viktor would handle admissions.

———•———

"Mr. Kvasterov will be present at Forensic Medicine from eight o'clock at night until six o'clock in the morning," Piggy Bank announced to the assembled staff in the conference room shortly before six p.m. He was standing behind a short fat man in a dark gray cardigan over a white shirt, projecting his speech out over the short man's head. "I am sure he will settle in quickly with your help, and I assume you will all firmly and fully support Mr. Kvasterov. Thank you very much."

"Call me Viktor, please," Viktor mumbled with an unhappy expression on his face.

Meanwhile, Piggy Bank had managed to increase the speed at which he disappeared from these meetings, which he detested, to Warp 3. Only the soft schluff-schluff of his loafer tassels lingered for a moment more, and then the conference room was silent.

I studied Viktor in depth. He was at most one meter sixty tall, shorter than the average woman; he was at least sixty years old and had an impressive beer belly. His arms were powerful, but with the sweat seeping through his shirt and cardigan and dripping off his temples to his neck, he did not look like he was going to be teaching any shady characters the meaning of fear. In other words, if someone wanted to pinch a corpse from the Institute for Forensic Medicine anytime soon, he'd just give Viktor a one-two. That'd sideline him long enough that body snatching would be no problem.

"Yes, well, welcome, Mr. Kvasterov," Katrin said, standing up and walking over to Viktor with an outstretched hand.

"Call me Viktor, please. Thank you," Viktor whispered, bowing deeply. It looked like he wanted to press his thick, moist lips onto her hand. The image I got of him suctioned to Katrin's skin like a leech turned my stomach. Katrin as well, apparently, because she pulled her hand back.

"Have you already seen where you'll be working? Did Piggy—uh—Mr. Forch show you everything?"

"Yes, the director showed me everything. Thank you." Viktor beamed at her. He was missing his upper left canine; the right canine shone shiny silver.

Katrin came to a dead stop, unable to decide what to do next while the staff got up from their seats. "Yes, well, we'll be seeing you."

"Thank you," Viktor said, bowing before each person as they left the room. "See you soon."

Martin didn't need to ask me, because I naturally rocketed over and down into the Basement around nine that night to see what the new guy was up to. He was in the back corner waiting to admit bodies. He sat on a rickety, old wooden chair at a rickety, old wooden table drinking jet-black tea out of a thermos. He was just staring around, eyelids half closed.

A woman was sitting next to him at the table. She had her head bent over a book and was reading, as I verified with a quick strafe, a medical textbook. As I hovered over the nape of her neck, I was immediately enveloped in a cloud of her perfume. Not like Birgit's perfume, which smells like a meadow of wildflowers, and not like Katrin's, which reminds me of a mixture of spices at the Asian grocery. Irina's cloud was heavier, earthier. Like how it smells under the covers right after screwing. Or right before. In any case, no flowers, no spices, only *babe*. Strong. Seductive. She lifted her head. Which offered me the opportunity to gaze upon both her extremely prominent and shapely cheekbones as well as everything else that was shapely, from her neck on down. *Oh, man!* All the movie starlets with their silicone melons are nothing in the face of such pure, natural glory. And I saw exactly that in her at first glance. If Birgit is a sporty Audi S4 and Katrin a custom-tuned Mercedes S-Class, this woman was a Bugatti Veyron. Parked in the Basement at the Institute for Forensic Medicine. Amid the bodies. Kind of at my place, in a sense . . .

I swirled around her clockwise and then counterclockwise, flew slalom through her bare toes in her light sandals, brushed up her narrow calves and down her naked arms and got lost in her thick hair. I stayed right with her, this woman who had eyes only for her book, until she said good-bye to her grandfather with a kiss to his cheek. Oh, God, how I wished I could feel that delicate kiss!

When she left, I followed her to the train and up to her tiny apartment in a huge building. She apparently lived there with her grandfather. Two bedrooms, one bath, full kitchen, front hallway. A tiny bedroom for Viktor, the larger for Irina. But even the larger bedroom was small. This princess deserved a palace but instead lived in a shoebox. At least there was running water and electricity. I watched Irina in the shower, inhaled the minty aroma of her toothpaste, snuck my way in between her hand and skin as she put lotion on, and watched from over her bed until she fell asleep.

My self-diagnosis was unambiguous: from the moment I first saw Irina, I had fallen totally and undyingly in love.

THREE

I went to see Martin early the next morning at the institute to get information on Viktor and thus also Irina, but Gregor had beaten me there. He was taking his last few irritated strides toward Martin's desk as I arrived.

"And nothing else? Come on, Martin, you've got to have something for me. Otherwise we don't have even one lead."

Martin shrugged. "I've run the blood type, a DNA sample, and a toxicological analysis for you. All of that from a single trace of blood that was a few hours old and not especially easy to isolate. There just isn't any more I can do at this point."

Aha, the two of them were talking about the stolen corpse. Apparently the lab results were finally in.

"Then run the tests one more time."

"The deceased was male, undetermined age, most likely Asian."

"I already knew all that from the CSI who picked him up off the street."

"We found traces of drugs in the blood, but so far the tox screens haven't IDed the specific drugs yet."

"But you are able to discern a sort of ballpark, right? Like, was it an anti-inflammatory? Cough syrup? Viagra?"

"Things are pointing to a sedative or analgesic, but right now there are just more questions than answers. We ended up having only a very small amount of blood to work with.

I'm sorry, but I just can't provide you with any new information right now."

Gregor growled in dissatisfaction. "We have a murder and not only no suspects but no corpse anymore, either—even though we *did* have one. How am I supposed to solve a case like that?"

Martin shrugged. Guilty conscience.

"And what is the lab saying about the evidence from the woman whose skin was peeled off by our John Doe?" Gregor asked. "Our current theory is it's the same perp who stole the murder victim's body. Just give us *some* piece of information we can use to go and find him."

"Don't you have any fingerprints?" Martin asked.

"No, otherwise I wouldn't be here riding your ass, would I?"

Martin sighed. "The laboratory is overloaded, and two pieces of equipment haven't been working properly since the move," Martin said. "We sent out the DNA samples . . ."

Gregor groaned. "Geez, nothing is working right, now." He blew a kiss over to Katrin and vanished.

Finally it was my turn.

"What do you know about Viktor?" I asked Martin.

"Nothing."

"Bullshit. Out with it."

Martin sighed. "Mr. Forch hired him as night watchman. That's all I know about him."

Martin was by now probably the only person at the institute never to call Piggy Bank "Piggy Bank," instead always referring to him by his proper name.

"And Katrin? Does she know anything?"

"No idea."

"Then ask her."

"No."

"Yes."

Martin put on his headset and started quietly dictating his autopsy report again. "The insufficient provision of liquids over the course of several months consequently resulted in . . ."

"ASK KATRIN!" appeared on his screen.

As you can see, I have figured out how to dictate capital letters. I hadn't interloped on Martin's wireless headset while he was using his speech-recognition software for a long time. The two of us have a deal. I don't interrupt him with my blibber-blabber while he's dictating his reports, and in exchange he leaves his computer on at night when he goes home so I can write. This is how I managed to write a complete account about the circumstances of my death and the solution of my murder and the investigation into the death of Sister Marlene. And send it to a publisher. It's totally easy because Martin's speech-recognition software can control any computer program. I just say, "compose e-mail," and the little window opens automatically. Then I dictate my text. For example: "Hi there, folks. I'm sending you the report about my death and the investigation into my murder case, attached here as a text file. It's all the honest truth; you can verify anything you like. It'd be great if you'd make a fancy book out of it. Later, Alligator, Pascha." And, presto, down the pipe.

I digress. Anyway, Martin was pissed now that I had interrupted him with my chatter, so he'd turned pigheaded. Normally he sticks it out with me for a pretty long while, but this time he had the misfortune of Katrin appearing right behind him and looking over his shoulder at the screen. She turned pale.

Katrin and Gregor both know that I exist. It's a long story I don't care to repeat here. In any case, those two swore to each other that they would ignore the fact that I exist. Even with Martin. But now Katrin was in a tough situation. She stared at the screen, read my exhortation, "ASK KATRIN," right there in the middle of Martin's medical report, and apparently was struggling to regain her composure.

"What did you want to ask me, Martin?"

Martin hadn't noticed she was there yet, so he winced. "Nothing, nothing." He broke out in a cold sweat.

I was glad to finally be able to communicate with Katrin directly. "What do you know about Viktor?" I wrote.

"Why do you want to know?" Katrin asked, turning to Martin. Geez, why wasn't she talking directly with me? Or at least the screen. Instead she was watching Martin, who was wriggling in his chair like a cat being dangled by its tail.

"I don't want anything at all," Martin said. He was fumbling around frantically with his headset, but you can't just switch it off with a button—you need to dictate to the program that it should switch it off. And as long as I was clogging the pipeline, that wouldn't work.

"Tell me everything you know about him, especially about Irina," I wrote.

"Irina?" Martin and Katrin asked, as though from a single mouth.

"She's the most beautiful woman in the world. Her boobs are as big as yours, but somehow rounder. More like apples. Not as point—"

Katrin turned pale; Martin turned red. He hammered around on his keyboard as if it were full of cockroaches he needed to kill. The result appeared on his screen like this: wqrss094kmmovdpivjwöek3r1m-lovkjäÜoApiu#fj+q.w,e-pofßj?mv.

"What the hell do you know about . . ." Katrin mumbled.

Martin dropped his head into his hands.

"Everything," I wrote. "So, what's up with Viktor?"

Katrin took a deep breath, folded her arms in front of her body, and got a kind of cantankerous look on her face. Nonetheless, she answered, "Nothing. Amazing, right? Even though Piggy Bank has me doing almost all of the administrative paperwork around here, I haven't heard or seen one word about this night watchman. No application materials, no employment contract, nothing."

"And Irina?" I asked, although I had already given up hope on that angle.

"I'd never heard that name until about ten seconds ago."

The phone over on Katrin's desk rang. She went over, listened briefly, and said, "Yes, I'll be right there," and hung up. "Ugh, yet another suicide who threw himself in front of a train. This is starting to take on alarming proportions. I've got to head over to . . ." She looked around the room uncertainly, probably thinking she might actually see me somewhere. It's really a pity that the two of us will never be able to fully enjoy each other . . .

I ended up accompanying Katrin to the train stop, because watching Martin speechifying reports is the bleakest thing in the whole world. Especially when you're not allowed to disturb him—and I'd already dramatically exceeded my disturbance quota for the day.

A dilacerated body is always a pretty exhausting thing to investigate. A normal dead guy is just lying around someplace in one piece, two dudes come and pack him into his to-go container, and then it's off to the Basement with him. Even a guy who just wanted to let it all hang out merely has to be snipped down from the beam or branch or wherever he slung up his tender soul—and, boom, you're done.

But these train Tucos bring a whole new meaning to the term "spaghetti western," and they create a phenomenal amount of work and stress. Now, any railroad locomotive is basically a particle accelerator. By which I don't mean anything to do with Higgs bosons or particleboard—I mean body parts, *very small body parts*. So when a German Class 407 ICE 3 high-speed locomotive strikes a human body at three hundred twenty kilometers an hour, everything is strewn around in smithereens. A head here (usually exploded), an arm there, individual sections of various members and organs. Sometimes you have to pluck the individual vertebrae out of the bushes. I always like to come along when Martin has to do one of those scenes because I can effortlessly zoom through the brambles along the railroad embankment, guiding Martin to more and more pieces that went astray. But when there are only his colleagues present, this is frustrating. I'm always finding something but can't draw their attention to it. That's why I followed Katrin for a while, watching her gather every conceivable kind of small bit, crawling through the brush getting twigs stuck in her hair, helplessly watching the cops and her trudge past half a hand only a meter away without seeing it, even though their eyes were wide open. Frustrated, I soon gave up on this and flew back to Martin, hoping he'd finally finished his tedious report. And I was in luck. For once!

Birgit was in his office. She had pulled her hair up into a tight bun, and her dark suit turned Beautiful Birgit into Boring Bank Broad. But her laugh was the way it always was, and her eyes were beaming. She had laid out several print-outs in front of Martin and was pointing at one of them.

"This one looks quite nice, don't you think?"

Martin picked up the sheet of paper and studied it thoroughly. I did, too. It was an apartment listing.

"You two are going to move in together?" I asked Martin. "Hey, that's great. That way it'll be a little more like *Three's Company* instead of *The Odd Couple*. Things'd get pretty bleak if it were just the two of us over the long haul." *Particularly given that one of us is such a wet blanket*, I thought—but didn't let him hear.

Martin dropped the paper and rubbed his temples. "It's an apartment for *two* people," he thought.

"I don't need a bed or any space in the medicine cabinet," I replied.

Birgit looked at Martin, astonished. "Don't you like it?" she asked.

"Yes, yes, I do," he replied. "It's just, uh, maybe we should . . ."

The thought that he still had to solve that pesky problem of spook protection popped up in his brain.

"Do you like this one better? It's also closer to your current apartment. If you'd rather stay in the same neighborhood . . ."

Birgit held out the next sheet of paper to him, and Martin again looked only briefly at it.

"I think I'd need to see . . ." Martin began, adding in his thoughts . . . *if I can make the apartment radiation-safe.*

These thoughts brought me down from my good mood faster than a seized piston'll sap your accelerator. "Are you having some kind of a mental backfire or something? Do you seriously think that you can wrap your entire apartment in your weird electrosmog netting?" I asked. "What are you going to do about the windows? And the front door? All the cracks everywhere I'll still be able to come through. What is that going to cost you? And how are you going to explain all that shit to Birgit?"

"Yeah, going to see it in person is a good idea. Should I make an appointment with the landlord?" Birgit asked.

Martin nodded spiritlessly.

"Well, I can see you're up to your ears in work. So I'd better let you get back to it. See you tonight." Birgit gave Martin a tender kiss, gathered up all the rental printouts, and left the office humming and happy as can be. What did this ray of sunshine see in Martin, the eternal drama queen?

"I'm not a drama queen," he snarled. "But I don't want you to move in with us. I don't want you violating Birgit's privacy."

"She'll never know," I said.

Martin only groaned.

Katrin was finally back from the railroad suicide scene. She had scratches from the brambles on her arms, she was all sweaty, and she had a splotch of dirt on the back of her neck that she'd presumably missed when washing up. The skin on her arms up to her elbows was still red from scrubbing. At a lot of discovery sites, forensic pathologists wish they had gloves that went up to their elbows. But there's no such thing. That may be a market niche for someone to fill.

"That's true," Martin thought, surprised. "Sometimes we'd really like to . . ."

"Oh my God! Oh my God, is it hot out there," Katrin moaned. "We walked for kilometers along the railroad embankment in the blazing sun looking for bits of flesh. I am dead on my feet."

Martin immediately brought her a refreshing moist towelette (he always kept such things in his desk drawer) and a tall glass of peppermint iced tea. He had been keeping some on hand at the office because peppermint is cooling. Or so he said.

Before Katrin could drink the tea or open the moist towelette, her office landline rang.

"This is Dr. Zange," she said.

Pause.

"My apologies—I thought this was an internal call . . . Yes, this is the Institute for Forensic Medicine. I'm Dr. Zange."

Pause.

"You want to rent a refrigerated morgue drawer? Well, uh, I'm not . . ."

Responsible for rentals, she had wanted to say, but the caller, who I could now hear because I'd found a nice spot between the receiver and her ear, said, "But I was given your name by the director's executive assistant. Ms., uh, Blaustein? She said that you are handling morgue drawer requests."

Katrin closed her eyes and rubbed her free hand over her forehead. "I'm so sorry, but there must be some mistake.

I have nothing to do with administrative matters whatsoever. I'm a medical doctor."

"Well then, uh, hmm, I don't know either."

"Just a moment, I'll transfer you to the *administrative office*," Katrin said. She uttered those last two words as though they were a brand-new disease or a cross between a biblical locust and giant Amazonian leech.

Martin watched her with a frown.

Katrin pressed the hold button, dialed the admin office to transfer the call, and swore as she waited for them to pick up. "Why am I the only one singing the 'Lonesome Johnny Blues' around here? Does Piggy Bank actually do any work in this place, apart from making my life difficult?"

Martin looked the way he always looks when someone in his vicinity throws a tantrum—uncomfortable and unhappy. And Katrin was bursting into tantrums more and more often.

On the other end of the line, Ms. Blaustein picked up. "Hi, it's Katrin Zange in Forensic Medicine. I've got someone on the line who'd like to rent a morgue drawer."

I started listening in again. Ms. Blaustein said, "Mr. Forch said that you'll be handling morgue drawer rentals."

"He is mistaken," Katrin growled. She took the caller off hold to put her through to the assistant and then slammed the receiver back into the cradle.

"That poor woman can't help it," Jochen said from the doorway. In his hand he was holding a large table fan. Apparently he'd overheard the conversation.

"I can't, either," Katrin countered, grabbing her bag and jumping up. "I'll be over in the Basement in case *anyone's* looking for me. And, Jochen, if you've got another one of those fans, I'll take one, too."

Naturally Katrin had anticipated who would be coming to look for her next, and only thirty seconds after her Oscar-worthy exit, he was standing in the doorway of the office staring stupidly at Katrin's empty desk.

"Where is Dr. Zange?" Piggy Bank asked, in his suit jacket and tie as always. Not a drop of sweat, not even a hint of moisture, glistened upon his smooth, tan skin.

"In the Basement," Jochen said, now seated again at his own desk. "I think she has an autopsy."

"Perfect. Then she can show and explain everything right away to the funeral director who just rented one of the drawers in the morgue." He added, "And when she returns, have her come see me."

"I'll put a note on her desk," Jochen said.

"Thank you."

Martin watched Jochen calmly boot up his computer and then plug in and switch on the fan he'd brought.

"The note," Martin reminded him.

"I put it on her desk," Jochen said. "The fan must have blown it away."

Martin sighed. "Acting defiant doesn't accomplish anything."

"Yes, it does," Jochen said with a smirk. "It's satisfying."

———•———

I zoomed to Katrin and watched her autopsy first an over-dose and then the pieces from the railroad embankment. It was hard. During an autopsy, usually you start by doing an external examination of the body, noting any bruises, lacerations, lesions, puncture wounds, and things like that.

Every centimeter of the skin is inspected with meticulous precision. This takes a pretty long time because a human being has just under two square meters of surface area. While that's going on, the gunk from under the ends of the fingernails is also secured, in case the dead person died fighting and there might be DNA evidence from the perpetrator under the nails. Then comes the opening of the three primary body cavities: the abdominal cavity, the thoracic (or chest) cavity, and the cranium (or skull).

In the case of the railway embankment body, however, the cavities had been opened already. The skull was shattered, and the abdominal cavity was split crosswise to just above the hip (or innominate or coxal) bone. Even so, it was obvious that there was a long suture extending from top to bottom over the whole abdomen. A surgical scar, still quite fresh. No more than a few days old. Katrin opened the suture and determined that the right kidney had been previously removed surgically.

"Kidney removed?" the colleague assisting her asked. "Cancer or something?"

Katrin shrugged. "An accident during a boxing lesson, or he fell off a ladder onto a mop bucket, a biking accident . . . we've seen it all before."

She examined the other organs, some of which were lying on the table in several pieces. Then she got to the bladder.

"Huh. Have you ever seen something like this?" Katrin whispered.

Her colleague looked up from his voice recorder. "Eee! What happened there?"

Together they peered at the bladder, which still had a puddle of urine in it. The urine was green.

"What is the DA's office requesting?" she asked her colleague, who was dictating the report. There was way less construction noise today.

"PM and tox," her colleague replied.

The district attorney's office, DA for short, are the people who decide how meticulous the coroners (or forensic pathologists) should be when doing the postmortem examination (or PM) of a "patient," as they are ironically called. For instance, if the DA's office is hunting for illegal drugs or toxins, they'll request genetic and toxicological (or tox) exams.

"It's good they ordered the tox," said Katrin. "But why did that even occur to them?"

See, a tox exam is actually ordered only if they already suspect there are toxic substances in the body. They factor in any prior information about the circumstances of the death. All of that is evaluated by the DA, and then they incorporate everything into the scope of the examination being requested. This can be of dramatic help to the forensic pathologists in their work.

"Because the engineer operating the train told the police that the victim staggered over the tracks, disoriented. Either totally boozed up or stoned, or otherwise on drugs."

"Wait a sec," Katrin suddenly said. "The engineer gave a statement?" Engineers who pulverize people because they can't bring their thousand-metric-ton trains to a full stop in only twelve meters typically end up in shock and don't say anything at all.

"He even wanted to keep driving," the colleague mumbled under his face mask. "But then the pleasant police officer pointed out to him that the shock might manifest later on, and so it would be more responsible to leave the rest of the trip to another engineer."

"And then?" Katrin asked while trying to find out whether the shinbone (or tibia) she was holding in her hand was the right or left one.

"And then the engineer covered the cop's uniform in puke from collar to socks and keeled over."

"How do you know all of this?" Katrin asked. "I was on the railway embankment in person and didn't catch wind of any of this." She decided it was the left.

"The cop is my brother-in-law."

"So your poor sister is stuck getting that uniform clean again."

"Nah." The colleague grinned. "Section one of the prenuptial agreement: puke-covered uniforms are the sole responsibility of the wearer."

Good grief, women's lib is really getting out of hand.

"I'm sorry to bother you . . ." said a strange voice from behind them.

The scalpel in Katrin's hand made a wild incision along the corpse's calf as she jumped. "How did you get in here?" she barked at a man in a black suit standing in the door to the autopsy room.

"The door was open," he said, embarrassed.

Katrin slammed the scalpel down on the autopsy table and stormed in long strides over to the poor man and past the morgue drawers toward the basement-lobby door. The electric lock wasn't working. No juice to the reader thingy that unlocks the door when you hold an access card in front of it. A hearse had parked on the ramp with its rear end to the door.

"Are you Dr. Zange?" asked the bashful man who had snuck up behind Katrin. (Note to my editor: no one says *sneaked*! Stop it with the red pen!) "I was told to find you and . . ."

"Just a moment," Katrin said, spinning on her heels to go back inside, but the guy followed her in like a puppy dog until she turned on him. "If you wouldn't mind waiting outside? This isn't a train station here."

The poor creature bowed slightly and slinked outside. Katrin pulled her cell phone out of her bag and speed-dialed a number.

"I want to speak to Forch," she said shortly afterward.

I hurried to get into position in the curve of her neck. This was going to be interesting.

I think her colleague was hoping so as well, because he was leaning in the doorway to the autopsy room, arms folded, watching Katrin with raised eyebrows. "I wouldn't want to be in his shoes just now," he murmured.

"Mr. Forch? Dr. Zange. The lock on the door down here isn't working again and the door is open."

Her intonation made it sound like Piggy Bank had left the door open himself—which was unlikely since he rarely to never set foot in the autopsy section.

"I have no idea what you're talking about," Forch said, "but shouldn't we be discussing your problem in a slightly more businesslike tone?"

"This issue is not *my* problem, Mr. Forch. It is the problem of the Institute for Forensic Medicine, of which you are the director, are you not?"

Uh-oh. When Katrin starts getting all sarcastic, her colleagues typically start hiding under their desks. I briefly considered zooming over and looking to see where Forch was hunkering down.

"Well, if you could get to the point, Dr. Zange. This conversation has been extremely inefficient to this point."

Katrin's cheeks glowed. "The door to autopsy section is open to anyone who cares to stroll in here, and a person unknown to me did that just now. It poses a risk to every person who has to work here and constitutes an unacceptable situation given that the bodies we examine here are evidence in crimes."

"And so in your view I should do what?" I thought Piggy Bank's voice sounded slightly mocking.

"Explain to me why the electronic lock is not working. And ensure that it is not deactivated again."

"Well, I don't think that I should have to explain anything to you, certainly when you are addressing me in such a tone. And furthermore, since you *are* on-site, it would be much easier for you to go over to the construction area and ask the contractor if they've cut another wire. So I'll be expecting your report."

Piggy Bank hung up, and Katrin gasped for air like she'd just taken a four-hundred-meter free dive.

"First take a breath, and then tell me what he said," her colleague said.

But Katrin did not calm down first and started talking right away. This time my editor deleted all of *Katrin's* naughty words. I swear—I'm really just the chronicler in this case.

"If I'm not mistaken, there *is* a backup power supply for the refrigeration," the colleague said. "I always thought that the door-access system was wired into that, but evidently that's not so. Come on, let's go upstairs and see the construction workers and find out what they can tell us."

Katrin's appearance in the realm of strong men with thick jackhammers created a bit of a stir. She had taken off her lab coat, and in her gauzy blouse and white linen pants she was hopping over the construction materials scattered everywhere. The workers whistled after her, making suggestive remarks and laughing, until Katrin flashed an unambiguous hand gesture at them. She denied herself a smile, but I could tell she was enjoying her performance.

Chicks just want to be hit on; it turns them on. *I knew it.*

"You've instantly made twelve strong friends," the contractor said, greeting Katrin with a wide grin. He was wearing jeans whose original color was presumably blue and a finely ribbed, olive-green wifebeater. He was kind of built like my favorite movie hero and even had a bright, multicolored snake tattoo that wound its way from shoulder to wrist on his left arm. Katrin gazed in fascination at this splendid slab of man, speechless for a moment.

"Hi, there," Katrin's colleague said, quickly jumping in. "Say, the electronic lock to the basement-lobby door downstairs is out again. Any idea why?" I was guessing he shared my worry that Katrin, given her mood, would pick a fight right off the bat with Mr. Cement Head here.

However, Cement Head did not give the impression that he was particularly upsettable. Certainly not by a woman, not even one standing before him with clenched fists and fury sparking from her eyes.

"Um, yeah. We cut the juice to the basement."

"Oh, just like that?" Katrin asked.

Cement Head smirked. "Yeah, imagine that, honey: just like that. You know we're *working* up here."

"We are too," Katrin retorted toxically. She was still under high voltage and looked about a millisecond away from taking the gorilla down. I wasn't sure who I'd bet on, frankly.

Cement Head shrugged. "We can reconnect the line in about an hour, so the lights'll be off until then. But that's what your backup power generators are for, right?"

"But the security system for the door . . ." Katrin's colleague objected.

"Oh, right!" Cement Head said, slapping his sweaty forehead with his hand—which was as big and dirty as the hubcap on an Audi Quattro fresh off the dirt roads at Rally Finland. "Now I see your problem. All right: Originally there were three separate backup power systems here. One for refrigeration, one for exterior door security, and one for air-conditioning and lighting. Our original contract was to swap out all three backup power systems for new ones. We've completed the backups for refrigeration and air-conditioning, but the contract for the third system was canceled."

Katrin's shoulders sagged. "By whom?" she asked, resigned. She already knew the answer.

"A Mr. Forch. He has final say in your shop, eh?"

Katrin and her colleague looked at each other, dispirited.

"But why . . . ?"

"He asked us how often we anticipated having to cut the power, or how often the backup power would need to be started up. We estimated two to three days per month. I think he said something like, uh, it wouldn't be 'efficient,' whatever that means."

"But you've already switched it off more than . . ."

"Well, honey . . ." He leaned back and folded his massive guns over his massive pecs. His forearms were as thick as my thigh had been, and as he moved his tattooed arms, the snake seemed to snap to life. Katrin gaped at the snake's wide-open jaw, as though she expected it to strike at any moment.

"It's pretty hard to accurately estimate how often we're going to have to cut the power in advance. Whenever you tear up some old joint like this, there're always going to be surprises."

"Did you give him your estimate of two to three days in writing?" Katrin's colleague asked.

"I may look like a lot of muscle and not much brains," Cement Head said with a smile and a bicep flex that made the snake dart its tongue at Katrin, "but even I'm not that stupid."

———•———

"That is most unconscionable, indeed," Martin said.

God, the words that guy knows! *Unconscionable?* I mean, when is the last time you said *unconscionable?* Anyway, what Martin was referring to was that Piggy Bank wasn't merely tolerating the lack of safety for the institute's employees and security for their clients' bodies but also actually *causing* it. (That's pretty fancy syntax there, huh? I've been getting quite familiar with professional communication now that I'm in the investigation business.)

"If that has been kept from the insurance company . . ." Jochen said, trailing off into silence.

The mood in the office went to hell again, and it felt like hell, too. Jochen's stench stirrer, a.k.a. fan, was pointlessly shifting the hot air in the room back and forth, but the mercury in the room never actually fell below hot-tub temperature.

"Phew, I do not envy you," Katrin said to Martin as they all powered down their computers, although Martin of course only pretended to. "And then going apartment hunting in heat like this . . ."

Martin winced because he would have preferred that topic to remain unmentioned in my presence.

"Aha," I chimed in. "What time is your appointment to look at the place? And where is it? I'm coming along. After all I want to take a look at my new pad, too."

"You are not coming along, and you are not moving in with us," Martin thought.

"But I'm part of the family."

"No, you're not. You're not part of mine or of Birgit's."

"We'll see about that," I replied defiantly.

It was of course a pain that he didn't tell me the time of the appointment, because now I had to tail him when he left the office. Martin got into his trash can, flapped up all the windows—you knew that 2CVs don't have roll-up windows, right?—and drove his creaking dinghy on wheels back to his apartment, where he met Birgit. They went upstairs, Martin changed, and then they got going. Hand in hand they walked down the street to Birgit's BMW. Past the pub where we had celebrated my birthday.

"Well, hello there! It's our noble benefactor," said a husky voice from behind Martin. A hand with fingernails painted bright red and decorated with tiny, twinkling cubic zirconia came to rest on Martin's upper arm. He looked back over his shoulder and jumped when he saw who it was.

"Uh, I think you've confused me for someone else," he mumbled.

Birgit had now turned around as well and looked at the only very scantily clad peroxide blonde who had gotten Martin to treat her to a few drinks the other night on the occasion of my birthday. Saskia. From TV.

"No way, sweetie! Say, why haven't I seen you back at the pub again? Or why haven't you stopped by for visit at my place? You did specifically ask me for my address . . ." She gave Martin a coquettish wink.

Martin blushed. Birgit eyed the slut with a mixture of interest and amazement.

"Really, you must have . . ."

"It was last week on Tuesday, and I wasn't drunk or high or anything else. I remember exactly what you were wearing. Like the shirt you have on now, only light blue."

Martin was wearing one of his favorite shirts: a short-sleeved shirt in a red-and-white kitchen-towel checker pattern.

Now that got Birgit's attention.

"Well, unfortunately I have to get going now," Martin said, taking the blonde's hand off his upper arm and pulling Birgit with him.

"Last Tuesday?" Birgit said. "The light blue checkered shirt? That was the night you suddenly had to leave at some ungodly hour and then smelled like pub the next day. Did you and your colleagues go out for a drink there?"

"Um . . ." Martin began.

"Now's your chance," I yelled. "Tell her about me. It was my birthday, man. I know she'll understand that you wanted to celebrate your best friend's . . ."

"*No*," Martin growled. Audibly.

"What, 'no'?" Birgit asked. She looked confused and not exactly cheerful, but not really angry either. Boy, she is a really extraordinary chick.

"*No* means he thinks he can lie to you for the rest of his life!" I yelled. Unfortunately, Birgit obviously couldn't hear me. "He thinks he can move in with you, marry you, have bonsai Birgits with you, grow old together with you—as old as his brain is right now—but *lie* to you the whole frigging time."

Martin began to shiver, even though it was still screaming hot out.

"Are you feeling OK?" Birgit asked.

"Everything's fine," Martin managed. They'd arrived at Birgit's cool convertible. "Well, let's go see if we can find ourselves a nice apartment."

His smile failed miserably, but Birgit planted a kiss on his cheek all the same. "I'm really happy we'll be moving in together soon."

I had to leave the two of them alone since it was already half past seven, which meant Viktor was going to go on duty soon—and with him, I was hoping, Irina. I definitely did not want to miss even one second of her, and so I zoomed over to the autopsy section.

Irina didn't show up until nine. For an entire, interminable hour I watched Viktor do *embroidery*. He had this huge, white cloth that could have been a sheet or a tablecloth, and white yarn that he was using to embroider a white pattern.

Every so often he would snip holes into the part of the cloth he had finished embroidering. He held the cloth over his dark trousers to make sure the dark material showed through the flower-shaped holes. I was stunned.

When Irina arrived, he put his embroidery away and beamed happily at her. I think we were both relieved. Me, because I didn't have to watch a grown man embroidering little white flowers onto a white cloth with white yarn anymore, and Viktor, because Irina had brought him his tea in a thermos.

"How was your day today, apple of my eye?" Viktor asked as Irina kissed him on the forehead.

"Fine, *Dyedulya*." (I'd originally written what I'd heard, which was namely *Jedoolia*, but my editor scrounged up an actual Russian translator who explained how to correctly transliterate what turns out to be an affectionate nickname for "grandpa.") "I got to assist on a very interesting operation, and I spent all afternoon at the doctor's office. They see some really amazing cases there."

"That's wonderful, Irotshka. I am vəəəry proud of you!" (Now that's my spelling, not the translator's. Clever, huh? And I should point out that, "I am vəəəry proud of you!" was *actually* Viktor's trademark phrase—even more so than, "Call me Viktor, please.")

Irina told him a few anecdotes from University Medical Center, where she was studying to be a doctor. Which meant she'd already been to college. Hmm, she had to be older than I'd thought. I couldn't totally make sense of their conversation because she was obviously not giving much context, since her grandpa already knew all that. Makes sense. Nevertheless, I drank her in, word by word, from her lovely, full, curved lips. I hung myself from her long, silky eye-lashes, the delicate little hairs tickling as though someone were running a down feather over me. I floated along her ears and studied every millimeter of the M-shaped hairline along the back of her neck. I perched in the curve of her neck, peering down her knocker knoll and snuggling into the small hollow where her collarbones met. Not a word she said escaped my notice. She had so little accent that you'd hardly have noticed it if you weren't watching her talk with Viktor. Her voice was low, just like her laugh, which jostled me slightly in my perch. So soothing . . . I'd never been able to tolerate the shrill screeching of some women.

"Do you have enough money?" Viktor asked her.

"Of course," she replied quickly. "You know I don't need anything."

Viktor nodded in relief and said once again he was "vəəəry proud" of her—and I was speechless. A chick who had enough money—I've never actually heard of such a thing. In evolutionary terms that is a whole new species. If I ever find myself in heaven and run into Charles Darwin, I'm going to tell him about this.

My excitement revved. For most of the rest of the night I forgot everything around me and had eyes and ears only for Irina: Irina the beautiful, Irina the noble, Irina the pure. I mean, there were other OK women, too—Katrin was hot, Birgit was totally groovy—but Irina was an angel. And I was pretty sure that the Good Lord, or whoever, had sent her just for me.

Viktor and Irina were interrupted twice. Once, the police brought in a new admit, and another time a funeral director came. The funeral director stared at Irina with

a nauseating lecherousness in his eyes. He'd almost completely slavered himself in drool. Upstairs and downstairs, if
you know what I mean. (My editor says that this hint should
be "abundantly and entirely" sufficient.)

"Fuck off, compost worm," I roared at him. (Now at this
point my editor noted in the margin of the manuscript that
I had surely meant to say "carrion beetle" or "burying beetle," and not "compost worm," but I'm not writing some kind
of update to *Brehm's Life of Animals* here, just so everyone
knows.) This guy was pissing me off with the drippy, thirsty
look on his face, complete with his tongue lolling out.

Viktor had him fill out the rental form; Irina helped him
copy the right morgue drawer number from the list of available drawers onto the form and then deleted the number
from the list. Finally, they stood side by side, supervising the
new tenant's move into its new home. The Worm had to take
his coffin back with him; coffin storage costs extra.

All of that was of marginal interest to me, and then only
to the extent that Irina was helping out her gramps. What
a woman! When she left the basement around midnight, I
went with her, following her through the dark streets, riding the streetcar with her for five stations, flying next to her
as she took long, firm strides home; and I perched on her
bedstead as she fell asleep. Then, all churned up inside, I
raced through the city, which seemed at once dirty, loud,
and full of humanity's basest instincts. I, by contrast, rev-
eled in pure, radiant, incandescent love. I was in the mood
for—poetry. There had to be words to describe my feelings.
To describe Irina's beauty. Words that I might like to say to
her or write to her at some point. I rocketed over to Martin's
office.

He'd left his computer on standby and his headset ready, as usual. I thought the designated command that woke the computer up and activated the speech-recognition software: "Wake up!"

Then I created a new text file, named it IRINA.txt, and stared at the blank page.

"Loving this angel at very first glance, Exciting flutterings deep in my . . ." was my first idea, which I rejected right away. It was nowhere near pure enough.

"O love of mine, Irina, thy tongue's tunes delight this dreamah."

That's better.

I spent hours versifying without coming up with anything I thought good enough to recite to her (or to have someone recite to her, since she can't hear me, of course). Or write to her. Somewhat disillusioned, I left the office and spent the hours until the start of Martin's workday in a strange state of restlessness that carried me, drifting through the whole city.

I was in love.

FOUR

"You've got to do me a favor," I told Martin as soon as he got to work. "You've got to . . ."

"There is nothing whatsoever that I've *got* to do," Martin countered.

God, sometimes it's really tiring always being dependent on someone like Martin. Like now, for example.

"This is really an absolutely exceptional situation," I said. "I . . . I'm in love!"

He stopped short, midmovement.

"In love?" he asked, so shocked and disbelieving as though, should anyone inquire, he would deny that I had even a limited capacity for sensitivity. As though I were a fleeting fog lingering over a meadow in autumn only to dissolve once struck by sunshine.

But I'm Pascha, a man in the prime of his afterlife and, in contrast to Martin, not impaired by a hormonal-drive disorder. I had fallen in love. Normal, right?

Martin had apparently gotten wind of my aggrieved swirl of thoughts because he then asked, in the faux friendliness he adopts whenever I'm furious, "With whom are you in love?"

"Irina," I whispered. I *sang*. I *rejoiced*.

"Irina?"

"Viktor's granddaughter. She keeps him company every night for a couple of hours while he's on night duty in the Basement. She brings him tea . . ."

A woman had never made me tea. Not anymore, anyway, ever since that time my mother tried to cure my first drunken stupor at the age of twelve with chamomile tea. I ended up puking piss-yellow, lukewarm water all over my bedroom.

Martin's gray matter was working overtime. *Is she single? Is it conceivable for Pascha to permanently latch onto this woman? Can I get rid of him this way?* This was of course complete nonsense, because as long as I can't communicate with anyone except Martin, I have no choice but to spend tons of time with him. Otherwise things'd look totally bleak for me. But I really held back so he couldn't read my thoughts.

"OK, so what do you want from me?" Oddly, he didn't sound as negative now.

"You've got to find out every possible thing about Irina," I said. "And about Viktor. At least as it relates to Irina. I mean, things like where do the two of them come from? Are Irina's parents still alive? How long has she been in Germany? Does she have a boyfriend? Has she ever had a boyfriend? Why'd she give him the boot? What does she like? Fast cars, chocolate, Crimean champagne . . . everything!"

Martin had wrinkled his eyebrows, trying to memorize my laundry list. "But if she's only there in the evening or at night, then I won't ever see her," he objected.

"Then just stop by tonight," I said.

Martin sighed. "But today is Friday and I wanted to take Birgit—"

"Another time."

He thought briefly of not doing it, but soon grasped that he'd get rid of me quickest by getting the information I wanted as fast as possible, and so he agreed. I remembered that Irina was doing whatever medical program at UMC to become a doctor, so I raced over to the university to look for her.

But I couldn't find her. In this throng of people, in this bustling bevy, half of whom were wearing white doctor's coats and face masks, how in the hell was I supposed to pick out one individual woman? Especially when I had no idea where to start looking? I zoomed through every corridor, in and out of every patient room, into an operating room— some blood sprayed right through me, which I found *nasty*, so I quickly put the kibosh on that approach; perhaps you remember my dislike of hospitals. So, I was torn. On the one hand, I was looking right where she should be, but on the other hand this place was total hell. I knew Martin and Katrin had three autopsies on their schedule that day, so I whooshed over to the Basement at the institute instead to see what they were up to.

Katrin was going off like a rocket, as usual. "I'm going to write a letter of complaint to the DA and demand that Piggy Bank immediately disappear from here and that we get a new, reasonable boss," she was grumbling at Martin as she slammed one of the morgue drawers so hard that I preferred not imagining how the body inside had been tossed around. That autopsy report would undoubtedly later read, "Evidence of postmortem blunt force trauma from impact against board-shaped object."

Martin was holding a list and standing next to one of the other morgue drawers that he had just pulled open. He checked the number on the tag tied to the corpse's toe, and then he tried to find this number on his list. His pen moved slowly down past the rows of text all the way to the bottom and then back up again.

"And?" Katrin asked.

"It's not on the current inventory. Strange."

"And the body we're looking for isn't in the drawer specified."

"What conclusion can we draw from this?" Martin asked.

"There must have been a mix-up and someone picked up the wrong body," Katrin mumbled. She crossed her arms, leaned back against the wall, and turned pale. "My God, this kind of thing just cannot happen. Never. Not even if we were melting in the heat of Death Valley at high noon in August."

"We had better do another sweep of all the morgue drawers," Martin said.

Although Katrin sighed, she nodded. "I'll start here at the upper left."

For a while all you could hear was stainless steel drawers being pulled out and clicking shut. Meanwhile, I was hanging out under the ceiling light, rooting for them to solve the riddle. I mean, if you're lying around here as a corpse, this whole experience is shocking enough by itself. But it's at least somewhat comforting to be treated as a human being, even if you're dead. So the idea of being stuck here having to watch these idiots jumble up their records and then lose track of who you are struck even me as creepy.

"Aha!" Katrin finally shouted. You could read the relief on her face. "Come over here and see if this is our man."

They both wiped the sweat off their foreheads once Martin finally confirmed they'd found their AWOL patient.

In the wrong drawer, yes, but still hale and hearty. If you can say that about a corpse. In addition to their documented clients, they also had a body whose toe tag had not been logged at all.

"We need to find out . . ." Martin began, but Katrin dismissed his thought with a wave of her hand.

"I'm not going to find out anything whatsoever, Martin. I'm on vacation starting tomorrow."

"I beg your pardon?" Martin asked in horror. "Who decided . . . ?"

"Piggy Bank, of course. He has no idea what's going on around here, so he signed my vacation request with a smile on his face, easy as pie."

"And you're leaving us?"

"Yes, I'm leaving all of you up shit's creek, all by yourselves," Katrin responded defiantly. "I've got to get out of here before I either stab Piggy Bank or keel over dead, myself. Gregor's been feeling the same way—he convinced his boss he was in desperate need of some time off, too. We're flying to Sweden last minute for two weeks. A lake, a couple of moose, and the two of us. No bodies, no Piggy Bank, and no mixing up funeral home clients with our own cases. And the maximum temperature will be a perfect twenty-one degrees Celsius."

Martin slouched in resignation. "I understand. Well, come on, let's finish the last two autopsies, and then I'll be the first to wish you *bon voyage*." He tried to force a smile and failed miserably.

I felt sorry for him.

"Here's the tox report on the railroad embankment guy," Katrin said. She added the folder to the stack on Martin's desk. There were several yellow sticky notes on each folder.

Martin skimmed each of the notes while also quickly taking in Katrin's additional explanations, and he grew paler and paler. Birgit had already called and asked when he was going to get off work, but in addition to his assignment from me to stop and check in with Irina later, he now had the awesome excuse of Katrin's vacation, which was forcing him to put in overtime, so Birgit went out with a friend for gelato instead.

"They did end up finding some pharmaceutical residues," Katrin said, "but they're not sure what exactly they are. Perhaps a sedative . . ."

"What? The same as with the missing corpse?" Martin asked.

"Who knows. Maybe it's a good thing that all of these cases are landing on your plate now," Katrin said with a wicked smile.

"Go ahead and laugh," Martin said, adding a friendly wink. "All right, now off with you. Have a fantastic trip."

He hugged her the way you would hug a snowman if you were out for a walk naked in the winter and happened to run into one. That is to say, with as much of a gap in between you as possible.

Personally I'd have . . .

"I thought all you'd been dreaming about is Irina," Martin thought snidely.

"Don't let Piggy Bank burn you out," Katrin said by way of good-bye, and then she was gone.

Martin picked up the case files on the deaths with the strange traces of pharmaceuticals and read each autopsy report and each tox report twice, word by word. "Conscientiously" is what you call that, my editor says. If she says so. Anyway, there were two cases: Katrin's railroad guy, and the guy who was admitted with a stab wound but stolen again that same night. The toxicologists hadn't been able narrow down the active substances far enough yet, but in both cases there was some kind of anesthetic with a "short elimination half-life." Whatever that means.

Around a quarter to nine I said, "Let's put this aside for now and head over to the Basement."

It always makes me nervous when Martin is reading, because he can read for hours upon hours, motionless like a salamander during its winter hibernation. But right now I was especially impatient because I wanted to finally see Irina again.

"So spirit your way on over there, already."

"No, you're coming with me."

"Fine, but you're not riding with me," Martin said.

See, I'd been banned from the 2CV ever since I recently disparaged the swaying trash can itself, criticized Martin's driving of it, and impugned the masculinity of trash can drivers generally.

"I'll fly behind you," I promised. As long as he finally got going.

At nine o'clock on the dot Martin arrived at the Basement. Viktor smiled warmly through the gap in his teeth at him, but there wasn't another soul in sight—Irina or anyone else.

"Uh, I, uh, wanted to stop by and see how things are going for you here, Mr. Kvasterov," Martin said.

"Call me Viktor, please."

"Oh, uh, yes."

"Yes, fine, fine. I have everything I need." Viktor pointed to the rickety wooden table with his embroidery, thermos of tea, and cup.

"Ask him where Irina is," I urged Martin.

"Aren't you bored down here alone all night?"

"No, not a problem. I have my needlework."

"Ask about Irina," I repeated somewhat more loudly.

"But no company," Martin tried.

"*Irina!*" I roared.

Martin winced. "I thought I noticed a young lady in here yesterday or the night before last, didn't I?"

Viktor's eyes widened. "You saw? This is allowed, yes? She is Irina, my granddaughter. Good child. Vəry good child. She is doing her residency at UMC and is already working as an aide at a doctor's office. Really, a vəry, vəəry good child. I am vəəəry proud."

"It's nice that you're not all alone here, then," Martin said, and he genuinely meant it. "Is she coming tonight as well?"

"Not tonight," Viktor said. "Unfortunately. But she is a young woman, it's Friday night, she goes out with friends."

A feeling of panic came over me. "Where is she going tonight?"

"Oh," Martin said. "Uh, then I guess I won't be able to meet her today."

"Not today, unfortunately," Viktor answered, shrugging regretfully.

"Where is she going?" I repeated.

"What are the young people up to this evening then?" Martin asked, trying and failing to be all nonchalant.

"Oh, she says she is out with some of the other residents. I do not approve of a young woman going out with people I do not know." He shrugged again, but this time it looked more like an apology. "But Irina says I must let her have some liberty, too."

Freedom, Martin mentally corrected him.

My God, Martin was a smart-ass.

"Well, then, have a good night," Martin said, turning to the door.

"Hey, just a second. You can still find out a few things about her life, at least."

Martin didn't even have to ask because Viktor had already started sharing, unsolicited. "You know, Irina doesn't have it very easy in life. Her parents are . . ." He cleared his throat. "Her mother, my beloved daughter, is dead. Father . . . well. I took her out of Russia . . ."

Father . . . well. What was that supposed to mean? Did the father bail on them? Or didn't Viktor like him? Or was he an unemployed painter, street artist, musician—or, worse yet, a poet?

"What's up with the father?" I asked.

"I can't ask him so directly," Martin protested. "It's none of my business."

"But it *is* mine. So what's up with the father?"

"It's also none of your business," Martin reprimanded me.

Fortunately Viktor was very forthcoming. "Irina's father, he does not have a good job. It would not have been good for Irina to grow up with him. So, I took her when she was ten, and I came here with her. In secret. To Germany. It is good here. Safe. Here Irina can live well. At the moment we do not have much money, but I have two jobs to help, and when she is done becoming a doctor, then she will lead a better life. I am vəəəry proud of Irina."

Martin nodded.

"Irina loves Germany. Everything is orderly and clean, the police are not corrupt, you can live here in peace."

Martin nodded again, this time impatiently. "I'm glad to hear it, Mr. Kvasterov, really . . ."

"Call me Viktor, please."

"And I look forward to stopping by next week to meet your granddaughter. But right now I have to get going."

Viktor winked conspiratorially at Martin. "Naturally, I understand. It is Friday evening, and you also have something planned. Do not worry about me. After all, I am here to keep watch. Good-bye."

Martin left the Basement for his trash can on wheels. I joined him because I wanted to be sure he got away from here safe and sound. It actually was a little creepy when the chop shop was quiet and empty. And not just because of the cemetery next door. Martin apparently didn't notice me because he was thinking, *I hope Pascha doesn't get wind that we're viewing an apartment tomorrow morning.*

I grinned. Virtually, obviously. I would be on-site punctually to stand at Martin's side as he toured the apartment.

But first, with yearning in my heart, I set out in search of Irina. She wasn't in her apartment or in any of the Russian clubs I knew, nor in Cologne's medieval Old Town, strolling along the Rhine under the stars. I was in no mood to revisit every pub and darkened movie theater filled with weeping chicks holding Kleenex instead of popcorn, so I gave up my search around midnight, totally depressed. I had found the woman of dreams, but she had fallen through my fingers. I felt lonelier than ever. The night was infinitely long and galactically boring, and the heat was getting to be too much, even for me.

The apartment the next morning was a hit. At least, that's what I thought. Birgit walked through the large, airy rooms, gazed out the tall windows at an actual patch of lawn, and beamed back at Martin again and again.

"The floor is quite fantastic—ship's deck hardwood," the agent rambled on, and Birgit's and Martin's eyes obediently turned downward.

"It's absolutely indestructible," the woman continued jabbering in a voice reminiscent of Homer Simpson on nitrous.

"It gives the room atmosphere and a cozy feel, don't you think?"

The cozy feel would not set in until after this whistling buoy was out of the tub, but actually she was right. This pad was a regular palace.

Martin waddled around with a woebegone expression, inspecting the size of the windows, the height of the ceilings, and the door to the balcony, and trying to imagine how he was going to seal the whole place off. Ghost-proof it. Against me. This was starting to piss me off.

"You can't get rid me," I told him.

He jumped in fright; apparently he hadn't noticed me before then. After the shock subsided, his face turned even more anxious.

"Don't you like the apartment?" Birgit asked, feeling insecure.

"No, yes I do," Martin stammered. "It's lovely."

"The high ceilings are great, don't you think? And the stucco rosette on the living room ceiling. It's so beautiful."

"Maybe I'll feel tingly when I rocket past it," I said. "Just a sec, let me just go test that right now . . ."

Martin suppressed a groan.

Birgit laid her hand on his arm. "What's wrong?"

"Nothing," Martin replied. "It's fine. I'm fine. But perhaps ceilings this high aren't ideal. Because of the heating costs. You know that all the heat rises and the floor stays cold unless you heat twice as much . . ."

"Well?"

The pout on Birgit's face pierced Martin right in the heart.

"Then again, maybe it won't be that bad . . ." he quickly added to reassure her, but not convincingly.

"Well, what do you say?" the agent asked. "I have a number of people interested in this property, so you should make up your minds quickly if you want the apartment."

Birgit gave Martin a radiant smile, with raised "Oh please" eyebrows and a "What do you say?" tilt to her head.

"Hmm, well, I can't just spontaneously . . ."

Birgit's shoulders sagged slightly. "No?"

"Um . . ."

"Thank you. We'll call you," Birgit told the agent, and then she said to Martin, "Come on, I'm taking you home.

I think maybe you're coming down with something. You're so pale."

I had to get out of this place, because otherwise I was going to get eye cancer from the misery oozing out around Martin. Birgit was plainly and simply the dream girl for Martin, the apartment was basically an affordable château, and Martin wanted the two of them to be happy together—just not with me. And he was apparently still hoping to find a way to swing that. He really had every reason to be happy now—he had a girlfriend living on the same plane of existence as he did, after all. I, by contrast, was an evanescent ghost who loved a woman made of solid, nicely shaped flesh and hot blood. Irina. Who still had not turned back up at her own apartment. My mood was starting to turn really foul.

I rocketed into Martin's office, where, as always, he had left his computer on for me. I connected to the Internet, went to the home page of a major search engine whose name I had better not mention (or so my editor advises me), and entered the name Kvasterov. I wanted to know everything about Irina. Was she on Facebook? Did she publish her most secret thoughts and wishes on a blog? Were there pictures of her online? Could I research her history and the history of her family? What was her cell number? Maybe I would eventually find the courage to just give her a call . . .

The search engine was operating at top form. Apparently every fifth vodka boozer in the world is named Kvasterov. I restricted the search by entering "Kvasterov," "Viktor," and "Cologne." Nothing. I went to the phone book site and entered the same data. Again, nothing. God, why hadn't I just made note of the street she lived on? "Kvasterov" and

"Irina." *Nada*. Unbelievable. Access to information is not exactly limited in Germany, after all. The cops here read your e-mail, listen to your phone calls, and know your bank balance better than you do—and then there's all those websites that publicly publish everyone's shoe size, sexual-performance rating, and pictures of wasted people dancing naked on the dining table—but somehow the Internet turned up exactly zilch about Irina.

There was nothing left to do besides shadow Viktor. That was not that difficult, because Saturday was apparently Viktor's laundry day. He had washed his wool socks by hand and was just hanging them on a line in his kitchen (!) when I arrived. Wool socks. During the worst heat wave that had hit the city of Cologne since the Middle Ages. A heat wave that had already claimed the lives of more than a hundred people in this county alone, if you believed the newspapers. Which everyone knows you shouldn't do, but who's going to come in and count the dead themselves?

It was already after five, and Viktor had now also washed a few pairs of underpants that must surely be listed as protected historical landmarks—the finely ribbed tighty-whitey kind with worn-out elastic and a functional fly—when the door swung open and Irina came in. Finally! She was apparently already familiar with the laundry line layout in the kitchen, because she didn't mention the unmentionables at all. But I couldn't tell whether she'd intentionally avoided looking. Which would be the normal impulse of a radiantly beautiful woman. To me, in any case, felted socks and baggy, farted-up underpants over the gas range do not convey the sense of warmth and security I expect inside my own abode. That could be mitigated expediently with just a few empty bottles of beer in the sink and a man-sized stack of pizza boxes next to the can for compostable waste. But Irina blinked her long, silky lashes, gave her little grandpa a kiss on his undoubtedly scratchy cheek, took her purchases out of her bag, and buttered a few slices of bread to have a late dinner of open-faced sandwiches with Viktor at the kitchen table.

"How was your trip?" Viktor asked.

"Nice, really, really nice," Irina answered with sparkling eyes. "We went up to the North Sea. The father of one my classmates has a vacation house up there." She did in fact look a bit tanner than she had yesterday, which made her even more appetizing.

Viktor looked sad. "Child, you know that you should not accept anything you cannot reciprocate."

What kind of logic was that? If you followed that advice you'd never get anywhere. Someone should quickly update Viktor on a few basic concepts of capitalism.

Irina laid her hand on his arm. She smiled. "Yes, you've taught me that, and it's good advice." (Bullshit!) "But I *was* able to reciprocate. I translated a medical journal article for him that ran in a Russian newspaper. If he had gone to a translation agency, he'd have been out of a few hundred euros."

Viktor beamed, cleared the empty plates, and washed them by hand with one of those mini neon-green toilet brushes, while Irina took a shower and changed. Guess who I decided to accompany?

Around six o'clock they both left the building together. Viktor had spruced himself up with a fresh red shirt pulled taut over his potbelly, and Irina was wearing jeans and a

T-shirt and no makeup, her hair tied back at the nape of her neck. She was definitely not planning on picking anyone up. And rightly so—she was my girl now, after all.

Their destination was the Russian expat club. Viktor scurried around the hall as chief cook and bottle washer while Irina helped out behind the bar. I didn't understand a word, of course, because everybody there was speaking Russian, but they gave Irina big smiles, which I could understand even without the words. Fortunately, the majority of the attendees were grizzled geezers and blubbery babushkas. Presumably the whole group of them were reveling in whatever shared memories, slurring out toasts or singing melancholy songs. No one was dancing that Cossack dance where the guys' knees keep collapsing like they have end-stage muscular dystrophy, but that was presumably because this crowd knew they'd never get back up again.

Irina tapped beer, slid vodka across the bar (in bottles! Shot glasses were nowhere to be seen in this crowd), and brewed charcoal-black tea in a strange contraption consisting of several stacked pots. How was she going to keep this level of activity up late into a Saturday tonight? *But that's fine,* I told myself. She couldn't get into any trouble here.

Until two young guys showed up and my practiced nose immediately smelled trouble. They were under thirty in flashy, pricey clothes, with watches they'd bought for either "two fitty" at the closest street corner or eight and a half thou in a small store with a doorbell and security. Or pinched from there—what do I know? They clearly worked out and had broad shoulders and narrow hips. They knew no one was going to pick a fight with them—but all the while probably hoped that some idiot might take a shot.

Irina's face seemed to darken when she saw them. They tried flirting with her, but all they got was an unambiguous brush-off. Still, Irina clearly knew the guys. Presumably only as regular shit-stirrers at the club, but maybe also because she knew them personally. Of course I didn't get what was really going on because they were all only speaking Russian with one another.

I kept my eyes on the two of them and would have followed them around after they left the club around midnight, too, if Irina hadn't been saddled with a pushy hundred-year-old, plastered off his rocker, proposing marriage to her. To everyone else there, this seemed unremarkable, since a number of men were jeering the old man good-naturedly while helping Viktor get the guy up off his knees. Finally everything was washed and put away, and the Saturday evening entertainment at the Russian expat club was finished. I accompanied Irina and Viktor home and perched upon Irina's nightstand until she fell asleep.

Irina worked on Sundays. Unlike almost anyone else in Germany, I might add. So I accompanied her to the hospital but didn't go in with her. I hate hospitals; I've mentioned that already, right? She spent that evening with a couple of female colleagues, first at a gelato café and then at the movies. When she went to bed around eleven, Viktor had already been snoring away in the next room for hours.

FIVE

"But who's filling in for Detective Sergeant Gregor Kreidler during his vacation?" Martin asked in a slightly irritated voice. He was stuck on the phone and annoyed when I floated into the office on Monday morning upon a soft cloud of pure, innocent love. Bodiless, selfless, undying love.

"No," Martin said into the phone. "I cannot tell you the name of the drug, but I can tell you the active substances, and then you will find . . ."

Martin rolled his eyes. That meant it had to be pretty bad, because while he's incredibly precise in his work, he never gets emotional. Rolled eyes bordered dangerously on a volcanic eruption for him.

"Listen, the body that was stolen from the autopsy section also had that substance in its blood, exactly like the suicide who had thrown himself in front of the train. In addition, I recall that we had a case like this a few months ago. A suicide after a surgical procedure, I think."

Brief pause, listening.

"I don't know whether you are still processing that older suicide case."

Pause.

"Under the current circumstances, I am quite certain, yes. Gregor Kreidler told me that you have not made any headway on the name of the deceased so far, and now I have a lead that might help someone find out his identity. So if you . . ."

He listened for a moment. "All right, yes, I will forward the tox results to you with a cover letter in which I refer to this possible connection again." He hung up emphatically.

Jochen blinked at him in surprise. "Are the police suddenly not interested in forensic leads anymore?"

"Well, Gregor's on vacation. Three of his colleagues called in sick this morning, and the others are just as dead tired as we are. And people in general seem to have grown dramatically more aggressive because of the heat, so the police and mental health officials are overwhelmed. At the moment apparently no one can deal with identifying one unknown deceased person whose body has gone missing."

"And the thing about the skin . . ."

"That case interests them even less."

"Oh, well." Jochen shrugged.

"But I have a terrible feeling about this pharmaceutical mixture, and if I'm right then we have a large number of similar cases still in-house," Martin said.

"I'm listening," Jochen said, moderately interested, though not enough to interrupt his own work.

"The tox lab found a mixture of drugs in the blood of two bodies over the past few days. In both cases, it's an anesthetic with propofol combined with a strong opioid painkiller. One of the bodies is a suicide who threw himself in front of the train. The other body was first killed and then stolen from our morgue."

"Anything else?"

"What do you know about general anesthesia?"

"Not much."

"General anesthesia consists of a sedative that immobilizes the patient, a narcotic or opioid that prevents pain sensation, and a muscle relaxant that allows the muscles to go limp."

Jochen nodded.

"The drug propofol is a so-called hypnotic or sleep-inducing agent and is commonly used in intravenous or injected anesthetic applications because it's relatively well tolerated and because the usual nausea after it wears off is significantly less pronounced than with an inhalational anesthetic. After prolonged application it can cause green-colored urine, which was key evidence for the tox lab in the railroad embankment case."

Jochen nodded politely.

"A few months ago, however, there was a theory going around in the medical journals that this anesthetic can trigger hallucinations or depression when combined with certain narcotics."

Now Jochen looked a bit more interested.

Martin raised two fingers and gave Jochen an urgent look. "Now we have two deceased with an almost-identical drug mix in their blood: one suicide, and one man who died in a knife fight . . ."

"So what exactly are you thinking? That we're facing a wave of suicides off of bridges and railroad embankments driven by post-op depression, or people whose hallucinations are getting out of control during wild knife fights?"

"Well, the way you phrase it, it does sound ridiculous."

"That's what I'm saying," Jochen said. "So write up your report and let the detectives do their work while you do yours. You've got more than enough on your plate."

"But if there really is a threat to the general public . . ."

"Man, Martin, once your report is written, your duty is done."

Martin shrugged but didn't abandon the idea. In professional matters he was a tough miniature Doberman that wouldn't let go once he got his jaws into something. And now he'd found something that aroused his suspicion. The words "anesthetic" and "post-op" were whirring around in his brain. *Post-op. Postoperative.* At that intersection, a new thought suddenly lit up: *If these people have been operated on shortly before their deaths they must also have been in a hospital. I will have to include that lead in my report for the detectives on the case because it could well be a means of identifying—*

Martin's landline rang. Jochen turned back to his own report, and Martin picked up the receiver. Piggy Bank summoned him to his office. Immediately.

"Mr. Gänsewein, thank you for coming right away."

Piggy Bank was again dressed to the nines and neat as a pin, whereas Martin had bands of sweat in his armpits and on his collar. Martin's office was fifteen degrees warmer than here in the supercooled Supercomputing Center.

Martin nodded, ill at ease. He still didn't know what the boss wanted from him. By contrast I had a clue, because I'd already flown behind Piggy Bank's desk and discovered something on his screen that didn't belong there.

An e-mail.

To martin.gaensewein@ifrm-koeln.de. But actually the e-mail was intended for me. It was from a publisher.

"Now, Mr. Gänsewein. Have you checked the inbox of your e-mail account today?" Piggy Bank asked.

Martin shook his head. "I haven't even g—"

"Then I can convey the good news to you myself." Piggy Bank crossed his left foot over his right knee and started rocking back and forth in his infernally expensive designer leather desk chair. "The publisher would like to publish your book."

"My book?" Martin asked hesitantly. Once again he was totally clueless.

"*My* book," I called to him. "They accepted my book! I'm going to be a writer—well, heck, I *am* a writer!"

Martin's face grew more and more confused. "What kind of book?" he asked me in thought.

"Well, my case, and the one with Marlene. You knew that I wrote them out . . ."

"Yes, your book." Piggy Bank tapped impatiently with the tips of his fingers on his left ankle. "Apparently you've invented a wild story about a ghost at an institute for forensic medicine who finds a woman's body in a car, and about a nun who burns to death in her convent—if I grasped the gist correctly from my quick perusal."

"You sent that to a publisher?" Martin asked me, aghast.

"Well, duh," I replied. "It's a fucking awesome story. Plus it's true. And this way the world will—"

"You see," Piggy Bank said as though to a three-year-old, "naturally you can live out your own artistic ambitions however you wish. But it really isn't acceptable for you to publish a tall tale like this as a factual report from the Institute of Forensic Medicine, nor for you to send e-mail about it from your institute account and using the institute's server."

"How does he know about all this?" I asked.

Martin seemed still unable to answer.

Piggy Bank looked questioningly at Martin. "Mr. Gänsewein, do you understand what I just said to you? Could you please respond?"

"Is Piggy Bank reading *all* of your e-mail?"

"*My* e-mail?" Martin thought in horror. "In this case it's *your* e-mail!"

"Well, the story's a lot more believable if it comes directly from a coroner at the institute," I continued. "That's why I used your address. Otherwise the chick at the publishing house will think I just made everything up."

Martin cleared his throat and put his hand to his forehead, covering his eyes. Slowly he said, "I don't know who is playing pranks here, but I can assure you that I have no aspirations to be a writer. Nor have I—"

"Now, Mr. Gänsewein, to borrow from the hobby writer's language of your own crime novel: all the evidence is against you, if I may say so."

Piggy Bank took great pleasure in the deliciousness of his own joke. *Hobby writer?* That from the yap of an effete, intellectually bereft coxcomb! I can wield a thesaurus with the best of them, asswipe.

Martin didn't say anything. He was wondering how he could have been so stupid as to let me have full access to his computer, and how he could have been even more stupid to believe my assurances that I was writing these reports only for myself, and how he could have been so absolutely, unfathomably brainless not to regularly check up on all the goings-on on his computer.

"I deleted the sent e-mail from its folder; you wouldn't have found it at all," I consoled him. My ambition was soaring on news of my impending posthumous career as a writer, so I couldn't exactly afford to be mad at Martin for all the nasty things he was suddenly thinking about me again.

"All right, Mr. Gänsewein. Basically this is how it is: the story naturally strikes me as rather far-fetched." (The guy has no idea!) "But it's apparently, uh, 'entertaining,' as the publisher writes." (Entertaining? This is the mind-blowingest megamurder story you'll ever read, so keep your stunted opinions to yourself, asshole!) "You may therefore publish it if you would like; the publisher does seem to be interested. But only under certain conditions, of course. First, all the names would have to be changed."

Martin nodded.

"And then I would have to require royalties from you on any income you earn from it."

Martin stared at Piggy Bank, stunned.

"Royalties?" he asked.

"Royalties?" I roared. "Has he been secretly huffing spray paint or something? He wants to earn money on my writing about *my* own deeply tragic, personal life story . . ."

"Naturally," replied Piggy Bank, unmoved. "If the name of the institute is mentioned and an incident from the institute's routine operations serves as the foundation of a novel, then it's obvious that the institute should have a stake in any revenue."

"Naturally," Martin whispered. He sounded exhausted. "Was that everything then?"

"In principle, yes," Piggy Bank said. "Naturally, I assume that I will also be mentioned in the acknowledgments."

Martin staggered out of his boss's office and made a bee-line for the break room, where he poured himself a glass of soy milk with extra calcium and magnesium from the fridge.

He had recently switched to this cholesterol- and lactose-free low-calorie bean slime, which Birgit had noticed with astonishment but without concern. Without concern because Martin guzzled only certified-organic free-range beans, of course. Not those genetic mutants taking over in Brazil's postrainforest agricultural era. I felt my esophagus do a loop-the-loop as he poured the snot-yellow liquid down his throat.

"You have abused my trust," he said as soon as he'd forced the first gulp down.

"Hey, we're going to be famous!"

"No one will take me seriously anymore if my name is connected with your sorry excuse for cut-and-paste writing."

"People will—"

"You have absolutely no idea what people will say," Martin roared, suddenly at full volume. "You've made my life into a living hell, but at least this hell has been my own private problem so far. If you publish this book I'll be a public laughingstock. I'll never be able to testify in court again as a coroner or expert witness, because all the lawyers and district attorneys and fingers will be pointing at me laughing. Birgit will leave me, I will lose my job, Katrin and Gregor will avoid me, and I can't even consider escaping by taking my own life for fear of ending up like you."

Martin stormed out of the break room in giant strides, maneuvering around Jochen in the middle of the corridor, who looked back at Martin in surprise, and snatching up his car keys and wallet from his desk.

"Martin," I called, whooshing behind him. "Martin, calm down. No one will be—"

"Shut your trap and fuck off," was the last thought he shared with me, still silently, before sealing all the hatches.

I let him go and slowly flew back to his office. In his haste, speedy Martin had forgotten to turn off the computer. I hovered in front of the screen and opened the e-mail from the publisher. Martin would calm down again, I thought, as I invoked the reply function. "Dear Ms. . . ."

Martin did not calm down. Not with me, in any case. He returned to the office two hours later, switched off the computer despite my protests, and then drove with Jochen to the Basement to do two autopsies. What he had been up to in the meantime I did not find out.

In the autopsy room, Martin had already opened the chest cavity of the body in front of him and lifted out the heart when someone started banging fiercely on the stainless steel door from outside. He was startled and reflexively squeezed the heart in his grip. The last remnant of blood that was left in it sprayed Jochen's face and hair.

"Aw, great," Jochen said, wiping the drops from the tip of his nose, glasses, forehead, and his antique-gray, shoulder-length rocker hair with the sleeve of his white jacket. "Typical case of high blood pressure."

Martin stared at him at first flabbergasted, and then he started to giggle. First only soft chortles and then less and less restrained. Finally tears of laughter were pouring down his cheeks, he doubled up over the body, and he had trouble keeping the heart from slipping out of his twitching hands. He couldn't stop. I was worried about his mental health. But Jochen was apparently not worried at all. He started giggling too.

As the two of them were laughing out loud, the door thundered again. Martin suddenly turned pale and serious.

"Open the door," Martin told Jochen. "I'll set the heart aside for now." He gave one more quiet chortle, like a baby burping, and then he pulled himself together.

"May we help you?" Jochen asked from the door.

There was a hearse backed up to the door on the ramp. The mole who had been pounding on the door bowed his head and looked up at Jochen. "Hello."

"Sorry, but the doorman is off today. Who shall I say is here?" Jochen asked, hiding his grin behind his face mask. Apparently this never-ending heat had permanently fried his noodle.

"I'd like to put a body into cold storage."

"Single or double?" Jochen asked through his nose. "Private bath, or shared? Continental breakfast, or breakfast and lunch?"

The mole forced a smile, but his eyes stayed on the floor. "Single, no extras, thank you."

"Very good, sir. If you would then be so kind as to write your contact information here."

Jochen and the bashful mole finished their paperwork, and then Jochen turned to Martin. "Would you help me for a second?"

"Of course."

Martin came and took hold of the head end of the gurney the body in the hearse was on.

"No, no, please don't bother—I'll do it!" the mole yelled in horror.

"The two of us have plenty of experience; we're a well-oiled machine," Jochen said and just pushed the small man aside, giving him a friendly nod, and hustled him back out the door. Martin and Jochen rolled the gurney in front of the intended morgue drawer and opened it.

The dead woman on the gurney was already prepared for her viewing and burial. She had some makeup on and was wearing a white summer dress. Her hands were folded over her stomach, and her hair was held off her forehead by a cheerfully colored hair band.

"Heave ho."

Together Martin and Jochen lifted the corpse into the drawer. Martin had touched the dead woman's shoulder and was now looking with interest at her neckline.

"Look at this; something's not right here," Martin said. He pointed to two tiny drops of blood that could be seen through her dress fabric on either side of her left breast.

"This is a rental corpse; there isn't anything wrong with it," Jochen said as he changed gloves and started walking back to the autopsy room.

Martin unbuttoned the dress.

"The implants are missing!" he cried after Jochen.

Jochen came back, looked at the body, and saw the thin incisions along the fold of skin below each breast. The way she was lying there, the grande dame was left with the tiniest tweakers imaginable, tatas so small you'd need to use nanotechnology to make a bra that would fit them. I mean, the waves of skin below her empty mini muffins looked like the tide coming in. She had enough yardage for three times her actual bust measurement.

"I see nothing—*nothing*!" Jochen said, bending over the body and redoing the buttons.

Martin stared at him.

"But her, uh, breast implants are missing . . ." Martin whispered.

"Everyone keeps some kind of souvenir of his darling," Jochen said. "A pocket watch, a lock of hair . . ."

"But this is . . ."

Jochen finished rebuttoning, vigorously shut the morgue drawer, returned to the door, and as he was about to open it, turned back to Martin. "Whatever this is, I want nothing to do with it," he declared, now very seriously. "I think Katrin already knows and that's why she got the hell out of here. And I'm going to handle it similarly: I do my job, but otherwise I keep my eyes and ears shut tight."

"But we can't just . . ." Martin mumbled.

"Yes, we can," Jochen said. "My employment contract does not specify anything about investigating every single rental corpse that comes in for irregularities." He stopped short. "My employment contract doesn't specify *anything* at all about rental corpses. If Piggy Bank wants to rent out morgue drawers, he can go right ahead. I will accept the bodies when necessary, but no more. I definitely do not feel like running after Piggy Bank everywhere, mopping up the psychotic shit that's dripping out the cuffs of his pants."

Aw, yeah! I made a mental note of that expression.

"All right," Martin said. "Well, let's finish the autopsy before yet another crisis befalls us."

In his confused, aggrieved, and scattered state, Martin let down his psychic wall just enough for me to follow his thoughts, which were not exactly casting Jochen in a positive light. Martin was wondering if Jochen had lost interest in his profession. And in solidarity with his colleagues. Or, worse yet, if he'd had something to do with the peculiar events of late at the institute. With the stolen skin? Or had he at least covered up for the thief? Like just now with the silicone implants?

"Give it a rest," I warned Martin. "Just because Jochen has a healthy instinct for self-preservation . . ."

"Oh, well, now that's something I know *you* can talk shop about with him," Martin shot back.

Man, oh, man, was he still hopping mad. But Jochen's approach did strike me as more sensible.

"Martin, come back down to earth, OK? First of all, life won't get any better if you guys start going at each other's throats, and plus I wrote the publisher . . ."

"I'm not interested in that now."

Fine, we'll just wait until later, I thought.

"I have my doubts I'll be interested in it later, either."

"I wasn't talking to you, Martin. I'm going to leave you alone right now until your blood pressure comes back down and we can have a conversation like two reasonable people."

That only pissed Martin off more. "You would dare to speak to me as though I were a defiant child?" He checked out from our conversation, his nerves shot to pieces.

He was right—normally this dialogue had always played exactly vice versa. *Strange . . .* I thought. *Can a ghost become more mature?*

———

Monday night at eight, Viktor showed up to work as usual in his cardigan with his embroidery. Irina came at nine. Finally! I hadn't seen her for almost twenty hours, and I thought she had grown even more beautiful in that time.

She set out the thermos of tea for her grandfather, pulled some books out of her bag, and sat down with him.

"How was your day, child?" Viktor asked.

"Fine, Grandpa. And yours?"

"Thank you, fine, as always. I saw a woman on TV again . . ."

TV, yes, that would also be an option for Irina. With her looks, she could be an actress. Play a doctor, for example. Or, if she really wants to be a serious professional, she could also create a medical show. Like that judge who plays herself.

My mental digressions meant I was no longer following her conversation, and I was surprised to find that it suddenly became quiet. Irina studied, Viktor embroidered. Shit. Now I'd learned nothing about her. And nothing about Viktor, who was apparently a TV celeb fetishist. And since Martin was still pissed, I didn't think he'd be coming by to visit them tonight. To the contrary. He wanted to view another apartment with Birgit and hadn't even given me an opportunity to talk about my e-mail to the publisher with him.

Irina left her grandfather around eleven, and of course I followed her home. All gentlemanlike. She had hardly walked in the door when her cell rang. At eleven thirty at night. I was excited to see who was calling at this hour.

Unfortunately I was unable to answer this question since Irina was speaking Russian. Oh, well, probably a friend. I zoomed closer to her cell phone, where of course I also came up close to her beautifully curved neck and her silky hair and . . .

The voice belonged either to a Russian woman with a considerable vocal cord disorder or—more likely—to a man.

This fact tore me rather abruptly out of my romantic musings and back to reality. I didn't want her talking to a man. Except her grandpa, and she spoke German with him. I hated the guy blabbing into Irina's ear with all my heart. Not just because I can't stand Russians. Those guys have caused a fair amount of trouble in my industry, so even when I was alive I was not favorably disposed to talking to them. But a man calling my Irina in the middle of the night totally pissed me off. Although, as I suddenly realized, I didn't exactly get the impression they were flirting. It seemed to be more a professional matter they were talking about. Maybe he was a classmate, a colleague? Yes, that could have been it. I would go with Irina to the hospital again to find out if one of her male colleagues was Russian.

"But how could this happen, Mr. Kvasterov?" Martin was asking Viktor when I finally found him the next morning. He hadn't been at the Basement or in his office. His computer was on, but not the speech-recognition software. I couldn't check my e-mail, and I was urgently expecting a response from the publisher. Which is why I'd set out to find Martin.

"Call me Viktor, please," Viktor said with an unhappy expression on his face. The two of them were sitting in the conference room at a large table; Jochen was sitting next to Martin.

"The funeral director said that he came this morning to pick up a deceased, but that body was already gone. And just now a second funeral director called to inform me that the casket his assistant had picked up contained a man and not a woman; his assistant had mistakenly thought 'Yannick' was only a woman's name and was later surprised to find he had received a male from the morgue drawer that you specified."

Viktor kept his eyes trained on the conference table.

"Mr. Kvasterov . . ."

"Call me Viktor, please."

"Viktor, please say something about this. We need to ensure that no further mix-ups arise in the future, and we need to be able to be sure that no one can tamper with a body that is part of a criminal investigation. You do understand that, right?"

"Yes."

Jochen rolled his eyes. "Viktor, you're really lucky that Pig—uh, Mr. Forch—hasn't found anything out about this problem yet. If you can assure us that there will be no further mix-ups, then we can overlook this. But to do that you have to tell us how this could happen."

Viktor shrugged and raised his head just enough to look at Jochen. "Perhaps I mixed up the numbers on the form. That was around three or four in the morning, because four deliveries arrived at the same time around then, and two of the people were, well, they were vəry unfriendly."

Martin made a face. Such vague speculations with fuzzy indications of time plus the emotional component don't do anything for a precision fetishist like him.

"Is everything else in order, Mr.—"

"Call me Viktor, please."

Martin sighed, then forced a smile. "Viktor. Fortunately for all parties involved, we were able to resolve this without irreparable harm. But we need to make sure this is the *only* problem. Can you assure us that no further irregularities have occurred apart from this mix-up?"

Viktor looked at Martin, hesitated, and finally nodded.

"He isn't sure," I told Martin.

"I can see that myself," he snapped back at me.

"I'll go right over to make sure everything is in order," Viktor said.

"And then, let's think about how we can avoid such incidents in the future," Martin said.

He was talking to Viktor as though he were a little kid, but that didn't appear to bother the Russian.

"Let's make clear right now that, even when there is a large rush, you allow only one individual at a time into the autopsy section and morgue. Handle all the formalities with that one person and oversee the body's placement into a drawer. You will check twice to make sure the number on the drawer is correct. Only then will you let the next person in. And if someone grows impatient or makes a big fuss, then call the police. OK?"

Viktor nodded eagerly. "Yes, yes, OK. I promise that this will not occur again. Starting immediately, everything will be done correctly. I will check everything two times, uh, *three* times."

"Good." Martin stood up and offered his hand to Viktor, who quickly jumped up onto his short legs to shake. Then Viktor practically ripped Jochen's hand off shaking it so vigorously before turning around and leaving the room.

"Man, you have the patience of an angel, little buddy," Jochen said. "You could have been a priest."

I have no idea why Martin thought of me at that moment.

"Martin," I called. "Turn on the speech-recognition . . ."

"Hello, Pascha," Martin thought, coolly. "I have a job for you."

"What? Am I a temp agency?" I griped. "I need to check my e-mail. The publisher may have already . . ."

"She did. But you will regain access to my computer only if you will promise to keep an eye on the autopsy section in the future."

"Fine," I said. "But you've already got a moonflower who's getting paid to do that."

"Apparently Viktor is unable to do it, as you just observed," Martin said. "In addition, he's here only from eight at night until six in the morning. After his shift is over and before the dissectors arrive in the morning, there are still one to two hours when no one is here. And what imposition is it on you to just make sure everything's in order a little more often?"

My poor little doctorito here was evidently suffering from some mental version of a hard-drive crash. "What, you think that I have nothing better to do than devote all my hours to hanging out in a tiled room with a couple of assholes hidden behind stainless steel doors?" *Shoot*—I was trying to avoid snarky comments so he couldn't claim I was being abusive, but that "assholes" comment just slipped out.

Martin shrugged. "Then unfortunately I cannot help you."

Now wait just a minute, I thought. *I am in no way dependent on your gracious condescension. As soon as you switch on your speech software . . .*

We had arrived in his office, and Martin sat down at his computer. But he did not switch the speech-recognition on, and he did not put the headset on. He was using the *keyboard*.

"Martin," Jochen said, baffled when he heard the clacking of the keys. "Since when do you type?"

"I felt like trying it out again so my fingers don't rust up," Martin told Jochen.

And to me he said: "I'll be typing a hundred eighty characters per minute again in no time. Have a nice day, Pascha."

I swirled around him for an hour, but I wasn't getting anywhere. Martin was typing on the keyboard, which is connected to the computer by a cable, and he was making calls on his landline, and had bulkheaded me out of his mind.

I was the loneliest person in the world.

———•———

For comfort I wanted to go see Irina, who I had accompanied to her job that morning at UMC. So I zoomed over and looked for her in the department where I'd parted ways with her, but she wasn't there. To cut to the chase: I did not find her. *God.* Martin had disowned me, Irina was unlocatable, and I was feeling so sorry for myself that I would presumably have bawled if I'd still possessed the requisite physical equipment to do so. Life as a dead guy is no picnic.

That afternoon I meekly snuck in to see Martin. "All right, fine. What do I have to do for you?"

He had walled himself off so thoroughly that I had to ask him three times before he even noticed me. Which had me pissed off all over again.

"You should merely make occasional, or rather, *regular* stopovers at the autopsy section and morgue and see what is going on over there."

"Uh-huh," I said with little enthusiasm.

"And in addition, could you also please keep your eyes peeled for any Asians who have a tattoo similar to this one."

He opened a photo on his screen. It showed a man lying on a sidewalk. Doubled over, one hand under his body, the other reaching way out, one leg slightly pulled in, the other stretched way out. He was wearing only a thin mesh tank top. The shirt was twisted and stretched down so far that the left shoulder blade was showing. The shoulder had a tattoo on it of a dragon breathing not fire but Chinese characters.

"Who's the guy?" I asked.

"This is the deceased with the stab wound who was purloined from the Basement."

Purloined!

"Where'd you get the picture?" I asked.

"Our CSI colleagues took it at the discovery site. Gregor's partner was kind enough to send it to me after I asked for her help identifying the body."

"For a soyback the guy's pretty fat, huh?"

Martin mentally scolded me.

"Perhaps he was a sumo wrestler," Martin suggested. "Maybe that's the first lead you could start looking into, then."

I was still able to control myself, but only just, and I swallowed without comment any snark about near-naked fat asses grasping each other between their oiled-up legs.

"So I should take a look under the shirt of any Asian guy I see and also make regular checks in the Basement to make sure all the bodies are lying in their beds? Like a boarding school teacher making sure the boys don't get to the girls . . ."

"Exactly," Martin said.

"Why aren't *you* taking care of all this crap?" I asked.

"Because our current work situation is intolerable," Martin said seriously. "And because the institute must take responsibility for losing a body that was entrusted to us, and we should therefore also recover it," he added, although more to himself.

"OK, I'll do it," I promised. "And now let me . . ."

"Tomorrow," Martin countered. "Only then will you have a turn on the computer."

And with that he dismissed me yet again.

———•———

The time until nine was dead boring, but Irina finally came, brought her grandpa his tea, and asked how his day was.

"Irina, it is so terrible, but I think I have had a mix-up," Viktor said. He told her the whole story. Whenever he got upset, his German became dramatically worse, but I was still (barely) able to follow him. He insisted they speak German together to practice the language of their adopted country, I suppose.

As Viktor recounted what had happened, Irina's face turned more and more worried. By the end she looked positively dismayed.

"I was so tired," Viktor said finally. "I fell asleep again, I think. But there wasn't anyone else here then."

Irina took a deep breath and grasped his hands, which he had been nervously kneading the whole time. "Two jobs are too much, Grandpa," she said. "When are you supposed to sleep? The few hours between your two jobs aren't enough. And we don't need the money. I told you from the start that I can get by without the extra money."

"But books are expensive, and you should also have a little something to live on."

"I was against you taking this job from the beginning."
Viktor nodded unhappily.

"Quit this job, *Dyedulya*, please. For my sake. You know
that you keep running into trouble because of your learning disability with numbers."

"Math and numbers were, uh, not even an issue when we
started," Viktor stammered. "Otherwise . . ."

The ensuing silence was somehow cringeworthy.

"I'll be done with my residency next year, and then I'll
be bringing home enough money that you can stop working
altogether."

"No," Viktor protested. "I want to work. I will not be supported by . . ."

"Oh, what would I do without you?" Irina asked, flatter-
ing him. She smiled at Viktor, but it was a troubled smile. "If
you'd like, you can shut your eyes for a little bit right now.
I'm here, after all. And when I leave in a little while you can
drink your tea. That'll perk you up."

I accompanied Irina home, waited until she fell blissfully asleep, and then zoomed back to Viktor. He was sleeping just as blissfully, although less comfortably. Pitifully, he
kept waking and falling back asleep over and over again,
each time his head slamming onto the tabletop. Around
four in the morning I noticed a dark figure lurking around
the building in the direction of Melaten Cemetery, just outside the institute. I followed the man, watching him climb
over the cemetery wall and following him another few minutes, but I wasn't supposed to be watching the cemetery, just
the Basement, so I did one more round there before checking in on Irina again.

She was fine. I only wished I could sneak into her dreams.

SIX

"Some lunatic dug up a fresh grave in the cemetery, took out the body, and pulled off the skin," Jochen was saying the next morning as Martin came into the office. Martin stood there behind his chair and did not move for a solid ten minutes.

"Could that be our thief?"

"Interestingly enough, he didn't take the whole body with him this time," Jochen said. "A visitor found her casually leaning against the Grim Reaper and fainted because she thought the woman had been buried alive and freed herself from her casket overnight."

(For people who don't know Cologne, I should explain that the Grim Reaper is a famous statue of a hooded skeleton that also serves as the official mascot of Melaten Cemetery, and it's only about fifty meters away from the institute.)

Martin nodded. A lot of people are afraid of being buried alive, but that fear makes no sense to forensic pathologists. It's in their nature to conscientiously hack a body to pieces before it gets stashed in the ground. I mean, even if you hadn't actually kicked it by the time you were served upon the pathologist's table, it wouldn't take more than an hour for you to become a large-scale version of an oven-ready fryer, thoroughly exsanguinated and complete with a little bag of giblets inside you.

"I'm guessing that the body they dug up didn't have a nice tattoo on it like on our Asian abscondee," I said, "but I'd like to point out verifying that detail would mean seriously upping our investigative workload."

Martin winced. "Speaking of tattoos . . ."

"Yes, I came up with an address where you can ask," I informed him graciously.

"Then tell me."

"First, your side of the bargain." Sometimes you just have stand up for your own dignity.

Martin started to object, but then he stopped and silently turned on his computer. He opened the speech-recognition software, plugged in the wireless headset, and watched eagle-eyed what I was up to on his screen. I opened the e-mail program and read the response from my publishing patroness. It was true: they wanted to publish my story! Both parts. I let out a jubilant scream that almost exploded Martin's braincase. He apparently hadn't counted on such spirited excitement because he hadn't lowered the office blinds. And now he was holding his dome in his hands.

"Another stunt like that and you'll be spending all eternity alone," he whisper-growled.

"I'm a writer!" I yelled. "I'm going to be famous."

"We'll talk about that later," Martin replied.

"They're going to sell my book in every bookstore with my name on the front cover. I wonder what my mother will say. And especially my father. He never did anything but cut me down . . ."

"That's not going to work," Martin replied, irritated. "First, Mr. Forch insisted that all the names in the book be changed, including yours, and second, you can't exactly write a book under your own name since you're dead."

"I can too, and now the world will finally find out everything."

"No, it won't," Martin said. "If you won't follow my rules, I'll write your publisher a letter rejecting her offer, and then the matter will be settled."

"But . . ." My dismay plunged so fast into the abyss I could hardly catch my breath.

Martin unplugged the headset. "So, next we're going to write a friendly reply." He was talking to me like I was an Alzheimer's patient and he was my butt-wiper: *How are we doing today, shall we shovel in some nice purée for breakfast? Oh, did we wet our bed again?* Made me want to puke.

He clicked on Reply and began typing. "Dear Ms. Blitzgescheit:"—name changing has since become second nature to me—"Thank you so much for your kind offer. I will return to that issue in a moment, but first I need to alert you to the fact that, when I wrote down the story, I accidentally used the actual, current names of actual, living persons. I would absolutely like to correct this error prior to publication. In addition, I would prefer not to come out publicly as an author. My anonymity must be strictly preserved; therefore, the book will need to be published under a pseudonym. How we proceed is dependent on your consent to these conditions. Thank you for your understanding. Sincerely yours . . ."

I glowed with anger, spinning a tornado around Martin, who was pretending not to notice.

"Should I send it?" he asked with feigned friendliness.

"No," I yelled. "You should write *my* name. I don't want any anonymojiggers. I don't want a psychonym. I want to see *my* name on the bestseller list."

Martin's finger glided over to the Delete key. "OK, then we'll turn the publisher down."

My clouds of rage imploded, and despair collapsed the fiery vortex of electrons into a kind of black hole. "No," I wailed. "Better a fake name than none at all."

Martin sent the e-mail. I could not stand to be around him anymore and went to look for Irina instead. Maybe she could make me feel better.

———

Finally I had a bit of good luck after being dogged for the last few days by nothing but bad. I found Irina at UMC just taking her white coat off and throwing her bag over her shoulder. Apparently she was off now. Although it was only just past noon. I observed with (virtual) eagle eyes who she said good-bye to. One woman kissed her on the cheek, which got me feeling pretty hot, and two male colleagues waved at her. One of them blew a kiss to her, but she reacted hesitantly with a smile that he really couldn't interpret as encouraging. I was relieved. Whoever the Russian-spewing, late-night telephone joker was, it wasn't one of the doctors here.

I followed Irina to the station and onto the train and suffered with her the unbearable heat that was making the air shimmer and driving stench out of the pores of her fellow riders. The car reeked to high heaven of armpit sweat, foot sweat, and perfume. And those were the smells that my editor didn't nix. Irina was standing by an open window, but that didn't help much. She suffered in silence.

I was so focused on Irina that I hadn't even noticed what direction we were heading, so I was somewhat surprised when we found ourselves almost downtown. She didn't live here. Did she have a date or something?

But she didn't go into a café bar or gelato place; instead she stepped into a nondescript building, and once inside she turned to the right down a short hallway. The wide door at the end was open, and behind it a number of people were sitting in a waiting room. Irina crossed the waiting room offering a friendly hello to everyone and no one in particular, as good German manners require, and then she opened the door at the far end of the room after giving it a loud knock. There, a huge doctor's office was divided into three individual exam areas separated by curtains, and there were several lockers lining the wall in back. A white-haired, vulture-like medicosaurus in a white lab coat was just accompanying an unbelievably tiny, shriveled old woman from one of the exam areas to the door. The woman walked so stooped you might think she was still tying her shoes as she went.

"Irina, how nice that you're here. We have a lot to do, as you can see."

No friendly cheek kiss, not even a handshake. As it should be.

Irina stuck her bag into the farthest locker, took a lab coat out along with one of those listening-spoon thingies that are always cold when they press them onto your back.

I hadn't seen such a cramped doctor's office since my last visit to my pediatrician, who actually treated me until I was thirteen and he quit medicine. My mother preferred to stick with him, dragging me there even though I thought

I was way too grown up to be seeing a kids' doctor. Even that one time I pulled a muscle during my loathsome gym class, I still found myself among the scared, sniveling diaper set, waiting in a room papered in dinosaurs while my classmates' parents had all long since started taking them to the regular hospital like *normal* people. And then my teacher of course had to loudly announce before the entire class that my *children's* doctor had exempted me from gym. God, I really wanted to seal his whistle in his mouth with the medicine ball.

"If you could take that one, that'd be a big help," said the Devonian dinobird, who had just said good-bye to the wizened woman.

"Certainly," Irina said with a warm smile. She pulled her lab coat on and went into the leftmost of the three cubicles. After that patient, it took hardly half a minute for an older man to appear next, and she put his broken finger into a splint. After that everything continued in quick succession. Old people, young people, men, women—most in headscarves—and with angelic patience Irina even patched up two squirmy little kids. At least half the patients spoke little to no German and had people with them to interpret, but the interpreters could hardly communicate in German, either. My wonderful Irina was helping all these poor people.

I watched her understanding eyes and dexterous fingers, I admired her knowledge, and I looked away only when she had to stick people someplace with a needle.

After four hours, I was starting to get tired. Of course I can't really get "tired," and Irina totally fascinated me, but at some point I just had to admit it's dead boring spending the whole day at a doctor's office. Even when the doctor is Irina. Once again I was torn, but I took it as a clear sign from above when a man came in around five thirty complaining of a boil. And in a very unpleasant location. He hemmed and hawed, and I wondered if he had an elephant zit on his ball sack or something—but in fact it was worse. "It's more toward the back," he mumbled, embarrassed, adding that he hadn't been able to sit properly for weeks . . . now *that* I really did not want to see. So I rocketed over to Martin's office.

I found him in the supercooled office of Monsieur Piggy Bank. Martin already had goose bumps you could have grated parmesan on, and his lips were suspiciously blue.

"Why is this body still here, then?" Piggy Bank was asking.

Martin was contorted over the desk, holding his head at an almost impossible angle, trying to catch a glimpse of the computer monitor. "That's the suicide from the railroad embankment, right?"

"Exactly. The autopsy report has been finalized and issued, so there isn't any reason for the body to still be here."

Martin flipped through his own notes. "That person has not been identified."

"So what?"

Martin did a double take. "What do you mean, 'So what'? A body remains here so long as it has not been identified."

"Whose job is it to complete the identification?" Piggy Bank asked in a tone that seemed simultaneously condescending, mocking, and irritated.

"The police," Martin said.

"Then the police should worry about the body, too," Piggy Bank replied. "Once we've completed the autopsy and autopsy report, our duty is done."

"But until a deceased can be buried, he or she remains here."

"Fine. Then the police will have to pay rent. Please ensure that the invoices are issued accordingly."

Piggy Bank dismissed Martin with a wave of his hand. Martin visibly hesitated, but finally his survival instinct won out, and he gathered up his folders and notes and left the office. I followed him into the break room, where he made himself some nice hot ginger tea.

Ginger is warming. You learn such things unintentionally when you have been familiar with Martin for a lengthy period of time. Peppermint is cooling, lemon balm is soothing, yerba mate is stimulating. So he was having ginger tea. When it was thirty-seven degrees Celsius outside.

"Have you gotten any further on identifying the suicide from the railroad embankment from last week?" Martin was asking Gregor's partner on the phone a few minutes later. I'd gotten to know her on my last case, when she flustered the suspect with her appearance. Very young, pretty, built for my tastes a bit too naïve, but that could only improve over time. She was still new.

"No," she replied, and even through the receiver her voice sounded clearly annoyed. "It's not really that easy to do without a photo of the face."

"And he didn't have any papers on him?"

"Dr. Gänsewein," the detective bunny replied, pronouncing Martin's last name as though it were an infectious disease involving oozing furuncles all over your body, "we are doing everything in our power, and it doesn't make our work easier if I have to explain myself to you now as—"

"No, no," Martin said. "Please don't feel like you need to justify yourself. Certainly not to me, of all people. But it's like this . . . uh, Mr. Forch is going to start billing Criminal Investigations to store unidentified bodies."

It was dead silent for a moment in the receiver. I squeezed through the small holes in the plastic housing all the way up to the speaker membrane because I thought I might have missed something—but that was not the case. The nice bunny was, quite simply, gobsmacked.

Martin stammered out a recap for her about the plan his boss had just come up with.

"All right . . ." the detective said after another short pause. "The CI admin office will deal with that. But all I can say is we haven't had a single lead on the ID, and a photo is obviously no longer possible by any stretch of the imagination. So I'm afraid that your morgue drawer is going to be occupied for some time. Or, you could arrange to have the body stolen, and then you'd have the drawer free again."

Ho-ho. That bunny could really lay into someone! My interest in her increased.

Martin squinched up his face but said nothing.

"If there won't be anything else . . ." she said.

"No, my apologies again. I really didn't intend to—well, uh, good-bye."

Jochen looked up from his desk and grinned. "Does Gregor's new partner make you nervous, little buddy?"

Martin blushed.

Jochen wasn't done yet, as shown by his widening smile. "I'll admit, she's pretty hot. But I always thought you were happy with Birgit . . ."

"That's what I thought, too," Birgit's voice rang out from the door.

Martin turned even redder. Birgit walked over to Martin's desk with a smile, pulled him playfully up by the ears and kissed him on the lips.

"Me too, me too!" Jochen called, raising his hand.

Birgit laughed. Incredible, this woman.

"Well, when are you finally going to be done today?" she asked Martin. "We wanted to go out to eat before we see the apartment."

Martin winced. "Ah, I'd almost forgotten."

Now Birgit's smile turned a little strained. "Martin, a woman might start getting the impression your heart and soul aren't really in the apartment search."

"No—yes, yes," Martin hastened to add. His heart was plenty in it; he was just troubled by an excess of soul.

"Yes indeed, sweetums," I cheerfully chimed in. "We are *very* much looking forward to *our* nice new apartment."

Martin broadcast a mental warning to me that prominently featured the word PUBLISHER.

Bastard.

"So, where do we want to go for dinner?" Birgit asked.

"I think I feel like noodles. Maybe Asian?" Martin suggested. "There's a little Taiwanese place I've been meaning to try."

"And you're coming with us," he ordered me in his thoughts.

What . . . ? Normally Martin was glad to have a break from me for a while, but now he was ordering me to come along? What on earth was wrong with him?

"We need to do a little investigating," he explained.

When the two of them were at last sitting at a rickety table on the sidewalk in front of the tiniest conceivable Chinese restaurant, Birgit looked around surprised.

"I've never been here before."

"I haven't either," Martin said. "But it comes recommended."

His inconspicuousness was so obvious that I smelled a rat.

"You're right," he thought. "Or maybe you recommended this place to me?"

"Makes sense," I said. "But not for the food."

I had taken Martin's assignment to heart and been visiting all of Cologne's tattoo parlors. In many of them, God knows I found it hard to keep on task. Especially when a female customer was getting a tattoo. I'd always considered a tramp stamp on the lower back to be pretty sexy. But you can also get tattoos on your inner thighs, around your nipples, or even—eh, I'm pretty sure you know who vetoed what I was going to say next.

But the good news was that in one parlor I saw this soyback who had a dragon on his shoulder. Virtually the brother of the dragon on our stolen corpse. This guy apparently worked as a tool for the tattoo artist, sitting around with him reciting entire epics in his incomprehensible *hu-cha wu-chi*. I had also followed him later on to the Chinese restaurant where Martin and Birgit were now sitting. He worked in the kitchen.

"All right," Martin said. "I'll show the picture of the tattoo around. *You* watch people's reactions."

"You can see for yourself how they react," I moaned.

"You will observe them once they're out of my field of vision," Martin clarified.

Birgit ordered for both of them. Vegetarian for Martin, duck for Birgit. Anyone who orders duck at a Chinese restaurant must really be a hopeless optimist.

"Taiwanese," Martin corrected me.

"It's the same thing," I grumbled. "Just get going with your tattoo."

Martin held up his picture for the young waitress who had taken the order. "I'm sorry to bother you, but I was wondering if you could tell me whether you've ever seen a tattoo like this before?"

At first she only casually glanced at the photo that Martin was holding up for her but then she stared at it.

"Do you know this man?" Martin asked.

"What?" Her head jerked up. "No, no. It's just a nice dragon."

She was lying. You could hear, smell, feel, and taste it.

"What do these characters mean?" Martin asked.

"Nothing." As she turned away, she added over her shoulder, "Those are just doodles that are supposed to look like Chinese characters."

Martin had no need to instruct me to follow the woman since her reaction was so clear.

She walked single-mindedly past the three empty standing tables indoors in the tiniest of tiny dining rooms and on into the kitchen. She could hardly squeeze in, the kitchen was so tiny. There were two kids sitting at a table coloring pigs blue in coloring books. Next to them sat a woman about 250 years old who was peeling various types of colorful vegetables and dicing the fodder into the tiniest of wok-ready snippets. Two more women in aprons and headscarves were wrapping some kind of vegetative matter in leaves that looked like parchment paper. An old man then gathered these packets and threw them into a deep fat fryer. Two young men were moving boxes of drinks back and forth. One of them had the brother dragon tattoo.

The waitress whistled and all motion instantly ceased. She said a few words or phrases—who knows with that weird language. Everyone set down everything that they were holding in their hands and ran out through the back exit. Within five seconds the kitchen was empty.

"Well, I guess you won't be having a meal here tonight," I explained when I was back with Martin. "The entire staff skedaddled out the back."

Martin stopped short, turned pale, jumped up, and scurried into the restaurant.

"Martin?" Birgit called after him. "Aren't you feeling well?"

"Everything's fine," Martin called back over his shoulder to her. Then he went into the kitchen.

The waitress was sitting on one of the chairs crying over the blue pigs. Martin pulled back. Then he called for Birgit.

"What on earth . . ." Birgit looked around in astonishment. The kitchen looked like a battlefield—the deep fat fryer was smoking so strongly now that it reeked of burned food. Birgit, ever practical, first pulled the basket out of the hot fat, and then she sat on the second chair and laid a hand on the waitress's arm.

"What's wrong? Is there anything I can do for you?"

"He didn't do anything wrong," the waitress wept.

As expected: deny everything first. Typical reaction for people who've got something to hide.

"No one has claimed otherwise," Martin said.

The waitress looked up and stared at Martin with a tear-veiled face. "Why are you looking for him then?"

Birgit looked uncomprehendingly back and forth between the waitress and Martin.

"Did you know that he's dead?" Martin asked.

The woman broke out into loud sobs. I wasn't clear on whether that meant yes or no, and if I was interpreting Martin's face correctly, he wasn't sure either.

"Listen, I'm a doctor. I'm not interested in residence permits, asylum applications, or anything like that. I'm interested only in finding out what the apparently very serious side effects are of a certain kind of drug. The young man . . . I'm sorry, what is his name?"

"Yan Yu," the waitress sobbed.

To me the name sounded like a noise you make when your nose is stuffed up, but Martin repeated the noise dead-seriously and without one twitch of his eyebrow.

"Yan Yu had a pharmaceutical, a drug, in his blood. Please tell me the name of the doctor he went to."

"Doctor? I don't know. Was he sick?"

Birgit offered the young woman a tissue, which she took but held in her hand unused. Didn't this little shumai know you have to *use* tissues for them to help?

"Where did you know Yan Yu from, then? Is he a relative?"

She shook her head and blushed. "Expats from the same country are always aware to each other."

Aware of *each other,* Martin mentally corrected her.

Even here in a sweltering hash house standing before a bawling Chinese girl, he cannot stop with the smart-assery.

"Chinese *woman,*" Martin corrected me.

You see?

"Would you be able to find out which doctor he went to? It's very important so that we can prevent future cases of people dying from this drug."

She shrugged and nodded at the same time.

"Here, take my card." Martin pressed a slightly crumpled business card with his contact information at the institute into her hand. Hopefully she wouldn't mistake it for the tissue now.

"Once you know the name of the doctor, you'll call me, OK? Please! It's really very important."

Martin and Birgit had to run to make their appointment to view the apartment, but they were both distracted and stank of grease and garlic even though they hadn't eaten a bite. The agent actually took a step back from them as she opened the door. When she saw Birgit's smeared mascara, I could tell she'd already written the two of them off.

"And he was murdered?" Birgit asked while the agent rather listlessly showed them the living room with its view out into a backyard paved with gray bricks.

"Stabbed," Martin confirmed.

The agent's forehead now reminded me of the pleated skirt my mother used to wear on special occasions.

"And this had something to do with the strange drugs?"

You could hear the doubt clearly in her voice. No wonder. Personally I'd never heard of a package insert that listed "fatal stabbing injuries" under a drug's side effects.

Then again, I'd rarely swallowed pills bought in packages with inserts . . .

"I had been thinking along those lines, until just now at least," Martin whispered back. "But maybe he was involved in a gang war, or maybe there was a history of drug addiction, or it was a personal matter . . . I don't know."

The agent's frown lines grew deeper upon hearing the words "gang war" and "history of drug addiction," and looking askance at the two potential lessees, she wrote a line through Birgit's name on her list.

"I'm not really hungry, but we should still eat a little something," Birgit said. "Anything but Chinese."

The agent seemed relieved when Birgit and Martin thanked her and left without expressing further interest.

SEVEN

"Are you finally going to Irina's tonight?" I asked when Martin and Birgit had managed to nab a table on the patio at a small pizza place.

Martin was startled out of his ruminations, which had been a mash-up of cohabitation, missing tattooed bodies, and drug cocktails. He was all mixed up inside, which isn't like him at all.

He must have been overwhelmed by the number of things he had going on all at once, or maybe the heat was softening his brain.

"Of all the things you could be musing about right now, it's cerebral softening," Martin thought, disgusted. Turns out that's an actual medical condition.

"It's not my fault that I don't have anything left on me that can go soft."

"I would like to spend just one normal evening off like a completely normal man. With my girlfriend. So please leave me alone tonight."

"Why are you looking so angry again?" Birgit asked. "You've been so . . . withdrawn lately. Have I done something wrong?"

Martin tried to smile. The result was creepy. "We've been having a very difficult time lately at the institute, actually. The new boss is driving us all mad, there's the chaos of having our temporary offices so far away from the autopsy section, and the heat has been unbearable."

"And that's all?"

Martin nodded unhappily. That was a lie, of course, but he still didn't want to tell her about me, so he couldn't also explain that he had personal demons, as it were, about moving in with her.

In reality, nothing was going to change if they moved in together anyway, since it made no difference to me if I observed Martin and Birgit at his or her apartment or in some new apartment they shared.

"But it matters to me," Martin thought defensively before quickly pulling his mental blinds back down.

But I'd caught the thought that he actually wanted to keep secret from me, namely that I not hang out so often when Birgit was there.

I thought about that at length.

Martin was right. Whenever I was looking for company, I zoomed into Martin's apartment—he's the only person I can shoot the breeze with, after all. If Martin wasn't home, I rarely looked for him at Birgit's because I knew he'd just mentally block me out there anyway. With our current arrangement, the two of them had a kind of private retreat at Birgit's, which I certainly *could* haunt but did only in the rarest of cases. If they moved in together, all that would probably be different.

"So, what about Irina?" I asked again, expecting to be blocked by Martin's thought lock.

"What are you offering in return?" Martin asked.

Ugh, he'd been picking up some decent negotiation skills.

"I'll stay the rest of the night at the institute and keep an eye on the cemetery. Maybe the skin freak will show back up."

Martin mentally wrung his hands, but finally he consented.

Birgit looked dispirited when he excused himself to run his errand.

Viktor turned pale when Martin entered the Basement. "Is something the matter?"

"Oh, everything's fine," Martin said. "I just stopped by to . . ."

Well, keep talking!

"I'm Dr. Gänsewein, good evening," Martin introduced himself to Irina with a handshake and the hint of a bow. People just don't do that anymore unless you're shaking the royal paw of the Queen, and then you don't shake and bow but kiss—which is why you bend over slightly.

Irina smiled at him. "Irina Yelinova."

"I am sorry, I would offer you seat, but unfortunately we have only two here," Viktor said, offering Martin his chair.

"No, no, please sit—I've spent the whole day . . ."

In the end, all three of them ended up standing there among the morgue drawers.

"Ask her if she has a boyfriend," I ordered Martin.

He turned red. "I can't just . . ."

"Oh, man, what the hell are you doing here then?" I asked.

"Are you enjoying the German summer?" Martin asked. I screamed.

"It didn't have to be *this* warm," Irina said, smiling. If she had thought Martin and his questions were stupid, I would have had to agree, but she didn't let on anything like that.

"Your grandfather mentioned you are doing your residency; is that right?"

Viktor almost burst with pride; Irina smiled.

Oh, the way her eyes beamed, her wide mouth and full lips revealing her beautiful, even white teeth with the slightly crooked canine that made her smile so unique, so somehow . . .

"Devilish," Martin thought.

That word choice was absolutely beyond the pale. Of all people, Martin ought to know that, due to my grievous, not-being-invited-into-the-light situation, I'm sensitive about references to hell and the devil. But—it *did* fit. Hmm. The canine turned Irina, my angel, into a delightfully *devilish* angel . . .

"Surgery," she said with a nod. "There are definitely parallels with your profession, in that we must make sure to patch the patients back up again correctly."

She sounded serious, but now the corner of her mouth pulled up slightly, showing a slight smile that Martin reciprocated after a moment's scare.

"Yes, we have it quite good," Martin said smiling. "We can't hurt anyone anymore."

"Well?" I interjected.

Martin winced.

"Get to asking her if she has a boyfriend."

"It's very kind of you to help your grandfather pass the time," Martin said. "Hopefully your boyfriend is understanding."

"I don't have a boyfriend," Irina said, continuing to smile. "I work at the university and I have lots of studying to do, so there's not much time for boyfriends."

"Who does she talk on the phone with at night in Russian?" I asked.

Martin ignored me.

"And you work at a doctor's office as well," Viktor added.

Irina gave a quick nod.

"Who is she talking to at night on the phone!" I yelled.

"And you're a forensic pathologist, right?" Irina asked. "Not a toxicologist, biologist, or . . ."

"Forensic pathologist, coroner, yes." Martin blushed. "And I love my job very much."

"Martin!" I yelled.

"Although it sounds like the situation at the institute is a bit, shall I say, tense at the moment?"

Martin was shocked. "How? What?" His eyes slid over to Viktor, who was staring at his granddaughter in dismay.

"I've heard that you're very busy because the funeral homes in the city don't have enough refrigerated storage," Irina said, blinking innocently. "And the heat wave is driving up the suicide rate."

I could feel Martin's relief spread through him like a warm wave. Not a word about the organizational chaos at the institute; no details about the stolen corpse, the impossible boss, or Viktor's failures; only information that had been in the newspaper. Martin *was* allowed to address events known to the public without fear of repercussions.

"Yes, it's really a difficult time. But the heat wave will pass."

"I'm sure."

There was an unpleasant pause.

"Who does she call!" I roared.

"Well, then, I should probably be going," Martin said.

"*No!* Ask her!"

"Do you need a ride anywhere?"

Viktor nodded vigorously. "It would be very nice of you if you could take Irina home."

"Oh, Grandpa, that's not necessary," Irina said. "I always take the train."

"But I always have a bad feeling when you are alone at night."

"It's no problem," Martin said. "Anywhere you like."

Well, now at least we still had a small chance that Martin would ask the questions we were here for in the more intimate setting of the car. A teensy chance. A nanochance.

Irina didn't have any physical response as Martin held the door to the trash can open for her. Nor when she sat on the "folding chair," as the passenger seat in this vehicle is officially known; nor as Martin flipped the little windows out and up. Not even when he turned the ignition. My stomach still turns any time I hear that noise. Virtually, of course, you understand.

"Who does she talk on the phone with at night in Russian?" I reminded Martin.

Irina told him her address, and Martin drove off. On the way she talked about the outdoor recreation opportunities the Cologne area had to offer. Nothing could have interested me less than the qualities of the various swimming pools and lakes, but Martin didn't say anything except for an occasional "hmm," "uh-huh," or "interesting." He ignored all my requests to ask Irina the really important questions. I howled with rage, but he switched off mentally. My powerlessness almost physically hurt me, even though that was impossible.

I followed Irina up to her apartment and was glad that I didn't have to listen to a phone call in Russian for once while I waited for her to fall asleep. After that I zoomed back to the institute. Martin didn't have to remind me a third time of my promise.

"We do have a few cases—naturally I can't comment on them specifically—where a drug cocktail was found of an anesthetic like propofol and an opioid, presumably buprenorphine. We can assume that these people had recently undergone surgical procedures, if I'm not mistaken."

Martin waited on the phone and checked off something on his notepad during the call.

"Now, in addition, we have the problem that some of the deceased affected by this have not been identified—and some are also no longer identifiable."

Some? What was that supposed to mean? It was true that the embankment body hadn't been IDed, and apart from a DNA match that wasn't going to be possible due to the condition of the body. But we had a name for the Asian guy now.

Short pause, but no writing.

"Exactly. My specific request therefore is this: we have one deceased with a very distinct tattoo who probably underwent a surgical procedure probably on the tenth or eleventh of July. What I'd like to do is send the data from our blood analysis over along with a photo of the tattoo, and then see if you can tell me whether you operated on this person."

"Martin!" I yelled. "The guy's name was Yan Yu."

"But he probably used a borrowed insurance card when he was in the hospital and may have been treated under a different name," Martin quickly thought at me as he simultaneously tried to listen closely to the voice on the phone.

Pause.

"For which the man was operated on? No, unfortunately I can't tell."

Pause.

"In addition, I'd also like to know if you may be missing any other patients who recently had surgical procedures done."

Short pause.

"By that I mean, people who have missed a follow-up appointment, haven't been in touch, didn't come to have their stitches removed, things like that."

Pause. Martin concentrated on his notepad but didn't write anything down. He nodded. "Yes, of course. I can have the detectives on the case send you their data as well. I just thought, among colleagues . . ."

Short pause.

"Yes, that's very kind. If you could let me know your e-mail address . . ."

He scribbled around on his notepad, said thank you, and hung up.

"Are you stealing work from the plainclothes?" I asked.

He had at least ten e-mail addresses all over his notepad.

"The detectives are standing idly by, and I'm increasingly worried about the side effects of this anesthetic. If in fact this agent is being used postoperatively . . ."

"Wait," I said. "Are you sure that all of these people were operated on? How do you know that from our former tattouchebag?"

"I don't know with any certainty because—"

"The body got pinched before you could examine it," I said, finishing his thought.

Martin sighed. In all his born days Martin would never get over this disgrace. Especially if he couldn't solve this mystery of the anesthetic in the blood.

"Where would he have gotten a mixture of anesthetics and painkillers in his blood if not from an operation?"

I moaned softly. "There is a flourishing trade in drugs of all kinds, dear Martin. You of all people should actually know that."

My point was that drugs of one kind or another were sloshing around in well over half of Martin's clients. Besides alcohol, which the slicers consider a drug (!), there tended to be a little of everything else you could imagine that could make you high, low, willing, happy, loud, wild, soft, or stupid. From leaves they smoked, to pills they swallowed, or liquids they injected.

"No one has ever turned up with this particular mixture before," he said as he sent all his e-mails out into the world.

There's a first time for everything, I thought, but I didn't comment further.

"Did anything happen last night?" he asked.

"I caught a couple screwing in a crypt, and another little couple wanted to play vampire and princess but then they didn't have the nerve. Otherwise, everything was quiet," I reported. I kept it to myself that Viktor had nodded off again. I'm not a rat, after all.

After his mass e-mail to all the local hospitals, Martin spent a while working quietly while I read the e-mail from my publisher, which Martin had printed out for me.

Dear Dr. Gänsewein:

The issue of discretion that you raised in your last e-mail is something we would be happy to ensure. A pseudonym is nothing out of the ordinary at all, and the concern about violating the privacy rights of third parties would have made it advisable to change the names of the characters in the novel in any case. On these points we could not agree with you more.

We look forward to discussing your novel with you further at your earliest convenience. Please feel free to give me a call at any time; you can reach me at extension . . .

"Martin," I yelled. "Call them! Right now!"

Martin shook his head. "I will not be making any calls at all until I have a plan for what we should do next. And I don't have any time for that at the moment."

I begged and whined, but Martin remained resolute. He's gotten pretty damn good at that.

I spent a while shooting through the city, but that gets boring pretty quickly since I don't have anyone to play with. Well, that's not quite true. During our case last spring, I actually managed to interface with a radio broadcast and manipulate a car's electronics, and I figured out I could do that with various cell phones as well, or alternatively slip in between an earpiece and a cell phone the way I can between Martin's wireless headset and the software on his computer. I had entertained myself for a good while with kid stuff like that, but first of all it tires me out locating the right combination of cell phone and earpiece, and second of all it actually isn't all that fun yakking into people's cell phones—because absolutely no one finds it weird or spooky. Everybody just thinks some technical error has switched the phone to a second call. People just unimaginatively say, "Hello? Hello? What are you doing on my line?" into the headset, and then they hang up. Dead boring.

But today I lucked out. I was hanging out at a beer garden when I suddenly became witness to a conversation that aroused my interest. It was about a museum.

No, no, I'm not actually a fan of museums, as you have quite rightly surmised, but I do enjoy setting off alarms that rely on capacitive magnetic-field sensors. I learned how to deal with this technology when Martin tried to jerry-rig a couple of Ghostbuster gimmicks in his apartment last spring. (Note to my editor: I don't care what's in your dictionary; *no one* actually says "jury-rigged." Jury-rigging is a felony; jerry-rigging is a craft.) The only one of these contraptions that's still around is the antielectrosmog mosquito netting over his bed.

Apart from playing around with their alarm systems, I think museums are dead boring. I don't like most of the pictures on their walls. With modern pieces you never know if it's a sandwich on the floor half-eaten by some animal, a forgotten hors d'oeuvre—or *Art*. Some great artist paints shit pictures that I could've surpassed in nursery school and then hangs them upside down on the wall. I mean, what about that involves *Art*? So in short, my stance on museums is they're great for people who need to get out of the rain, but that really just doesn't apply to me anymore.

So back to the beer garden. This guy mentioned a museum that actually sounded interesting. And interesting to me, specifically. There was no art in the pseudocultural sense; what there was, was the opportunity to test the laws of nature. Yeah, I know—anyone can test gravity just by hurling himself off the roof of any old building. That's not what I mean. In this museum, you could move objects with your thoughts. At least, that's what the guy in the beer garden claimed. I had to put in another half hour of listening to the guy yammer on about pedagogical implications and didactic thingamobutions, but *finally* he mentioned the name of the place: the Odysseum.

I zoomed over to Kalk—yet another one of Cologne's creatively named boroughs, on the right bank of the Rhine—because that's where this awesome place was supposed to be. I got there in the nick of time to join a whole horde of Cub Scouts who looked like an ad for IKEA in their twisted yellow-and-blue neckerchiefs. The littler ones were wearing them regulation-style around their collars; the cooler boys had tied them Rambo-style around their heads. They all looked ridiculous.

I whooshed through the lobby and past the ticket booth, because obviously I don't have to pay for tickets anymore. In the central hall a shiny silver basketball was hanging from a superlong cable over a sort of low circular table with a compass star painted on it. The ball was swaying back and forth in what appeared to be a straight line, but over time it was knocking over these little tubes set up domino-style in a circle along the outer edge of the table, which was about a meter and a half wide. Slowly, one by one, the ball knocked them down in a clockwise direction. Huh. I was a little bowled over, myself.

"A Foucault pendulum," a bright-eyed pip-squeak said.

"That's exactly right," the den mother said. "It demonstrates the rotation of the earth."

No way, dude, I thought and then zoomed closer to observe this nonsense up close. In the middle of the circular table was a small red light. As I came closer, I felt an electromagnetic pulse. It tickled. I flew over the light one more time, and then orbited it in wider and wider and then smaller and smaller circles. And here's the kicker: the pendulum swayed off course. Whenever I flew right in front of the pendulum over the red light, it put a little curve into the ball's path. It took barely two minutes for the pendulum to start dithering in the circle like it was stoned and stop knocking over the little tubes. A black-clad museum crow with a little name tag and nervously jingling key ring hanging around her neck raced over, gave the Cub Scouts a dirty look, and stopped the pendulum. The kids were ushered into the next hall for the first of several "World of Experience" exhibits so the drunken pendulum could sober up. I was already digging this museum.

There were a couple of dinosaurs roaring in the first World of Experience, but I couldn't find a way to control them. I had more fun in the second World of Experience, though. Up on a screen they were showing what TV program the people on Saturn would be watching today, taking into account how long it takes television signal waves from earth to get there. The awesome puppet version of *Jim Button and Luke the Engine Driver* was older than me, and I was overcome with a short wave of sentimentality. But then all of a sudden I wondered whether I could travel around in space, too. After all, I was something akin to a radio wave. The very idea ripped through my electrons in a shudder, though. I wasn't sure if I wanted to think about that again, let alone try it out, ever. I mean, what if I didn't come back? Things down here on earth would definitely be on the lonely side if Martin blocked me out again, but compared to being the only spiritual being in the infinite vastness of space? Or . . . maybe I wasn't alone, actually. But what had me even more scared shitless was the idea of running into alien ghosts of slimy creepy-crawlies from Mars, or anywhere else for that matter. With my virtual tail still between my virtual legs, I moved on, envying the bonsais who could actually try out the astronaut's spinning whiplash seat.

At some point I came across a rectangular see-through box that didn't have anything inside.

What was the educational point of displaying an empty box? The name on the sign for the thing said Cloud Chamber, but there weren't any clouds inside it at all. I flashed into the box to take a look around firsthand, as it were, and I suddenly felt a kind of coldness all around me. I quickly exited the box, rising above it a good half meter for safety, and then I looked back—and froze.

You could clearly see the curve of the path I had just flown through the box, and then it faded before my eyes and disappeared. *But it had been there.* You could see the exact trajectory I had drawn through the nothingness, even if only very briefly. I tried again. I drew a circle. Fine, it was more of an egg, but it was *my* trail. Now as I looked more closely, I could see other, tiny traces. Something would flicker up and disappear in one spot, and then it would reappear briefly in another spot. Like tiny contrails from tiny airplanes.

I started to tremble. I had seen a trail I had caused, and I had also seen other trails that I had not caused. I was faced with the question: Who made the other trails?

Very carefully, very slowly, and with the kind of excitement I used to feel before, oh, say, stealing a Ferrari
Testarossa, I approached the box again, dove in, and tried
to make contact with the others. *Zoop*, one just flashed past
me. But so fast and so low-energy and so—well, I can't think
of the word. Maybe I should just say *so substanceless*—that
for a moment I thought I was deluding myself. But then a
trail passed by me again. Slightly stronger than the first,
but again totally vacant. Whatever that was, it didn't have a
consciousness.

On the one hand I was relieved; on the other I was
totally disappointed. I needed a break, and so I zoomed out
of this creepy dark World of Experience and into the next
one: Cyberspace. Tons of games from Mindball to the Light
Speed Bicycle that you could play against computers—but
only if you could press buttons or push pedals.

Bored, I moved to the next exhibit, which tested whether
radio and Wi-Fi signals could penetrate various substances.
They had several little recesses with antennae in them, and
a computer screen above showed you the signal strength
for each antenna. Visitors would then cover the recesses
with various materials to test how well they insulated the
antennae from the radio signal. The material options didn't
include anything like Martin's antielectrosmog netting,
incidentally; they had only wood, plaster, plastic, and metal.

I watched for a while, bored again, until I suddenly wondered where they had hidden the transmitter, which obviously had to be out in the hall somewhere. Probably on the
ceiling, so I sauntered along the rafters and found it.

Once I found the transmitter and started interfering
with the signals, the readings at the exhibit started to go

haywire, which again caught the eye of the museum crow, who swooped down onto the scene. I had Finagle's Law in mind, like when you have a toothache that goes away by the time you get in to see the dentist, so I didn't interfere with the experiment as long as the crow was hovering nearby. Accordingly, I made the signal strength read zero when the reception antennae were *uncovered*, and vice versa. There were two little boys who started bawling at their overwhelmed mother because the exhibit didn't work—which was hilarious. But it's also seriously tiring to intercept radio signals for more than a little while.

I spent another few hours in the various other Worlds of Experience, but I didn't find another experiment I could control or impact myself. Contemplatively, I did a few more runs through the cloud chamber before I dashed back out into the heat of the city and leisurely followed the scantily clad Colognistas along the Rhine. All the while, I couldn't stop wondering: What was up with that cloud chamber?

By now, it'd gotten pretty late, and I kept on cruising aimlessly through the hot summer night until I ran into an urgent blue-light parade. Whenever you see several squad cars racing through the night, it pretty much means something entertaining is in store. And then two streets ahead, when another ambulance turned the corner and joined the parade, I knew I'd struck gold.

After all, it remained possible that one day I might meet another soul that couldn't find its way into the light. Marlene had been a soul like that, but ultimately she did find an exit from this strange netherworld where I've been stuck dancing the limbo, and not in a good way. I had encountered other souls right at the moment of their deaths, but they would all flash past me toward heaven or hell, no idea which. So my hope of finding a soul mate (!) wasn't that great anymore, but if I didn't have anything better planned, I still followed the blue-light caravans and ambulances to see what, or who, went down.

There was no need for the ambulance to be speeding since the guy lying on his back with his legs splayed out was definitely dead. As far as I was concerned, at least. The whole front of his nightshirt was bloody. It wasn't hard to see where all the blood had come from, either: his throat had been cleanly slit wide open.

But paramedics are a special breed. I've never seen them arrive only to shrug and bail after seeing all the mess. Nope, they are always hands-on.

Two guys rushed over to the man, each wearing emergency gear so heavy I had no doubt that in this heat it had probably caused one or two paramedic fatalities, as well. One of them slipped in the pool of blood and landed rudely on top of the victim.

"He's still warm," he announced drily.

The only thing you could hear after that was the paramedics doing compressions and breathing harder and harder while they started heart massage. The first attempt at resuscitation made the blood bubble from the slit throat. A few minutes later they finally capitulated and cleaned up their equipment.

"Detective Jenny Gerstenmüller," said Gregor's pretty young detective partner after climbing out of a squad car and holding out her hand to one of the uniforms on scene. She was wearing shorts and a colorful blouse that was knotted up over her stomach, making her look more like a waitress at a trendy beach bar than a police detective. "Who found him?"

"His dog," replied another uniform. "He was barking so loudly that a woman who lives here threw a bag of ice cubes at the mutt. From way up there."

The policeman pointed up at the back of a building in which two windows on the top two floors faced the dark, narrow side street where the dead guy was lying. All the other surrounding walls were windowless.

"Ice cubes?"

"Apparently she didn't have anything else handy. In any case, she saw two people wrestling next to a car. She threw the ice cubes, then one fled in the car, and the other fell down and stayed down."

"And the car?"

"Dark color. No make, no plate, nothing."

Jenny sighed. "Good place for a murder. " She added, "If it hadn't been for the dog . . . and where is he?"

The uniform pointed to the backseat of a squad car. Inside the car's window a fur ball was jumping around like crazy with flecks of blood all over his flue. "Get him to the animal shelter right away. But first let's move everyone back behind the cordon so CSI and the coroners can do their work."

Apparently Jochen was on call tonight. He arrived ten minutes later, said hi to everyone there, and then knelt next to the body. He followed the usual procedure. He stuck the guy's hands in paper bags (the first of which ripped because Jochen was being clumsy) to secure any fingerprints or DNA evidence under the fingernails. He took photos and samples from the wound (a couple of dog hairs were sticking out of the slit throat like whiskers); he studied the entire corpse with a magnifying glass for other evidence (dog licks through the blood on the chest, a *lot* more dog hair); and he documented the discovery position to decide later where the perp might have been standing (behind the vic), how tall the perp had been (around a hundred eighty centimeters), and whether he was right- or left-handed (left). Jochen held a lengthy succession of less-than-glamorous yoga poses, and of course I was totally bored since this was all old hat to me.

Until they moved the dead guy.

He had been lying on top of the murder weapon, which now lay in full shining splendor on the dark asphalt. A scalpel. A well-balanced blue handle, a blade like on a butcher's knife, product ID "PM40" embossed in the handle. PM for "postmortem." Exactly the kind of thing they use at the Institute for Forensic Medicine. Jochen turned pale and looked back over his shoulder at Jenny, but she didn't happen to be looking his way.

There's always a lot of ruckus that takes over whenever you find the murder weapon, and there was in this case as well. But apart from Jochen (and me!), apparently no one else had noticed the connection to the institute. I couldn't share my observation with anyone, and Jochen evidently didn't want to, either. He informed the police of his find— but he did not let on that his fellow skin slicers use the same model.

CSI arrived and pushed Jochen aside. They photographed the weapon up close; they documented its position; they assigned a pro number (in CSI speak "pro" or "production" means "evidence"); they took more pictures from two meters away; and then finally they stuck the item into a prelabeled bag, which in this case had to be put into multiple layers of bags so that the frigging-sharp blade didn't slice through the plastic and create another victim.

Jochen hadn't uttered one peep since he'd found the scalpel. I wondered why he was keeping his trap shut so tight. Surely he didn't have anything to do with what had been going on at the institute?

"I'd like to have the autopsy report on my desk first thing tomorrow morning," Detective Jenny told Jochen, giving him her toughest expression.

He stared at her in disbelief.

"In writing. You can submit the tox and other lab results as soon as possible thereafter."

Jochen slumped. "You're the boss."

I waited with Jochen for the buzzardmobile, and then I accompanied the body to the institute. When Jochen arrived shortly afterward, Viktor already had the paperwork ready and was sitting back at his table again. His response to being invited to watch the autopsy was a quick sign of the cross from his right to left shoulder. The second slicer on call was a new colleague, who brought the dissector in right away. As soon as all three of them had their scrubs and masks on, it got going.

The start of any autopsy consists of visually examining the body in its delivered form and then removing its clothes. By now, the nightshirt was kind of glued onto the dead guy, so Jochen had to be very careful peeling the thing off.

"The deceased is clad in a *jellabiya* and trousers with an elastic waist and a drawstring; both appear to be made of cotton," Jochen's assisting colleague dictated. "There is no evidence of damage to the clothing."

"What did you say he's wearing?" Jochen asked.

The dissector also stared wide-eyed at the nightshirt, which she had just set to the side.

"An Arab outer garment. What did you think it was?"

Jochen didn't say he thought it was a nightshirt, and of course I didn't know whether he did since I can't read his mind.

Once the dead guy was finally lying on the stainless steel table in all his naked glory, the pathologist started scouring the body centimeter by centimeter for external evidence of any kind. This part is pretty boring because the expert examination of two square meters of skin including all fingernails and toenails, the scalp, and every fold of skin takes a frigging long time. But slicers are a special breed, as I think I've mentioned. If a dead guy has a pinhole in his ass crack, then they will find it.

They didn't find any external irregularities on this evening's nightshirt aficionado apart from athlete's foot. But just then the crazed roar of what sounded like a scrap metal compactor boomed out from the basement lobby where Viktor was supposed to be on guard against any violations of morality and decency in the morgue.

The three living souls in the autopsy room were terrified. A couple of weeks ago they might have been taken aback or mildly annoyed and gone to check what all the noise was, but now all three faces were frozen in panic. I zoomed out and arrived just in time to see Viktor frantically trying to squeeze his fleshy, sock-clad feet into his shoes. But before he had even one shoe on, a guy disguised from head to foot approached him and pressed a giant cotton ball over Viktor's mouth and nose. Viktor went limp and collapsed forward, his upper torso landing on his rickety table. The masked man broke Viktor's fall, because otherwise he'd have broken his nose.

Two more black-clad figures ran right on through to the morgue, past the morgue drawers, and then turned right. Into the autopsy room. I whooshed along behind them, screaming, but I couldn't do anything to prevent the awful thing that happened next.

Jochen and his two colleagues had thawed out of their terror and carefully crept toward the door. As the two masked men raced past, they effortlessly bowled Jochen and his horrified colleagues over. The three of them toppled over onto each other, landing in a human knot on the floor. They slowly tried to disentangle themselves.

Meanwhile the two intruders unrolled something that looked like a giant hammock, grabbed the dead guy on the table by the head and feet, heaved him off the autopsy table in unison, and laid him on the giant cloth. Then they tucked in the sides of the fabric, each grabbed an end, and they were on their way.

Stupidly, Jochen had just gotten back up onto his feet. Even more stupidly, he staggered. And most stupidly of all, in doing so he fell into the first of the two fleeing body snatchers. Jochen's hands reflexively tried to grab hold of something, and what they found was the neck of the intruder. He could easily have shaken Jochen off and kept running, but instead he stopped. He took one hand off the end of the improvised body bag that was slung over his shoulder; then he grabbed the blackjack dangling from his belt—and struck. Jochen sank to the floor, this time falling onto the guy's feet, and that apparently *really* pissed him off. He laid a serious kick into Jochen's skull and two more into his ribs. Finally Jochen stopped moving, and the two body snatchers vanished as fast as they had come.

The second pathologist and the dissector still lay huddled together on the floor with their heads down and had hardly seen anything. It was only after they heard the invaders' steps in the corridor fade, an engine start up on the ramp outside, and squeaky tires peel away, that they dared move. They looked awkwardly at each other, unwound themselves, and then looked around and discovered Jochen.

He was bleeding. From a wound over his ear and from his nose.

The dissector chick shrieked hysterically until her colleague slapped her on the cheek.

"You dial one-one-two and I'll see what I can do for Jochen," he ordered her.

She nodded. She fumbled her cell out of her pocket and called the cops.

Her colleague started tending to Jochen. He felt Jochen's pulse, got a flashlight and shone it into his eyes. He felt his skull. He determined that a clear fluid was dripping out of Jochen's ears.

"Oh my God, an open skull fracture," he whispered and made a sign of the cross.

I felt sick. I couldn't bear it hanging around here, so I rocketed over to Martin and tried to wake him up, but I couldn't get through his frigging antielectrosmog setup. I roared, cried, and shrieked my soul out, virtually of course, but Martin kept on snoozing while his colleague Jochen was snuffing it over in the Basement.

It made me sick.

And I couldn't do anything other than passively watch things at the hospital and see how Jochen did.

———

Martin was still not quite awake and out of his safety net when I started exploding ugly words out around his head. "Selfish asshole" was one of the tamer expressions; as you may have anticipated, my editor has eliminated the rest.

"We had this problem with your shitty netting once before, if you recall," I bellowed at him.

Martin blushed. That time someone had almost kidnapped Birgit; now Jochen was the victim. "What on earth is wrong?"

Oh, right—apart from yelling insults I hadn't updated him on anything yet. So, I laid out the events of the previous night in all their hideousness before him. Martin nervously fiddled around with his pajama collar and turned paler and paler.

"And where is Jochen now?" he asked.

"UMC."

"How is he?"

"Hellishly bad." The words almost stuck in my throat, because as you know I'm a little sensitive about words like that, but in this case "hellish" was a dramatic understatement. Jochen was fighting for his life.

"That bad?" Martin whispered as he took in the images and thoughts from my mind, unfiltered. Jochen with his open skull fracture, emergency surgery, the intensive care unit with all the gizmos and tubes and nurses monitoring his vital signs with furrowed brows and anxious faces. I had visited there only briefly and very cautiously—because my track record with medical devices is not the best: we tend to interfere with each other.

Martin took a shower, which I didn't watch, because the way he hops around under the shower with his slice of artisan-made curd soap and flosses in between his toes with his washcloth is neither exhilarating nor exciting. It's just ridiculous, actually.

When he emerged from the bathroom, Birgit was already in the kitchen making Martin some peppermint tea and some coffee for herself. Martin drank *her* espresso in one big gulp while staring vacantly into space.

Birgit stared at him. "What is wrong with you?"

"Jochen was assaulted last night. At the institute. He . . ." Martin stopped and a tear ran down his cheek.

"How do you know that?" Birgit gasped. Then she opened her blue eyes wide. "Did his ghost appear to you?"

Martin had once told Birgit that ghosts sometimes talk to him. So she thought he was like a medium or something. And now she thought a dead Jochen had spoken to him. Ugh. No wonder she looked like she'd just made a five-liter blood donation.

"No, no, Jochen isn't dead. At least, he was still alive two hours ago. I was actually notified of all this by a, well, you know . . ."

"By a ghost," Birgit whispered.

Martin nodded.

"Are you going straight to the hospital?"

Martin shook his head. "They won't tell me anything there, and I can't do anything for him. I'm going to drive out to the office and see if I can't shed a little light on this whole, terrible story." Martin looked prepared to go to any length to help. And that's the kind of guy he is, too. Well, until the first teensy problem turns up.

"That is not true," Martin rebuked me. "I almost died solving both your and Marlene's murders."

Well, with Marlene he had risked *other* people's lives.

"For the love of God just shut your trap for once if you can't make a sensible contribution to solving this."

Once again he was making it seem like I was to blame for everything. Fine. I was familiar with this dynamic; it's always been this way. I cleared out. As soon as he needed my help, he would be reminded yet again that having a ghost up your sleeve can be quite useful. Then I'd let him beg for forgiveness on bended knee and offer terms that he'd have to give one hell of a hard look at. I was going to have to give some thought to what my demands would be . . .

I rocketed to the hospital to see how Jochen was doing, but apparently there was no change so I zoomed back over to the Basement. Things had settled down again there. The two cops, now hunkered down in their blue-light special next to the basement ramp entry, were bored.

So I zoomed back out to the temporary offices. Martin had just made it in. He was sitting at his desk staring blankly at Jochen's desk. He didn't hear the knock on the open door. I let him daydream and instead focused on the worried face of Detective Jenny, who knocked a second time.

"Dr. Gänsewein!"

Martin winced.

"I'm sorry to bother you, but I have to ask you a few questions."

"Of course."

Jenny looked good enough to eat. She had changed out of her beach-bar duds and into black linen slacks and a white linen blouse and put up her hair. The circles under her eyes marred the impression a bit, but she was still young, and they'd fade again soon enough.

"It's about the events of last night. I apologize for seeming in a hurry, but as I'm sure you know, speed is the best investigator."

That sounded suspiciously like textbook talk, but Martin just nodded.

"Who has information about the coroners' duty schedules?"

"For that you'd actually have to ask the boss up . . ."

"Mr. Forch isn't in the building, and his secretary, Ms. Blaustein, said that you can best explain all the procedures within the institute since you are the most senior coroner on staff right now."

"I am by no means the . . ." *Most senior,* Martin wanted to say, but he bit his tongue. The coroner with the most seniority was currently in the ICU fighting desperately to keep death at bay.

"The department heads draw up the schedules. If someone doesn't want, or is unable, to take on a specific shift for personal reasons, he or she must then find a colleague who is willing to swap."

"Was Jochen Beckmann scheduled to be on duty last night, or had someone swapped with him?"

"He was scheduled."

"And who is familiar with, or has access to, the schedules?"

Martin puffed out his cheeks while he thought. "Every doctor, every dissector, every assistant, every secretary, the boss . . . certainly more than thirty people in total. And the schedules are not really a secret. A colleague or two may well have the schedule posted on the refrigerator at home, no idea."

"Do you have the schedule on your refrigerator?"

"No."

"Have you ever had trouble in the past from people or groups who refuse autopsies on religious grounds?"

Martin froze. "No," he said to Jenny. Then to me: "What's that question all about?"

"No idea," I replied. Actually I had meant to sulk and ignore him a bit more, but I was so surprised that I dropped my previous plan.

"A message in Arabic was found. It had been left behind in the basement lobby of Forensic Medicine," Jenny explained. "It explains that the dead man needed to be 'saved before being mutilated by the infidels.' "

Martin is a precise person who thinks before he comments on a topic. Even on a subject as ridiculous as this one. So he thought. He pondered whether he had ever heard the next of kin of Muslim bodies expressing any opposition to an autopsy. He considered whether Islam even had a prohibition on autopsies. He considered whether the events of recent weeks could have something to with people of certain religious convictions. Then he came to a conclusion.

"Don't be ridiculous."

Jenny's tired face couldn't quite conceal a teensy-tiny smile. "That doesn't sound much like the words of a scientist."

"I'm not a religious scholar but a forensic pathologist; on this issue I thus have at most a personal opinion to offer, nothing more. But if you want a more aesthetically pleasing wording, then I would say: I am unaware of any cases in which congregants or representatives of Muslim groups or organizations have mentioned any Islamic doctrine that opposes autopsies. Although Article Two of the German Constitution guarantees the right of physical integrity, and although Muslim decedents are usually buried within twenty-four hours of death, autopsies are accepted in Islam if necessary to punish a murderer or clear innocent parties."

Jenny stared at him in surprise. She apparently didn't know him well enough to realize that the conscientiousness with which Martin practices his profession also applies to his actively studying the doctrines and dogmas of the world's great religions and philosophers.

"Nor does anything I know about the events of last night point to that sort of doctrinal basis," Martin added.

"How do you have so much background on last night already?" Jenny asked, suddenly suspicious.

Martin cursed himself for this gaffe. He quickly summarized all the information that he'd heard that morning on the radio. "I know that there was a violent break-in and that Jochen was brutally beaten. That doesn't sound like something a devout family would undertake for the salvation of a relative's soul."

"No." Jenny shook her head, which she held bowed over her notepad. Suddenly a tear dripped onto the paper. She quickly wiped her face.

Martin opened his drawer and offered her a snot rag faster than most men can say "crybaby." He is prepared for anything. At the same time, there was some confusion in his cranium. Why had the detective suddenly started bawling?

Had he said something wrong? Was she overwhelmed by the case? Overtired? Was she secretly in love with Jo—no. Martin pulled himself together. He really couldn't imagine that.

"What's the matter?" he asked softly.

"If I hadn't ordered him to start the autopsy right away . . ." Jenny sniffled into the tissue. "And this time I really wanted to do everything right, since I failed to call in a coroner the last time I found a . . ."

Wow, this was some emotional backfire that Jenny was spewing out her tailpipe—what a stellar addition to CI she was!

My virtually rolled eyes naturally drew a rebuke from Martin the Compassionate, who laid his hand on her arm. "What happened to Jochen is not your fault, Detective," he said quietly. "You did your job. That's your duty. You cannot accept responsibility for what happened. The people who did this to Jochen are the bad guys. You have to catch them, OK?"

Jenny sniffled and nodded. "I'm sorry."

"Think nothing of it," Martin said.

"I think I have everything, then," Jenny said, collecting her things and walking to the door. Martin walked with her. Not halfway into the hall, Jenny turned around, pulled Martin's right arm around her neck, and kissed him on the cheek. Then she quickly left.

Yet again I couldn't believe it. Martin is so galactically über-awkward, but there's something about him that women find sweet. Like a teddy bear with an owie, something about him compels women to hug him and give him a kiss on his smooth-shaven cheek . . . because he's so understanding, because he took care of them and comforted them so nicely.

Actually, it's kind of a beautiful thing.

The only unfortunate part was that Birgit saw the whole scene from the far end of the hallway. She froze, opened and closed her mouth a couple of times, turned around, and left the building in vehement strides.

EIGHT

Martin worked through the weekend because without Katrin or Jochen they were hopelessly backlogged with autopsies. He didn't notice that Birgit was extremely curt with him on the phone when he explained that he had no time to view apartments. He also passively accepted that she didn't have time for him in the evenings, which was quite unlike her, so ultimately he devoted himself to his old-street-map hobby, cataloging street names from the period prior to 1870.

Although my hope was to stay close to Irina, she went missing Friday night through Sunday night. She visited the seaside, as I learned when she finally turned up again. I was glowing with rage that I'd missed yet another one of her weekend trips. I was seriously starting to worry about our relationship. Now I had to look truth in the eye: she probably had a secret lover.

And come Monday morning I found that not only my mood but also the mood at the institute in general was glum. Martin was now sitting all alone in his office. Katrin was still sunbathing on the shore of a hopefully mosquito-infested Scandinavian wastewater holding pond, while Jochen continued to fight for his life in the ICU. So the wake-up call from the institute's director for everyone to meet in the conference room actually suited Martin just fine. At least now he had a reason to leave his deserted office and mingle with the living. Although I clearly sensed that Martin was awaiting the expected news with mixed feelings.

"All of you have heard about recent events," began Piggy Bank, who showed up ten minutes after the appointed time—his new habit—which gave the staff a chance to whisper gossip among themselves about the latest crisis. "Naturally these events have taken a toll on our business operations."

Martin tried to sit up a bit straighter, ready to accept the boss's praise for the twenty hours of overtime he'd put in over the weekend, but Forch just kept on talking—and Martin slouched back down again.

"We're already seeing cancellations on morgue drawer reservations."

The colleagues exhaled collectively.

That doesn't actually have anything to do with our work, Martin thought. *On the contrary, I'd be glad to be rid of all the drama with the funeral homes on top of everything else. The constant body-in/body-out rigmarole is getting on all our nerves.*

"I would therefore like to ask you all to refrain from making any negative statements about the institute, the situation in the basement lobby, or the security conditions in-house. Gossip and tittle-tattle on these topics are undesirable. This applies to the offices, the break rooms, and the hallways. You are prohibited from talking to the media. You are prohibited from talking to family members, friends, and acquaintances on these topics as well. If any of you should be asked about these topics, please state that you cannot comment on internal matters."

The academics assembled in the room sat frozen in their seats.

"I'm sure the police will also be contacting some of you," Forch continued. "Any police contact must be referred to me immediately. Any questions?"

Martin raised his hand. "If an investigator with full police authority calls and asks me where I was at a certain time, may I then provide him or her with that information, or not?"

"No," Piggy Bank replied. "You will inform the official that any inquiry, any request, any investigative activity must pass through my office first. I will then contact you insofar as this is necessary."

Martin didn't nod. He didn't say anything. He only stared at Piggy Bank. To Piggy Bank, this amounted to insubordination of the first degree.

"Have you all understood these instructions?" Piggy Bank asked, looking each staff member in turn in the eye. Most nodded more or less clearly. Finally Piggy Bank looked at Martin.

Martin slowly nodded while the words "That is not legal; that cannot be legal!" raced through his brain.

"Any contravention will result in a disciplinary warning letter. Behavior injurious to the institute may be punished by suspension or, in serious cases, by termination. If you come to have knowledge of such behavior by colleagues, I expect a report."

Disgust swept through the conference room like an icy wind.

"In conclusion, one more piece of very good news."

A glimmer of hope appeared on most of their faces.

Jochen has improved, Martin thought.

"The security situation in the basement lobby has been rectified. Starting immediately, the electronic access control has been disabled and the new door will be equipped with a traditional security lock. This means you will continue to need your magnetic cards to enter the offices, but your cards will no longer work to enter the basement lobby and autopsy section. Each of you who has a need to enter that facility will be issued a key. Please pick up these keys in the main office. Thank you for your cooperation."

With these words, Piggy Bank rose and tasseled his way out.

The coroners, pathologists, dissectors, assistants, biologists, chemists, toxicologists, lab rats, and admin employees remained where they were, thunderstruck. They all looked at each other. Some looked worried or were sneering; others looked shocked and furious. They were all trapped in the mire now.

"I thought he was going to say something about Jochen," said a guy whose name I didn't know. A biologist, I think. "Instead he praises the stupid keys as though they were our souls' salvation."

"Prohibited from speaking! I can't believe it!" a woman yelled. A chemist, I think.

Martin kept quiet. But he was thinking quite unambiguously: *All trust, all collegiality, all sense of community are now destroyed.*

"Why?" I asked him. "You're all in the same boat."

"No," Martin countered. "Even though we all get along well together usually, starting now everyone will be afraid that everyone else is angling for the boss's good graces. So everyone will mistrust everyone else; we will no longer be able to talk with each other without the concern that someone will tattle. We've been denied every natural and healthy outlet to vent our frustrations, so we will be stuck, pent up and afraid not only of our boss but also of betrayal by our colleagues."

"Wow, Martin, you're a regular psychologist!"

He didn't smile. "I only wonder what Piggy Bank was thinking when he came up with this plan . . ."

———

The mood at the offices and in the Basement not only sank but plummeted. Martin blathered his reports into his computer, he stopped going into the break room, and all the colleagues limited their conversations to technical and professional topics. Whenever Martin had a bit of free time, he would brood over the files about the anesthetized corpses or research that topic online. However, this didn't turn up much.

The atmosphere was really bugging me and getting me down, because even though Martin occasionally claims I'm a heartless monster, it's not true. The bad mood was pissing me off. So, I left the institute and rocketed over to Irina. Or rather I went to look for her. I couldn't find her at University Medical Center, and so I whooshed over to her doctor's office. *Bingo.*

She was again patching up heaps of people with all kinds of infirmities. Usually bad things. Broken arms and legs, open wounds, a young man who seemed pretty healthy and reminded me of a famous Latino actor, actually, who apparently had some problem with a kidney. He hit the floor in devastation when Irina gave him his diagnosis, but she offered consolation right away: "You can get surgery for this."

At first, the good-looking Latino didn't get it. His buddy translated.

"But . . ." he began once he'd finally understood what "surgery" meant.

"No buts," Irina said. "Don't worry; it's a routine procedure."

"But . . ." he said again, making the internationally known gesture for "money."

"No," Irina said. "It won't cost anything. I'll get in touch with you when we have a date."

The buddy translated, and the guy looked like he was going to kiss her feet.

My Irina! Yes, indeed, she was a regular angel.

———•———

Viktor arrived at work right on time that evening. Apart from the white gauze turban that made his fat head look even fatter, he acted as though nothing had happened. Which was not that easy, because even though they'd installed new entry doors, you could still clearly see black streaks on the door frames and the wall from the break-in explosion. Plus, there was still the blue-light special staking out the entry.

Martin had driven home after work, sorted a few city maps, and accidentally fallen asleep on the couch. That's why he didn't notice when Birgit didn't call or stop by—again.

Life was bleak, and it was all bumming me out pretty bad, so I hung out at the movies and took in some action flicks that I'd already seen, and then I tried a Harry Potter movie marathon, although I cannot *stand* those movies because Harry is such a self-centered little prick of a fraidy-pants, and the way he looks at you with his suffering eyes pisses me off big-time.

But Quidditch: I wouldn't mind playing that sometime. I meet all the prerequisites: I'm airworthy, fast, nimble, and mean. Unfortunately, I'm alone. This is a considerable impediment to team sports, but it didn't keep me from spending the rest of the night training. If I ever met another soul, I'd immediately pick them for my team. At least if said soul turned out to be someone other than a nun this time.

———

At seven o'clock the next morning, Martin was sitting at his desk, excitedly dictating an e-mail.

"Hey, what's going on?" I called.

"The issue of the drug victims . . ." Martin thought briefly in my direction. "I've come up with an idea. So far I've only tried to find hospitals that might recall having these patients, but a second approach occurred to me. I'm trying to find out which hospitals actually use this anesthetic mixture."

"Not the dumbest idea," I replied. Even Martin needs praise once in a while, and my ruminations on team sports had once again reminded me of my loneliness. So maybe I was a bit nicer to him than usual. And because I remembered the publisher again.

"I don't have time right now to deal with that," Martin said, mentally raining on my parade. "First I have to . . ."

"But after that—first thing," I stated.

Martin sighed. "OK."

Of course nothing came of it; I should have known. Because Detective Jenny turned up in Martin's office.

"Hello, Dr. Gänsewein," she said with a shy smile. "I had a couple more questions for you. May I come in?"

Martin stared at her like the rabbit at the snake.

"Dr. Gänsewein?" she asked cautiously.

"Uh, well, do you have an appointment?"

Detective Jenny furrowed her brow. "An appointment? With you? No. You knew that already, right?"

"Mr. Forch has prohibited us from speaking with the police without his prior knowledge and consent. If you haven't checked in with him, then I'm not allowed to . . ."

Her look quickly transitioned from surprised, taking a quick tour through disbelieving and stunned, and then moved right on to volcanically pre-eruptive. And whereas a moment before she had just been coyly leaning on the office door like a girl, now she was stomping back down the hallway like a testy rhinoceros cow.

"Uh, I'm sorry . . ." Martin called after her from the door.

She waved him off.

Martin turned around and almost died from shock. Standing directly in front of him was Birgit.

"Hmm, did you two have a fight?"

Her sarcastic tone flew completely over Martin's head of course. "I informed her of the latest directive by the management of the institute, and she was understandably a bit underwhelmed."

"Directive?" Birgit said, confused.

"Mr. Forch has prohibited us from any interaction with the police. Every investigation, every questioning of an individual, must be passed by him first."

"Police?" Birgit said, now totally stunned.

"Detective Gerstenmüller." Martin pointed with his right hand vaguely down the hallway in the direction the panzer rhino had stomped off in.

"And what did she want from you on Friday?" Birgit asked.

It never occurred to Martin even once that Birgit knew about that visit, his thoughts were so focused on Piggy Bank's dumbass directive.

"The same as today. To ask me a few questions about the assault on Jochen."

"Tell her that the detective felt guilty," I advised Martin.

He wondered briefly why he should do this, but then on their way into the office he told Birgit the whole story about the bawling detective bunny on his visitor's chair.

"And you consoled her and for that she gave you a kiss good-bye," Birgit said with only a very teensy-tiny furrow of the brow.

Martin nodded. Again he didn't get that Birgit apparently already knew all this from somewhere, although he hadn't told her any of it before.

"All right," Birgit said, though her smile wasn't quite as happy and beaming as usual. "So what's the current status of the investigation?"

"I'm not allowed to say anything about it," Martin mumbled. " 'You spout, you're out,' " he said running his index finger under his chin.

"That's ridiculous," Birgit said.

She looked genuinely indignant. But whether because of the gag order in general or because Martin was applying the gag order to her, I couldn't tell.

"No," Martin agreed, dead serious. "It's terrible."

"Martin," Birgit said the way a strict schoolmarm does before explaining that you should not steal a classmate's sandwich or punch him in the nose just because he has the coolest brand of tennis shoes, which you really wish you had. "Mr. Forch is not the boss of your mouth. You can talk to me about anything."

Martin looked at her sadly. "I guess," he said, lowering his voice to a whisper. "But not here."

"We can talk about it tonight—after we look at the apartment." Birgit set a printout on Martin's desk.

Martin's shoulders sagged even further.

"I'll come pick you up at six." With that Birgit planted a kiss on Martin's cheek and disappeared.

Detective Jenny didn't turn back up. Weird.

"Perhaps Mr. Forch answered her questions directly," Martin suggested.

"Yeah, right," I replied sarcastically. "Because he really knows his way around forensic medicine. Honestly I think by now I know more than he does."

Wait—why wasn't Martin contradicting me? Wow, he was *actually* refusing to back his boss up on this. God, that is about as disloyal as you can get, and disloyalty was something I had previously thought Martin totally incapable of. *Hmm* . . . Martin, my little goose, was teetering on the brink of revolution.

"Certainly not," he said, dismissing the notion.

"I wasn't entertaining the idea *seriously*," I admitted.

The apartment viewing that evening dragged on just like all the previous ones, and Birgit was slowly but surely wearing down.

"Martin, what is the problem? I feel like we're never going to find an apartment you like. You're not usually so . . ."

"Pissy" was the term that occurred to me, but unfortunately I couldn't feed Birgit her lines.

"My mind is just really somewhere else right now," Martin said, trying to talk his way out of his predicament. Sadly that was not well received.

"You've been very absentminded lately."

Nope, his problem was more, shall we say, spiritual than psychological . . .

"I'm starting to wonder if you even want to move with me at all."

There. Now it was out. Martin turned pale, the cold sweat seeped from all his pores, and he fidgeted unhappily on his chair in the gelato café. "No . . ."

"No?" Birgit yelled. "Does that mean you want to break up with me?"

"No, no, Birgit. For heaven's sake, that's, uh, that's not what I meant," Martin stammered. "I just meant that I, uh, well . . ."

Good grief, what an embarrassing sight.

Birgit stared at him silently.

"I'm just really terribly worried at the moment, and from morning to night I'm thinking about the strange things going on at the institute. I'm worried about Jochen, and to be honest I'm worried about everyone who works in the autopsy section. Myself included. I'm . . . I'm scared."

What a wuss, whining like a girl. *Be a man*, I thought. *You can't say that!*

Birgit stood up straight. Yep, she was doing exactly the right thing. You can't be seen with a whiner like that. *You tell him to call you once he's put on a pair of dry pants.*

But no. Birgit stepped over next to Martin's chair and hugged him tightly. "I'm sure the police will . . ." Birgit started, but Martin shook his head. "The police are just as understaffed as we are. Detective Gerstenmüller is totally overwhelmed by the case. No one over there has even an inkling of what's going on at the institute. And they're not looking at the big picture, which I believe connects these individual cases."

"Then let's go home and clearly write out all of the events including all of the information that you've got. Maybe we'll notice something that we can give the police."

Martin nodded, relieved.

I let the two of them head off alone. Based on my experience, Martin would take a pad of graph paper, delineate various columns and rows with his ruler, neatly label them, and then start documenting every individual fart that anyone has let slip based on its color, odor, and combustibility. Which is to say: I was happy to let the two of them handle the details without my help. I'd check back in on them later to add a final touch to the whole shebang. Until then, I went looking for Irina.

I found her in the Basement with Viktor. My heart skipped a beat once again just seeing her. I cuddled into her neck, perched on her shoulder, drew in the scent of her perfume and shampoo, and zigzagged around her long, strong, slender fingers. I felt electrified, just like when I'd ended up in the radar antenna at the airport, or in the microwave beam from the top of the broadcast truck. Each individual particle that I was made of twinkled with sweet excitement. I couldn't believe she was unable to perceive me. Shouldn't her hair stand on end, the way it does from static electricity? But no. Absolutely and totally nothing. I sighed.

I couldn't stand being in her presence, having her standing right there in front of me but totally out of reach. I had to find an outlet for my overwhelming feelings, otherwise I'd explode in all directions and evaporate like a cloud of gas. I zoomed over to Martin's office in the minuscule hope that he'd left his computer on. After all, there was a chance that his paranoia had subsided, since I'd hardly spent any time with him for a couple of days, getting all up in his business. So maybe he'd gone back to his old habit of leaving it on for me. I was shaking with excitement as I approached his desk and could hardly contain my happiness when I saw the faint glow of the light on the headset. It was on and ready to use.

I woke up the computer and tried to check my e-mail first, but it didn't work. Weird. I couldn't open the e-mail program. I couldn't connect to the Internet either. Even so, the speech-recognition software *was* running; I could tell that from the little icon in the menu bar. I tried the word processor, and behold—I could open the file named IRINA.txt. Martin must have found a way to limit my access to the programs he didn't mind me accessing. Well, at least I could try my hand at a few more poems. I gathered my thoughts and feelings, and wrote:

The loveliest swan on earth, our home,
or anywhere under heaven's dome,
is Irina, the pure, the fair.
Forever dwell in this, my prayer:
Whatever I do, wherever I lean,

I'll be with you, Irina my queen.
Czarina from a faraway land,
Come, Irina, take my hand.
I will adore you in my private shrine,
I can never die, but I'm yours to refine.
You are my only joy in this existence,
I see but you alone, from necessary distance.
And should your death ever draw near,
I'll be with you, have no fear.
Lying in wait, I'll welcome your soul,
and we'll be always together, never unwhole.

Even I was almost moved to tears. Virtually, of course. I saved the text as I had my previous attempts at poetry in the folder 05_Sent_Reports_Archive, but I changed the file name from IRINA.txt to the standard format Yelinova_Irina.txt. The autopsy reports in this folder had been completed long ago; nobody did anything with these files anymore. That's why I was sure that no one would find my file. But if they did, the old file name IRINA.txt wouldn't leap out to them right away as an obviously personal file.

When I came back to the Basement, Irina was gone. Even though it had been almost unbearable to be in her presence a moment ago, now the loneliness broke my heart. I raced out to search for her. She was already at home in bed, where she lay blissfully asleep with her cell phone in her hand. I'd have liked to hide that gizmo from her, because it was still switched on and actually she shouldn't have had it irradiating everything near it, such as her brain, for hours on end, but unfortunately I couldn't do that, of course. I watched over her as she slept for a while and then did my rounds through the city.

The appeal of all the scantily clad chicas everywhere was fading. For weeks now every girl had been showing off every conceivable tattoo, from shoulder to belly button to ankle. I'd pretty much seen everything by now. Chinese characters (which probably meant "sweet-and-sour pork" or "down with Mao"); flowers and other shrubbery; Chinese dragons, fantasy dragons, and dragon boats; every stop up and down the Milky Way; men's names, women's names; Celtic friendship symbols; and pretty much any and every other insipid, tacky thing that exists. The thrill of seeing such things diminished more and more each day, and honestly mortals in general were getting more and more on my nerves. Hardly any resident of Cologne had been able to get a reasonable amount of sleep for weeks, and it was starting to show in people's behavior. Women were bitching each other out; men were coldcocking each other—or their whores—for trivial reasons; and blue-light specials were scuttling back and forth across the city to pick up yet more psychos. The city's stress level was way, way up.

Normally none of this would bother me. Wherever there are a lot of fights, that's where the action is, and I like betting with myself on the winner—but tonight everything was just pissing me off. I flashed through various people's living rooms until I found a chick who had exceeded her sell-by date by at least ten years. She was hunkered down with a two-liter carton of low-calorie ice cream and a truckload of snot wipes (fresh ones on the left, used ones on the right) on the living room couch, transfixed by some late-night tearjerker. I'm reluctant to admit this, but I stayed and watched the boob tube with her, choosing to hunker down on the side with the unused Kleenex.

Unbelievable how deep I'd sunk. And all because of Irina, who of course had no idea about any of this—and never would, I was convinced. Until the last movie of the night— *Contact* with Jodie Foster and Matthew McChloroform, or however you say his name—when an idea came to me . . .

Eventually Annette Schmaltzette, or whatever my ice-cream-inhaling companion was named, dozed off to dream of her own romantic heroes. At some point around dawn, I realized that Birgit and Martin's investigative work had totally slipped my mind. So I rocketed over to Martin's and found their carefully graphed and labeled pages laid out on the table so that I could read them. He must have done that intentionally because normally Martin is a complete neat freak who never lets anything lie around unnecessarily. Apparently, he wanted to have my assessment of events to date. I studied the data line by line, which listed every individual irregularity at the institute with the date and type of event.

There was the female body whose skin had been peeled off, which unfortunately also lacked any fingerprints or DNA evidence from the perpetrator. Then there was the tattooed body of Yan Yu, the Asian guy whose body had been stolen. Most salient characteristic: traces of both an anesthetic and a painkiller in his blood. Katrin's railroad embankment body came up next. Most salient characteristic: the same mixture of drugs in the blood as in that of the tattooee. On the next page, Martin had noted the small number of details known about the body that was stolen midautopsy, when Jochen was assaulted.

Next to that was a list of cases from the last few months in each of which some combination of drugs had played a role. Martin had even included suicide by alcohol and sleeping pills, ecstasy overdose with an over-the-counter cold remedy, anaphylactic shock with an antibiotic, and one traffic accident that had apparently been caused by a delayed reaction time after the driver had taken the wrong combination of pills for some rare disease with a rather hard-to-pronounce name.

Martin has the most phenomenal memory I've ever seen outside of *Who Wants to Be a Millionaire?*, and he had neatly listed these nine cases from memory. Next to some of them he'd even included the official case number!

I spent quite a while floating over these lists, but nothing rang any bells for me. I saw no connection, no pattern, not even a toehold for anything other than a coincidental convergence of unfortunate events. A normal amount of drug abuse or medical malpractice; inattentive staff at the institute; a necrophiliac; and a couple of religious fanatics whose brains had been boiled crazy by the current heat wave. That was the only connection. The heat. Nothing else.

I was already perched on her nightstand when Irina's alarm clock rang, and I wished her a good morning. I left her in the bathroom alone until I heard the flush of the toilet, then I showered with her and followed her to the university. I left her there after wishing her a nice day. I don't like hospitals, even if the woman of my dreams works in one.

Of course Martin was already sitting at his desk when I arrived, checking his e-mail.

"Speaking of e-mail," I said.

Martin winced.

"Apparently the speech-recognition software is not working correctly. Last night I couldn't send any e-mail at all . . ."

"Then it's working perfectly."

"And I couldn't get online . . ."

"Good, good."

Oh, great. Here it is just after eight in the morning and he's already eaten me for breakfast.

"Fine. If that's the way you're going to treat me, then I'm not going to tell you what I figured out from looking at your lists of clues."

"OK."

Man, this is lame, I thought. *Even idle threats aren't fun anymore.*

"I've come up with a good lead, actually," Martin said. "In fact, I'm on the verge of something explosive."

"Bowel trouble?" I tried, but he didn't react. He just kept checking his e-mail. *His* e-mail. My e-mail didn't seem to exist anymore. I received e-mail only by the grace of Martin. Made me want to puke. I was going to have to find a way to access the Internet somewhere else.

I really wanted to sulk, but Martin was so excited about his successful hunt and I couldn't keep my electronitos from buzzing around him to see what was up, so I finally gave in and just asked, "OK, so what did you find out?"

"I found out who's using that anesthetic."

"Huh?"

"The drug that the toxicologists found in the railroad body. The drug I suspect may trigger depressive—"

"So who is it?"

"Well, if we disregard the veterinary hospitals . . ."

Ha! That would be something! A veterinarian gone mad who started occasionally practicing his craft on bipeds . . .

". . . then we're left with the Clinic on the Park." Martin pretended that was all there was to say.

"What park?" I finally asked.

"I don't know," he muttered.

I've always shied away from physical violence, except when it is truly called for, but at that moment I imagined holding Martin's head in both my ethereal hands and thwacking it several times against his desktop and then asking him in my friendliest voice, "What fucking park?"

I must have actually thought the question because Martin replied that that *was* the actual name of the hospital. The Clinic on the Park. Period. Then he opened a website. The Clinic on the Park.

"Nice," I said. "And now?"

"Now you go and check the place out."

Surely I'd heard wrong. But I hadn't heard wrong.

"I'm just supposed to check the place out? Don't you have any other problems you want me to handle? I mean, you're withholding my e-mail from me, Internet access . . ."

"I'll restore your access to those once you've gone to see what's going on over there."

Well, apparently he thought this clinic was pretty important if he was voluntarily offering that. There had to be a catch.

"On one condition," I whispered.

Martin sent out waves of denial at an intensity that almost blew me to the wall.

"Fine, then I'm not going." I pretended to switch off and bail.

"All right, what sort of condition?"

Aha, look who's talking now. "You are going to take Irina to the Odysseum."

Now Martin was flabbergasted. "You mean that new science museum . . ."

"Exactly. I'll give you the details when we're that far. Of course I'll be coming along; that's the whole reason for the exercise."

Martin frantically considered what sort of veiled trap might be built into my proposal, but he couldn't come up with anything.

"Well . . ."

"Yes or no," I said.

"Oh . . . all right."

"OK. Tell me what to do."

———•———

The Clinic on the Park was a giant behemoth of a building that definitely wasn't built in modern times. Turrets, small oriels, scrolls and flourishes all over the stone façade, wrought-iron railings in front of the supertall, skinny windows. No prefab concrete slabs. No 1970s charm like the asbestos pit where Martin had spent the last few years, no glass-and-steel cubism like medical facilities of a more recent date. This was a stately prewar building, perhaps a onetime manor house, abutting what could only generously be termed a "park." A minipark. More like, there used to be a park here before the clinic hogged up all the space. There were a couple of token trees left here and there on the grounds. No idea what kind of trees. (That was a stupid

182

question my editor asked. She said readers will want to know what kind of trees they were so they can picture the park. Fine: trunk on bottom, leaves on top. Or needles. Or needle leaves, what do I care?) So, if four trees along the street made a boulevard, then these thirty trees made a park.

I wove my way through the main entrance and then hung frozen in midair for a moment. This was supposed to be a clinic? The marble floors were covered with immense Persian rugs, and suspended from the two-story-high ceiling was one of those ginormous chandeliers that looks like a glazier had swept up all the shards of glass from his workshop floor, threaded them together on thin strings, and hung the whole thing up so the shards would dangle around the stupid lightbulb. There was a counter by the wall on the far left, and some women in dark pantsuits were standing behind it smiling warmly. I mean, I must have screwed up my flight path, because this was clearly a hotel.

After a couple in-depth tours of the entry hall, I started to suspect I might be in the right place after all. Because instead of signs labeling conference rooms I kept finding signs labeling WING 1, WING 2, and WING 3. *Wings?* I wondered, recalling the square structure of the manor house, but I followed the signs. And then finally behind the swinging door that led from the top of the swanky grand staircase to the second floor, the space at least vaguely resembled a hospital. The few doors that led off the hallway were as wide as they are in hospitals, although the walls and door frames didn't have the plastic protectors on them to keep the hospital beds from scuffing things up. Here, the pale yellow walls featured large-format canvasses of the cuttingest-edged examples of splatterism and spray-paint daubism. The doors to the rooms had numbers on them but no names. I zoomed into one of them and found myself in a suite. There was a hospital bed in one corner, a reading chair, a coffee table, and a desk in the other corner. The door to the bathroom stood ajar; inside, everything was made of marble, granite, and gold. In the hospital bed lay a person who had an immense plaster mask on their face. *Must be at least a broken nose*, I thought. Until I saw the pictures on the wall. Pictures of a woman with a nose in the middle of her face. Normal. Although the noses were different in each picture. One was wider, one was narrower; some had bumps, others didn't; some were snub noses, others not. I had a bad feeling about this.

I spent the rest of the morning cruising leisurely through the hospital rooms. Silicone tits were in the lead over nose jobs and liposuction. Full facelifts, eyelid lifts, and (wait for it!) ball sack lifts were in the middle of the field. And bringing up the rear were ear pinnings, cheekbone shavings, and leg-bone lengthenings. And there were a few hideous men lying pale in their beds, not looking like a highly gifted surgeon had done their looks any favors. Maybe these were the "before" guys?

I reported on everything to Martin during his lunch break, which he spent at his desk. He'd spread out a cloth napkin over his desk pad, upon which he'd set a hand-lathed Italian olive-wood platter, upon which he'd arranged his meal: a sandwich with red-pepper spread on two slices of whole-grain bread that together held a once-green leaf of lettuce in a tight grip. Plus radishes, grated carrot, and a few raw broccoli florets. For dessert he indulged in an unsweetened fruit yogurt. As if all that weren't bad enough, he rinsed this hamster feed down with a very special sparkling mineral water that he bought in glass bottles at the organic market at almost three euros per liter. I mean, that's more than the SuperPlus at the gas station.

My report gave him some food for thought, at least.

"Now I wouldn't have suspected that."

"Why not?" I asked. "Nothing more logical, really. You mentioned post-op depression. Maybe the guy didn't like his new nose. Or his freshly hoisted ball sack, or . . ."

"But the railroad body had had a kidney procedure," Martin thought. "And it's highly unlikely that the undocumented Taiwanese man went there for cosmetic surgery."

"Liposuction?" I suggested.

"In the photo it didn't look like he'd had any fat tissue suctioned out."

Hmm. There was something suspicious about that case, actually.

"Would you please go back and . . ." Martin said.

I pretended to hesitate, but actually I was already planning on keeping an eye on the clinic on an ongoing basis. Or more specifically, on the patients. On the female patients. And especially the ones who were having new silicone implants installed in their high beams. That was one interesting thing they had going on over there. Not the installation itself—yee-ech—I didn't want to see one bit of that. But the before-and-after comparison was definitely interesting. This morning one chick had checked in who wanted to get herself some new double-Ds. What she came in with was no more than an *a* (lowercase!). I wanted to experience this transformation with her. So I told Martin yes.

After the lunch break, I briefly checked in on Birgit—who was hard at work pulling up apartment ads on the Internet—then zoomed back over to the park clinic. I watched a doctor in a starched white coat, who was apparently the mammary meister. He welcomed one not-very-well-endowed chick after another into his office, each in turn laying her T-shirt, blouse, or top carefully over a waiting stool, and then undoing the clasps on her bra. And then gravity did its terrible deed. OK, well gravity had no effect on some of them because it can only exert force on matter that is actually present. The tit smith used a red felt-tip marker to draw lines all over the skin and presented an array of implants in various shapes: conical, round as a ball, pear-shaped. Some women seemed embarrassed by one model or another, while others picked up the pouches of goo in their hands, kneaded them, and asked about sturdier or softer fillings.

Saskia from TV, who had raised a glass in honor of my birthday with Martin the other night, had just arrived for a follow-up exam. I patted myself on the back because I had been able tell from the get-go that those things weren't the real thing. She, too, took off her T-shirt and bra, let the meister finger the almost-invisible scar, and gave him a smile that I supposed she considered provocative. The doctor, not so much.

I hung from the ceiling light, my mouth agape, and I knew for the first time in my life that I'd missed my calling. Popping cars was cool and all, but this here was heaven on earth—and the white coat was just sitting here in his little office like Adam in paradise.

Only with difficulty was I eventually able to tear myself away. The afternoon sun had gotten pretty low in the sky during my visit, and for the first time in weeks I could make out clouds on the horizon that promised rain. *Look out*, I thought. *Not just rain*—because from somewhere over the Eifel Mountains to the southwest of Cologne I could already hear thunder rumbling. The rain starting pummeling down the very moment I wanted to leave the clinic.

I don't like to fly around when it's raining. Especially not during thunderstorms, because I'm afraid of lightning. Incidentally, I didn't develop this fear until after I died. Right around the time I grasped that I'm really just some kind of electromagnetic wave. A bolt of lightning is a physical phenomenon involving an enormous amount of electrical energy. Whenever lightning strikes a tree, the leftover pile of wood catches fire. Whenever lightning hits a power line, the lights go out. The potential result of lightning hitting me is something I do not care to imagine. So I prefer staying inside during storms.

So I hung out in the clinic a little while longer, watching the small, potbellied janitor frantically scurrying around the patio in his little gray coat, gathering up the striped cushions from the outdoor furniture and rearranging the deck chairs on the *Titanic*, really, because it looked like pretty much everything around here was going to be inundated before long. As it let loose in torrents, I watched the dwarf scuttling around with shoulders stooped in a fruitless effort to stay dry . . . and at that moment his bandy-legged waddle struck me as familiar. I zoomed from one window to the next, keeping an eye on him from inside, and when he opened the door to his storage shed with the last cushion under his arm, a blast of wind ripped the door from his hand and, startled, he jumped out of the way. And I recognized him: *Viktor.*

NINE

Lightning may as well have struck me. I couldn't think clearly. I tried to calm down. I knew that Viktor had several jobs, so why couldn't he be a janitor at a clinic, too? Or a gardener, a handyman, or whatever else. In any case, Viktor definitely didn't have anything to do with whatever anesthetics Martin suspected were driving people into depression and to suicide. Viktor probably couldn't even spell the word "anesthetic." The fact that Martin had zeroed in on this clinic through his research and that the night watchman at the institute worked here by day was a coincidence, nothing more.

Right?

I circled the ugly chandeliers in the entry hall like a fly and tried to think. That's why it took me so long to notice that the storm had passed. The streets were already starting to dry when I left the clinic and zoomed over to Martin. I still hadn't decided whether I should even tell him about Viktor's job at the clinic, but when I arrived at Martin's office, it was empty, anyway.

At first I was disappointed, but then I recognized the situation as an opportunity to finally get some work done on Martin's computer, since the headset was set up and the e-mail program was open. So I hovered in front of the screen and read my e-mail. If I was not mistaken, there should have been a response waiting from my publisher. And bingo! I found the e-mail that Martin had been withholding from me for days, in an e-mail folder sensibly labeled PUBLISHER. Sometimes, it's actually superconvenient that Martin is such a neat freak.

The content, in a nutshell, made me happy. I was a writer. The publisher sent me a contract; I needed only sign it, and then my un-brake-able career would catapult me right to the top of the bestseller lists.

Speaking of signatures, there was still the one small problem of getting Martin to do that for me. My excitement evaporated. And it wasn't rekindled by Martin's arrival. To the contrary. The first thing he did was yell at me for using his computer.

"No problem," I replied. "Set me up with my own account somewhere, and then I won't have to always use yours."

He didn't answer and instead closed the e-mail program, switched off the headset, and started pressing on the keys with his slightly oily fingers. I rolled my figurative eyes. How many men do you know who apply hand lotion every single time they finish washing their mitts?

Martin didn't actually get around to typing anything since Piggy Bank had appeared unnoticed at the door.

"Mr. Gänsewein, I'd like to discuss your attitude toward work."

Martin turned pale as a ghost (ha!). "My attitude toward work? Is there an issue I should be aware of?"

Naturally there was an issue he should be aware of: he worked too much. As long as there was work, he did it. Even evenings, nights, or weekends. There was actually a whole range of issues he should have been aware of. However, I didn't think Piggy Bank intended to raise that kind of complaint, and I was right.

"I noticed that you have been researching the origin of a certain anesthetic that has turned up on a few of the toxicological reports."

Martin nodded.

"Are you being paid to do this?"

Yet again Martin grasped nothing. "Paid?"

"That actually isn't part of the scope of your position as a coroner; am I correct?"

Head shaking.

"Then I must ask you to refrain from this research."

"But I suspect that this particular anesthetic poses a hazard . . ."

"Mr. Gänsewein, allow me to explain to you once again what my duties are as director of this institution. My job specifies that I should lead this institution with the greatest possible efficiency. Efficiency means that everyone performs exactly those duties that are required of his or her position and, in addition, that everyone performs them with the greatest possible efficiency. It is the very definition of *inefficiency* to perform work that is not part of the clearly defined scope of your position. Such work is not remunerated. Therefore, you are costing the institute time and money. You are preventing us from doing the tasks we have been assigned to do and for which we are being paid."

But it's important . . . Martin thought, but he said nothing.

"I assume that I have expressed myself clearly, but I might do well to state it once again so there will be no misunderstandings: I demand that you do your work as a coroner.

No less, but also no more. Not one bit more. I expect you to immediately terminate all research activities that you have undertaken with regard to this drug."

Martin sat silently in his chair, regarding Piggy Bank with a petrified look on his face.

"I will also record this warning in writing and add it to your personnel file."

Martin's eyes widened.

"Now, I don't wish to keep you from your work any further. From your real work, mind you."

Piggy turned and loafered away; Martin sat frozen in his chair staring after him. The word "warning" was haunting his brain.

I preferred to clear out. But I couldn't take being so alone. So I went in search of Irina, but I couldn't find her. Not at UMC, not at the doctor's office, and not at home. I could have cried. Irina was living her life without knowing about me, without knowing how much she was loved. This could not continue. I remembered the idea I'd come up with a couple of days ago and rocketed back over to Martin. This time his participation was required.

"What am I supposed to do with Irina at the Odysseum?" he asked after grudgingly acknowledging me.

"You're going to go with her to certain science exhibits so that I can communicate with her."

"You want to communicate with her?" In Martin's brain the shrill sirens of Cologne's fire, police, ambulance, disaster response, and civil defense vehicles all started screeching simultaneously.

"You talk with Birgit; I want to talk with Irina."

"But that is totally different."

"No it's not."

"But you can't, uh, you can't . . ."

It occurred to Martin that I was occasionally able to infiltrate cell phone calls, although that trick only worked with some phones, plus Irina didn't have a Bluetooth headset for her cell. And besides—I confess this only with extreme reluctance—I didn't know what I was going to talk to her about. It's not like I could just pour out all my love as an anonymous voice on the phone. She'd think I was some perv and hang up. No, I wanted to confess my love to her in a different way. I already had an idea how.

Martin didn't say anything, paralyzed in sheer horror. He was having these nasty fantasies again in which the world learns about me and ridicules him or locks him up in the psych ward or points at him like a monster in a circus freak show . . .

"First of all, I can't invite Irina to visit a museum with me just out of the blue. I hardly know her."

"It's not like you're going to take her to a peep show or something . . ."

"And second of all, I'm sure she won't want to go with me."

"OK, then I won't be able to keep helping you with your investigation. Although I did find out something very, very interesting at the Clinic on the Park today."

"What?"

"I'm not saying."

Martin hesitated and wavered and writhed mentally back and forth, trying to write off the whole thing, but he really could not let the mystery of the stupid anesthetic go. So finally he caved. We agreed that he would visit Irina as soon as possible that evening in the Basement and that he would invite her to the Odysseum Saturday afternoon. Then, he wanted to know what I'd found out.

I had the upper hand for once. "I will tell you that on Saturday after the museum," I advised him, grinning. Then I cleared out for a couple of hours. My favorite primetime shows were just starting in the nation's living rooms; I didn't want to miss them.

Watching Martin ask someone on a date was like watching a ten-car pileup in slow-mo, as expected. If Viktor hadn't enthusiastically said yes on her behalf, Irina would never in her wildest dreams have agreed to go to a science museum with Martin. But Viktor had already accepted the invitation with beaming eyes, and it seemed that Irina couldn't find a way to get out of it. It didn't matter to me. To the contrary. It would have worried me far more if she had eagerly accepted an invitation from Martin (!) to go to a museum (!) and were looking forward to it. Instead, I would be reveling in Martin's awkwardness until he finally wrapped up his date with Irina. Because only afterward could he go home and flop onto the couch next to Birgit, completely exhausted. Saturday nights he's not good for much in the way of entertainment anymore.

I was looking forward to Saturday with Irina so much that Thursday and Friday kind of passed by me in a blur.

Martin spent Saturday morning looking at apartments, which had become his usual pastime lately. Birgit had set up three appointments, dragging Martin everywhere from hey to diddle-diddle, the corners of her mouth drooping ever lower from appointment to appointment.

"I don't understand why you haven't shown even an inkling of liking any of these apartments," she said around noon. "I would never have thought you would be so . . ."

"Finicky"? "Whiny"? "Pouty"? Which word would she have likely chosen? Granted, Birgit has the patience of a saint, but even saints apparently get their fill of bullshit at some point. And to me it appeared that Birgit was about to reach that point.

I was starting to worry, so I whispered to Martin: "Any of these pads is a thousand times better than the places I used to live; I don't understand—"

"I do not want a ménage à trois," Martin interrupted me, harshly.

Incidentally, I had to spend an hour searching for that stupid term online before I figured out how to spell it, let alone what it means. Don't even get me started. Why was Martin suddenly speaking Frog? What he meant to say was simple: he wanted to live with Birgit and not with me, blah blah blah. But if that were the reason he kept nixing any apartment that Birgit served up for him on a silver platter, he may as well have nixed the idea of living with her, too.

Suddenly Birgit's cell rang, and after some brief banter she jotted down an address.

"That's good. We've got another appointment to view an apartment at two. Online this one looked like the best one of all. You want to stop and get a bite to eat until then?" Birgit's eyes were glowing again and she seemed to have already forgotten her mild disgruntlement from before.

"Unfortunately this afternoon I can't," Martin muttered. "I, uh, I've got . . ."

"Oh," she said with a pout. "More overtime already? Evenings, nights, and now Saturdays?"

Martin lowered his head. Guilty conscience, I suspected.

"Well, I suppose I could go take a look at it alone," Birgit said. "And if I like it, we'll definitely find a time when you can see it, too."

———

Finally it was time. Martin had picked up Irina, Viktor had waved good-bye to them with wet hands from washing his wool socks, and then they made it to the Odysseum. The first thing I did was show Martin my trick with the pendulum. He didn't get it.

"They don't need an electromagnet in the table for that," Martin thought.

Irina was standing there looking bored. *Perfect.*

"Let's go to the second World," I ordered Martin, but embodied beings have to laboriously travel from one theme world exhibit to the next, and Martin didn't trust himself to just hustle Irina past the dinosaurs and on to the next exhibit. So they ran around wearing fake dinosaur feet in sand, got a good scare by the dino, played Gene Flipper, and after the nice little movie, finally emerged next to the cloud chamber.

"Over here," I directed Martin. "Pay attention: now you guys look inside the box, and I'll write something."

Martin and Irina peered into the cloud chamber (you know, where all the little contrails briefly appear and vanish again). I took a running start and flew the outlines of the racetrack at the Nürburgring—well, only the grand prix track, actually, minus the north curve.

"Wow," Irina said with mild interest. "That's a very clear stripe."

As soon as I'd appeared in the fog, Martin had frantically read the information card for the scientific explanation of the phenomenon.

"They call it a 'cloud chamber,' but the fog inside is actually made of an alcohol that makes alpha and beta radiation visible."

"Huh," Irina said.

"That's the radiation that comes directly from the sun," Martin continued. "It consists of individual negatively charged electrons and positively charged helium atoms. They're everywhere, but here the alcohol fog allows us to see them."

My God, how boring. Still, Irina's eyes didn't stray from the cloud chamber.

"Now I'll write something," I announced to Martin, breathlessly. "You'll have to look closely."

I made every effort to spell out *Irina*, in cursive.

"What's that?" some snotty little miss suddenly asked, banging her greasy fingers onto the glass pane and holding her nose too close over the box so that it fogged up from her warm lollipop breath. Irina was briefly distracted, and I had only just finished the *i* and a little squiggle off of it that was going to turn into the *r*.

"Fuck off, you rug rat!" I yelled.

Now I'd forgotten where I was. Does the next stroke go up or down? It's pretty frigging hard to write properly when you're inside the letters themselves. You're not looking down at the letters, so you have to decide whether to zoom straight or around to the right or left.

"Let me start again," I told Martin. "Keep looking."

I started with the *I* again. That's also the easiest one, since it's just a straight line. Then a sharp left into the curve, then a straight line, then a one-eighty to the right, the same way back to the top, then you turn right . . .

"Me too."

"Me too!"

"Me too!!"

"Mama, I can't see anything at all . . ."

No frigging way. A kid's birthday party at the museum. Didn't people take them to McDick's and feed them greasy fries anymore? Did these fart dumplings have to be here *right now?*

"Oh, aren't you Dr. Gänsewein?" the mom slurred as she tried to pull the sticky hand of the little pest in her arm out of her mouth.

Martin looked at her, irritated.

"I work with Birgit Arend at the bank. We met a few weeks ago."

"Ah, yes, of course," Martin said.

"Oh, please, take my spot," Irina said politely from next to Martin and then took two steps back.

"*No!*" I yelled. "Martin, you've got to . . ."

"Shall I perhaps grab her by the back of the neck and press her face against the chamber?" he asked, exasperated.

"*Yes.*"

"Oh, thank you so much, that's very kind," said the mom, who pressed forward next to Martin as her head was pulled backward. Three brat fingers were now stuck in her nose.

Oh, shit, now they've been totally sidetracked, I thought. *Well, we'll just have to try it again later.*

I followed Martin and Irina through the whole World; they watched a couple of Paleolithic TV shows and pressed a thousand buttons; Martin read every word of information that he could find and explained everything to Irina, although she didn't ask about anything. Well, she did ask a few questions, but I was sure that was purely to be polite. I kept my eye on the cloud chamber.

"Now!" I roared when the coast was clear again.

"Let's take another look at that cloud chamber," Martin suggested.

"Oh, we already saw that."

Martin's desperate look softened Irina's heart. "All right."

"Now!" I said and began writing: the straight line up, sharp left into the curve, then a straight line, a right one-eighty, same way back to the top, right there, slight swing to the left for the small *i*, then—hey, what was that? I'd just flown through a comet storm of consciousless electrons. And my next bombardment got me totally off track. *These aren't just a couple of lightweight electrons,* I thought. *These are thicker and heavier. Damn it, they are getting totally—*

"Pascha?" Martin asked.

Had he felt that, too? I felt like I was dissolving, a truly terrifying sensation. I'd never experienced anything like that before. Not in the radar antenna at the airport; not in the microwave beam with the radio show. This was my naked existence. I was shaking.

"The sun must have emitted some kind of particle burst," Martin told me. "I think we'd better end the experiment now."

No was what I wanted to yell. *I want Irina to be able to see me, I want to write her a love letter and poems, I want to* . . . but I couldn't get any sound out. I'd been scared, well, to death.

I followed Martin and Irina apathetically through the exhibits, and the more depressed I felt, the more relaxed Martin got. He was a scientist in his element, trying the various games and experiments. As for Irina, she wasn't overflowing with enthusiasm or anything. And why would she have been? I never would have dragged her here for *that*. She was supposed to see *me*. I wanted to tell her that I loved her. But I had nothing. Devastated, I spent the rest of the weekend in a grave, moribund mood.

"We're baaack!" Katrin sang when she burst back into the office on Monday morning, and Martin rose from his desk chair to give her a hug.

"Thank God," Martin said, pulling a strand of Katrin's hair from his teeth and then pressing his hands into her kidneys. This was nonhazardous terrain: there wasn't a bra clasp in the vicinity, and the kidneys aren't close enough to the tailbone or butt cheek that a touch could be easily misconstrued. Martin knew exactly where the kidneys were located in the human body, and he loved them for their innocuousness.

"Bring me up to date," Katrin said as she plopped onto her chair.

Wow, she looked hot. Katrin's always a real hottie, but now with a line-free tan that I could see through her white linen pants and blouse . . . my God . . . I thought about what Gregor and she must have been getting up to on that lonely lake in Sweden . . . or was it Finland? Oh well, geographical details were not what interested me on this question . . .

Martin shut me down with a stern mental rebuke, then laid out all the recent developments for Katrin. Katrin grew paler and paler with every word out of his mouth. When he described the assault on Jochen, any and all remaining color drained from her face.

"How is he?" she whispered, horrified.

"He's well enough to receive visitors," Martin said. "I want to go see him this afternoon. Then I'll know more."

Katrin nodded, shocked.

"And otherwise? Piggy Bank . . . ?"

Martin reported on his investigation into the anesthetic and on Piggy Bank's ban on Martin pursuing any further work in that regard whatsoever.

"A private hospital?" Katrin asked.

"The Clinic on the Park," Martin replied. He was about to give further details when Katrin smiled wide.

"Cologne's famous tit shop? For all the B-listers on local TV?"

Martin blushed.

"Don't tell me you've never heard of the place?"

Head shaking.

"Typical Martin." Katrin jabbed him in the side.

And Viktor works as a janitor at such a trendy clinic, with TV celebrities coming in and out?

Shoot. I'd let that thought slip—and Martin picked up on it instantly.

"Viktor is the janitor at the Clinic on the Park?"

"Or gardener or . . ."

Together Martin's and my thoughts sounded like a flock of birds all twittering like crazy in one tree. The words "anesthetic" and "Viktor" popped up in his brain somehow connected together—but a vigorous shake of his head split them apart again. Slowly but surely, Martin began to organize the chaos in the folds of his brain. I was anxious and afraid when I saw what direction his thoughts were headed.

"Why would Viktor have anything to do with the body snatchings?" I asked, dismayed.

"Well, think about it," smarty-pants Martin said.

Of course I'd been trying to do that since I'd made the discovery.

"If this clinic is botching its anesthetics," he said, "then forensic medicine should be able to detect the botch jobs."

Huh?

"And to keep the issue swept under the rug, Viktor is stealing the bodies that . . ."

"Martin?" Katrin asked cautiously. "What about you?"

Oh, right. She couldn't follow our conversation. To her it just looked like Martin had started staring glassy-eyed into space for a second.

"Martin," I said, interrupting his wild fantasies. "You identified the anesthetic in the railroad body and no one pinched that one."

"But the tattooed murder victim . . ."

"Was stolen before Viktor started working here. And we think by the same guy who pulled the skin off of those two women's bodies."

"And the issue with Jochen . . . ?"

"You know," I said, "when the second body was stolen, Viktor took a one-two to the head just like Jochen. And we don't know about any anesthetics in that one's blood. And then there were those religious slogans the police found . . ."

Suddenly I remembered the scalpel that that guy in the nightshirt with the dog had been killed with. With mind-boggling effort I was able to keep that thought secret from Martin. But what did that scalpel prove? It was only one tiny, insignificant piece of evidence. It didn't necessarily have anything to do with Viktor. Anyone who went in or out of the institute—or some other hospital or forensics lab, for that matter—could have nabbed it.

"Martin?" Katrin asked again. By now she was standing right in front of him and waving her hand in front of his eyes.

"Oh, yes, everything's fine. I just remembered something else," Martin mumbled.

Katrin exhaled.

"It turns out Viktor . . ."

"*No!*" I yelled. As long as we were clueless about what connected the various events at the institute—if anything did at all—then I saw no need to mention Viktor's name. I just didn't want to believe for a second that Irina's beloved grandpa had his fat fingers in whatever dirty business was going on. Casting suspicion on him would implode Irina's entire world. "Not Viktor!"

"What about Viktor?" Katrin asked.

"He's the janitor at the Clinic on the Park, too," Martin whispered, more to himself than to her. But Katrin had already gotten that.

After performing two autopsies with Katrin, Martin visited Jochen. During his lunch break, Martin had drawn a "get well soon" card and collected signatures from all of the colleagues who were available. He would even have tried to get Piggy Bank to sign, but the boss was working out of the office. To go with the card, Martin packed a bottle of red grape juice and a couple of butter-free, cream-free, sugar-free and in fact chocolate-free vegan chocolates that it would clearly not be possible to implicate in the development of any future arterial or coronary thrombosis: tofu truffles or whey balls or whatever other stuff that could potentially help you live longer, all the while leaving you desperately wondering what the heck for.

Jochen looked authentically happy, actually, even though his smile was still pretty crooked. The bandage around his hand, the neck brace, and the thick bandage around his chest to stabilize his broken ribs prevented him really moving at all, and they still couldn't switch off his pain completely.

"What are the doctors saying?" Martin asked.

Medical terminology flew back and forth—they were both doctors, after all. I could read in Martin's head how disturbing he found it that he was chatting about life-threatening bone fractures, contusions, hematomas, and other such things he could not see, and yet he was very familiar with how they looked when you peeled back the layers of skin impeding your view to get a first-hand look at the damage on the inside. In this case, however, the diagnosed injuries were inside his colleague—inside Jochen's body—not in some random corpse on a stainless steel table, unable to feel pain anymore. Martin shuddered.

"How are things going at the institute?" Jochen wanted to know.

"I would be interested in knowing that as well, but right now this is about you," boomed a deep voice from the doorway.

Gregor and Detective Jenny entered the hospital room, which was now totally over capacity. Gregor literally dove at Martin from behind and hugged him with wild abandon, which made Martin blush. Martin politely shook Jenny's hand and straightened his shirt, which Gregor's attack had caused to come untucked.

"Good day, law enforcement," Jochen said with a forced grin. "I should have known the two of you would show up the minute the doctors declared me of sound mind again."

He was trying to sound cool, but Jochen wasn't as casual as he was acting. He was probably embarrassed to be seen by pretty Jenny in his drab plaid pajamas.

Gregor perched on the windowsill resting his feet on a chair, the front third of which Detective Jenny utilized as seating. She took out a notepad from her bag, laid it on her knee and stared at it, her head lowered. Martin leaned against the wall.

"Why don't you tell us first in your own words what you remember. If anything is unclear, we'll follow up on it."

Jochen nodded and started with the phone call dispatching him to the murder victim. He described how everything proceeded the way I'd observed it, at least up until the moment his lights went out.

"Could you hear the attackers speaking among themselves?" Gregor asked.

"No."

"Could you hear them saying anything about Viktor?"

"No."

The game went like that for quite a while longer. Gregor asked for further details, Jochen had no clue.

"What was the situation with the murder victim?" Martin suddenly intervened. "How far had you all gotten with the autopsy?"

Gregor gave Martin a thumbs-up, and Detective Jenny also looked up with interest from her notes. When she met Jochen's eyes, she quickly looked back down at her notepad. Was she still suffering from a guilty conscience?

Jochen ruminated for a moment. "He was dressed in Arab clothes, and apart from signs of the attack per se we had not detected any external abnormalities at all."

"Your colleague already said that," Gregor confirmed.

"We had drawn some blood for the tox . . ."

"No specific findings," Gregor added.

"Someone should have been able to get prints . . ." Jochen muttered.

Detective Jenny shook her head. "You did put the body's hands into paper bags at the discovery site, and the dactyloscope" (that, incidentally, is the nickname for the fingerprint specialist at Criminal Investigations, because in Germany coroners are not responsible for a body's mitts) "was supposed to run the prints the next day . . ." She was almost whispering and kept her face down. Martin felt for her, of course. Martin, my sweet little goose, likes to suffer along with others.

Except with me.

"I'd rather not comment on that right now," he thought my way.

Bastard.

"But . . ." Jochen started rubbing the bridge of his nose with his thumb and index finger, but he quickly abandoned that with a soft groan. Hadn't he seen himself in the mirror yet? His face, or what of it you could see, looked like a color palette for a beginner's course in meditative watercolor painting. "I remember when I stuck his hands into the bags at the discovery site, I was having some trouble. I stuck his right hand in a bag, but then it ripped. I stuck the bag in my coroner's case so I could throw it away along with my gloves and the rest of the garbage back at the institute. But I never got that far . . ."

Gregor beamed at Jochen. "Bingo. We'll check up on your coroner's case first thing back at the institute."

"And then there was the scalpel . . ."

"No prints, unfortunately," Gregor said. "Right now we're trying to find out where it could have come from."

Jochen stared at Gregor. "Well, from the Institute for Forensic Medicine, I strongly suspect. At least, it's exactly the kind we use."

Shit. Now it was out. The room froze. Detective Jenny's pen froze in the air; Martin's hand froze on his neck where he had just been wiping off some sweat; and Gregor was perched crookedly on the windowsill with one foot still on the chair and the other on the floor midway to standing.

Viktor, was the first thought that shot through Martin's head.

"Don't talk such bullshit!" I screamed.

"Are you the only ones who use those things?" Gregor asked.

Jochen tried to shake his head, but he gave that up after half a shake and a shriek of pain.

Martin jumped in. "No. Those postmortem blades are also used in Anatomy and Pathology."

Gregor nodded and prodded Jenny to note that new information.

Gregor and Jenny drove with Martin back to the Basement, got Jochen's coroner's case out of his locker where his colleagues had put it after the accident, and took the evidence with them back to HQ. Martin returned to his office, and I set out in search of Irina. If Martin so strongly suspected Viktor in the anesthetic cases, then Irina would be needing me more than ever.

TEN

"How many cases of this have we seen now, actually?" Gregor asked, tired and annoyed.

He was leaning on Jochen's desk, Katrin was sitting at hers, and Martin at his. It was already after eight, and the offices were empty. Viktor was sitting in the basement; Irina was still at home, where she was getting ready and making him some tea before coming to visit him in the Basement around nine.

"First, there are these two cases with the anesthetic . . ." Martin started.

Gregor waved for him to be quiet. "That isn't ready for Criminal Investigations—it's a scientific theory at most."

Martin shrugged.

"As of now, two murder victims have been stolen from the institute, correct?" Katrin said.

Martin and Gregor nodded.

"Neither murder has been solved, and it's very unfortunate that neither body has been IDed yet."

"But one of them . . ." Martin began, then bit his tongue. He still hadn't told anyone yet about the results of his investigation at the Asian eatery.

"Spit it out," Gregor said. He leaned forward and waited for Martin's lips to open, which were currently still pressed tightly together. Gregor is a pretty frigging smart cop. And he's known Martin for ages. He can totally tell when his buddy is keeping something interesting a secret from him.

"The name of the man with the, uh, tattoo on his shoulder is Yan Yu . . ." he stammered, then laid out the whole spiel about his personal research, the restaurant, and so on. He grew meeker and meeker the angrier and angrier Gregor's face got.

"Damn it, Martin, you're not a cop. Why didn't you inform CI?"

"I tried, but they told me that they were too short-staffed and they didn't have any leads, and you were on vacation, and Fräulein Gerstenmüller . . ."

"*Frau!*" Gregor and Katrin both yelled at the same time to correct him. I giggled. I wondered if there were anyone left anywhere in the world apart from Martin who still seriously used the word "Fräulein." I think I might have heard a friend of my grandfather's use it once when I was about four . . .

Martin fell silent.

Gregor sighed. "OK. I acknowledge that CI failed to devote the necessary attention to this case."

Martin nodded with bowed head.

"What else would you like to tell me?"

"Don't tell him about Viktor's janitor job," I yelled, but I was too late.

Martin was eager to share every shred of information he'd painstakingly amassed over the past few weeks. About the anesthetic (which made Gregor roll his eyes); the connection with the Clinic on the Park; and Katrin and Martin's suspicion that Viktor was covering up or removing evidence at the institute whenever the clinic botched up with the anesthetic.

Gregor's face was one big question mark. "But there are only two cases involving anesthetic: the railroad body and the tattooee who was killed in a knife fight, right?"

Martin nodded.

"Now wait. I thought the tattooed stabbee had been stolen by skin fetishists?" Katrin interrupted. "Also, Viktor wasn't working here yet when that happened."

Martin shrugged.

"God, what a mess," Gregor groaned.

The meeting was soon over, and Martin drove off to get some gelato with Birgit. Once again they walked past the corner pub where we'd celebrated my birthday, and once again that blonde, Saskia, greeted Martin like an old friend. Birgit didn't look thrilled but said nothing. Her usual smile wasn't really anywhere to be seen, actually. At some point, even Martin himself noticed how quiet Birgit was being.

"I am really mad," she said in response to his inquiry.

Martin made a guilty face.

Birgit smiled. "No, not at you." But then she froze for a moment. "Or is there some reason I should be mad at you?"

Martin shook his head hesitantly. The words "apartment search" were zipping through his brain, but he quickly suppressed them.

"OK, get a load of what our marketing unit has come up with."

Birgit works for a bank, and it turns out even banks market products too, which they call "financial products." Weird, right? Usually I tune out when Birgit starts talking about banking, because I just don't get most of that crap. But this time I was able to follow her. So their latest product was a special kind of loan.

"They call them cosmetic surgery loans."

The tone that Birgit said that in would also have worked if she'd said "slave trade loans."

"Apparently there is a clinic here in town that specializes in cosmetic procedures. Now they want to offer their clients installment payments. Using loans taken out from us."

"The Clinic on the Park," Martin said.

"You know it?" Birgit asked.

"We've heard that name at the institute in connection with, uh, no, well, never mind."

"Don't say 'never mind,' " Birgit said, indignantly. "If this clinic is cause for concern, then I would like to know. Aren't they trustworthy? Is their work not good? Have there been deaths from the clinic?"

"No," Martin quickly said, squirming around uncomfortably. "The name just came up in connection with a theory that so far doesn't hold water."

Birgit considered him with a skeptical look on her face. "If something concrete pans out, will you tell me?"

Martin nodded. "Do you think you could, uh, let me know what you know about this clinic, um, you know, only publicly . . ."

"Sure," Birgit said. Finally her usual smile brightened her face again. "I feel like we're a good team, you and I."

Martin smiled and took her hand.

So much schmaltzy togetherness meant this probably wasn't the place for me, so I cleared out. I accompanied Irina home, listened in on her Russian phone call, which made my already-bad mood even worse—especially since I had no clue who she was chatting with—and stayed with her until she fell asleep. Then I spent the whole night in front of someone's boob tube somewhere where they had left a sports channel on. Not really fulfilling since sweaty men in colorful shirts don't do it for me, but better than nothing.

Early the next morning, I did a rocket round through the city. There was a fresh breeze for the first time in weeks. I don't know why, but these early hours of the morning totally bum me out.

Back when I was alive I had no idea that the world even existed before nine o'clock. Well, more like ten—sometimes even eleven. When I was in school I was aware of the hours between breakfast and lunch, obviously, as I was during my aborted automotive apprenticeship. But after that, my daily rhythm shifted considerably later. And now I don't sleep anymore at all, since the dead don't doze. This is one aspect of my current limbotic condition that is particularly unpleasant, but it can't be changed. And the period right after sunrise is exactly what sends me into full-blown depression every day. Maybe because people are slowly waking up everywhere—but not me. Maybe also because the early morning is so thoroughly and utterly *human*. No drama, no phones, TVs, or iPods. Just humanness. Pure and unadorned.

But whatever the reason, I didn't like this time of day, and I'd had little success in just ignoring it so far. I get restless at sunrise. So, I usually did a round through the largely empty streets where only a certain kind of person tended to be out and about: garbage collectors, bums, bakers, newsboys, and . . .

Stretch limos.

Huh? I couldn't exactly rub my eyes, so you just have to imagine my equivalent. I'd been rocketing around haphazardly and realized I actually wasn't far from the Clinic on the Park. Beneath me a convoy of seven stretch limos was moving through the quiet streets.

So, people like to call Cologne the "media capital" of Germany. It's a lame name, I know, but there are actually tons of movie and TV production companies here, plus the headquarters for several major national radio and TV channels, not to mention all the starlets who are affiliated with show business in some way or another. Starlets as well as wannabe starlets, like Saskia. So it's totally not unusual to see a stretch limo in Cologne, usually transporting various B- or C-listers around, as opposed to the really big fish.

But here were seven swanky stretches, each long enough to compensate for any underendowment, heading in a convoy toward the clinic on a hotter-than-average morning. Had one of the third-rate TV channels gotten a volume discount for its anchorettes at the tit smith's? Had they booked an operating room equipped with a conveyor belt? I followed the phalanx of false-phallus fill-ins, which was indeed driving to the clinic, where the limos swooped in formation onto the light gray gravel of the driveway. Disembarking from the first car was a buxom chick wearing what looked like a short little white-and-blue nurse's dress and an expensive-looking hat, followed by a fat old man. The doors of the last limo opened, releasing a fat old trout wearing—I had to look twice—a fur coat, followed by a whole horde of people of both sexes ranging from ages five to twenty-five. Only the nurse, the fur ball, and the fat bastard went into the clinic; the others all stretched and looked around with tired eyes, most of them lighting up a coffin nail. Judging by the stench, they'd harvested the tobacco leaves themselves on their way here. In the vicinity of the off-leash park.

I could not imagine that the fat bastard was here to straighten his nose, but when I zoomed into the entry hall to listen in at reception, there was no one to be seen. Boy oh boy were they quick at check-in here. I thought about taking a little spin through the facility to look for the group, but I decided not to. My aversion to hospitals is particularly strong in the morning, so instead I slipped away over to Martin's.

Martin isn't exactly a mood elevator in the morning, either, but Birgit had finally spent the night again, and I really do like to see her in the mornings.

I was looking forward to the new apartment so that every morning I—

"Not a ghost of a chance," Martin thought.

Not this again!

"We really need to have a serious talk about the future, Pascha."

"My future is with you," I said. "And with Birgit. And with your kids, and your kids' kids, and your kids' kids' kids, and . . ."

Martin rubbed his temples, moaning.

"Oh no, aren't you feeling well?" Birgit asked lovingly, putting a cool hand on Martin's forehead.

It's a mystery to me how Birgit's hands can be so completely different from the hands of other women. Usually, women have cold hands. Then they stick these under men's sweaters or in their pants and get all mad when the guy cries out and removes the icy paw with all available force. In many situations, however, women have hot hands—and then also usually sweaty. They paw the guy all over his face with them even if he's already sweating. Same reaction, same drama.

If I didn't happen to know that angels don't exist, then that's exactly what I'd say Birgit is.

"Oh, yes there are angels," Martin whispered with his eyes closed and such a blissful expression on his face that he looked stupid.

"What are you mumbling about over there?" Birgit gasped.

"You're an angel," he repeated.

Birgit laughed. "Unfortunately I've got to get going. Are we seeing each other after work? We could go out for pizza again."

Martin nodded happily as Birgit said good-bye with a long kiss.

Yes, it was going to be a lovely time, just the three of us.

"Mr. Gänsewein, I've been informed that you had a conversation with a detective about the events at the institute, although I made it explicitly clear to you that any contact with outside agencies must be run through me first. For this reason I have prepared a warning letter for you, already your second. I'm sure I don't need to remind you that a third warning will be grounds for termination."

The happy smile that Martin had worn into the office and that had persisted for a few minutes after his arrival because Katrin was there had now vanished. Totally. In its place, sepulchral despair.

"Uh, I, my apologies . . ."

Forch's phone was ringing. He snatched it up. "Yes?"

Pause.

"Who? Detective? Kreidler? Never heard of him."

The door flung open, and Gregor stormed in. "Detective Sergeant Gregor Kreidler, Mr. Forch. Pleased to meet you. We have not met before, but I'm investigating several murders that are in one way or another connected with your institute, given that you are storing, stored, or autopsied the bodies. I have a few important questions; it would be very nice if we could get right down to business."

While he was speaking, Gregor gave Martin a quick, inconspicuous wink, but otherwise he pretended not to notice him at all.

"Excuse me," Martin muttered. "If you don't have anything further, I'll head back to the . . ."

"Yes, but please remember what I just said."

Martin nodded and slinked out of the boss's office like a beaten dog.

Forch's secretary scowled at him very sternly over the frames of her reading glasses.

Martin snorted disapprovingly through his nose. That did the trick. The secretary turned back to her computer, although she then jerked her head back over her shoulder to give Martin a final look that'd have frozen him to ice if he'd seen it.

Now I just had to decide if I should follow Martin to his autopsy, or . . .

"It'd be really nice, Pascha, if you could sit in on the questioning of—"

"All right." I turned around and kept Gregor and Piggy Bank company.

". . . no reason why Criminal Investigations should be looking into my institute."

"Well, key evidence has been stolen from here, after all."

"Evidence?" Forch said as he tugged each of the cuffs of his shirt slightly out of his jacket sleeve.

"Yes. The bodies of murder victims must be treated as evidence."

I just knew Gregor was secretly totally enjoying this interview. I bet Katrin was the one who complained about Piggy Bank to him—not proper, rule-compliant Martin. And Gregor was having fun laying into the prick, which was not normally Gregor's style at all. But now here Gregor was, sitting back in his chair all cool-like and egging Piggy Bank on. The black T-shirt and jeans he had on suited the scene perfectly. Emblazoned across his chest were the words MAD PIG and below that was a drawing of a wild boar's head with red eyes and giant horns poking through its cop's hat.

"Well, yes, I did report the theft," Piggy Bank said.

Gregor laughed sardonically. "Reported? That's rich. The DA is considering taking action against you, and you are making reports?"

Piggy Bank tugged again at his cuffs, now somewhat more frantically. "Action?"

Gregor leaned forward. "Legal action. You are subject to statutory evidence management rules, which you are apparently guilty of criminally neglecting."

"Criminally?" Tug, tug, tug.

"Yes, a punishable offense, Mr. Forch. So, let's start from the top. I need a full listing for each entry and departure of a body over the past four weeks. Each body with its full name, case number, and a note describing whether the body was under the DA's jurisdiction because it was part of a criminal investigation or under the jurisdiction of private law for investigation of insurance claims or malpractice suits and the like. And of course a listing of all bodies being stored for funeral homes. Please e-mail me that list within the next half hour."

"I will have a staff member immediately . . ."

"Of course. However, I'm going to have to borrow Dr. Gänsewein and Dr. Zange from you briefly; you won't have access to them for the next two hours."

Tug, tug. "What does that mean, 'borrow'? Questioning of staff may be carried out only in my presence . . ."

"No, Mr. Forch. Questioning of staff will definitely be carried out *without* your presence. And to ensure as much I will be taking both of them with me down to HQ. We will be able to take their statements right away, and that will expedite the matter. Good day."

I was still laughing when I caught up with Martin and Katrin in their office.

"Field trip, field trip!" I sang.

"Field trip?" Martin asked aloud.

Katrin looked at him surprised. "What? A field trip? Where to?"

"To the gelato café," Gregor replied, grinning from the door. "Double time, let's go. Police order."

Martin needed some coaxing, of course, because he had so much work to do and he really didn't like playing hooky in the middle of the day . . .

"We're not playing hooky," Gregor said. "It's a legal matter and you're coming, so let's go."

They piled into Gregor's company car and stopped first at a gelato place near HQ, and then they went up to Gregor's office.

"What's all the hubbub?" Katrin asked. She had a dollop of whipped cream on the tip of her nose and a drop of chocolate gelato leaking from the tip of her cone, which Gregor stared at openmouthed. I do believe he and I were having the same fantasy involving wet skin . . .

"I'm probably going to get my third warning letter and then I'll be fired," Martin whined.

"Nonsense," Gregor said. "All right, let's get down to business."

Martin and Katrin sat up somewhat straighter.

"The unenviable task has fallen to me of splitting up your body mingle-mangle into clearly recognizable individual cases because no one here at HQ can make heads or tails of what exactly we're actually dealing with."

Collective nodding from the panel from Forensic Medicine.

"Let's do it."

I did not care to listen yet again to the enumeration of the various crimes and misdemeanors, so instead I went in search of Irina. Of course it was already late enough that she had to be either at the hospital or at that doctor's office, but my yearning for her was stronger than my disinclination for asylums for the infirm, so I rocketed through the long corridors until I finally found her. In an operating room. She was just stitching up a huge abdomen that sooner belonged to a whale than a person—although I couldn't be sure since green surgical cloths covered the rest of the bundle of blubber.

Irina's suturing was beautiful, in any case, unlike Martin's suturing of the ginormous incision in my abdomen at the end of my autopsy. And I had no doubt Irina had put the whale's organs *neatly* back inside where they belonged, as well.

When I got back to police HQ, Martin and Katrin were already gone. Gregor seemed to be studying the list of body admissions and discharges, which he had apparently received, and he was jotting down a bunch of things for himself.

Dead boring.

I raced to the Basement, where I found Martin and Katrin full of excitement.

"This one, too," Katrin said, vigorously pushing a morgue drawer shut. Then she wrote a check mark after the corresponding name on the list.

"What's wrong?" I asked Martin.

He winced.

Good grief, at some point he was going to have to get used to me just turning up. It's not like I can stomp my feet or cough conspicuously as I approach.

"Several of the bodies are missing their eyes."

"You look like your eyes are about to fall out, too," I said.

"Don't be daft."

Whenever Martin goes all monosyllabic, that's a bad sign. As long as he's curmudgeoning, it means he's still doing reasonably OK. But when his sentences shrink to a couple of words or less, you'd better start worrying. I was worrying.

"What does that mean?"

"Removed."

Geez, why couldn't the man just say what the deal is?

"MARTIN!" I yelled. "WHAT DOES THAT MEAN?"

"Stolen!"

I was speechless for a moment. I totally grasp that there are psychopaths out there who've got an irreparable crack in their cylinder-head gasket. They peel skin off of corpses and pull it over their own stomachs because they think it's cool. Whatever. But an eyeball? What are you going to do with that? Wear it in your belly button?

"Actually," Martin said, "corneas are very much in demand."

Ah, full sentences again. Things were on the upswing.

"Corneas?" I echoed.

"Haven't you ever heard of organ donation?" he asked. And then he thought, rather rudely: "You were probably on the verge of needing one, what with your overboozed liver."

Whenever I make comments of that type, Martin berates me for being a disrespectful bully and/or for having bad diction. But when he says something like that, then it's—

"Simply a medical fact."

"Fine, I get it, man."

I wasn't sure if I should keep sulking or ask more questions, but Katrin took care of my decision for me.

"Someone has been here and removed all of the eyes from the fresher bodies. Here, in our institute! I just don't believe it."

She tousled her long hair—which she actually had to pull out of her ponytail at the nape of her neck in order to tousle. Then she stood with arms akimbo, shaking her head. Katrin is totally hot on a bad day, but when she gets agitated she's a complete bombshell. If I were Gregor, I'd annoy her from dawn to dusk just to see her eyes smolder. And once I'd annoyed her enough, then I'd—

"Enough!" Martin said.

Prude.

"Didn't you see anything at all?" he asked.

"No." Uh-oh, now we were back down to one-word sentences.

"Did you not see anything because nothing happened here, or did not you see anything because you weren't here?"

"Because I wasn't here," I replied.

"But I asked you . . ."

"You asked me to pay attention, and I've been doing that. That is by no means the same thing as hanging out here 24–7, month in and month out, while Viktor gets paid for snoozing half the night."

Whoopsie. Now it was out. I actually hadn't meant to say that.

"Viktor snoozes?" Martin asked loudly and clearly. *Diction.*

"What?" Katrin asked.

Martin looked at her scared, then he started talking quickly. "What if Viktor has been sleeping while he's on duty?"

Katrin looked around, incredulously. She looked at the rickety wooden table with the two rickety chairs. "Here?"

Martin shrugged.

"Maybe you envision him lying down in a morgue drawer instead?" Katrin teased, smiling.

"I'm being serious," Martin said. "What if he's been sleeping?"

Katrin stopped smiling. "Much more interesting is the question: What if he hasn't been sleeping?"

———•———

"Why would someone want to steal eyeballs?" Gregor asked two hours later.

"For the corneas," Martin explained. "I'm no eye surgeon, so there's no way I could do a reasonable job removing a cornea. But removing an entire eye and then passing it on to a specialist so he or she could prepare the cornea— that's something I could do."

"And then what does this hardworking hypothetical collector do . . ." Gregor said, looking at a piece of paper on his desk in front of him, "with sixteen corneas?"

"Sell them."

"Sell them?" Gregor echoed, unconvinced.

"Of course. You can sell anything. I've been boning up on it this afternoon."

He presented Gregor a list with body parts on the left and prices on the right. Gregor looked at it and whistled through his teeth.

I already knew about the list since I hadn't strayed from Martin's side since he mentioned the ridiculous idea that Viktor was dealing in corneas. Viktor, Irina's grandfather, did not slaughter people.

"He wouldn't need to slaughter people at all," Martin corrected me. "People arrive here dead already, after all."

"And the two bodies that got nicked?" I said. "He sold them for parts?"

"Well, you've been advocating the theory of *different* perpetrators for each of the incidents. The tattooed man ended up with the skin fetishist, and the Arab . . ."

"*Mohammed* personally spared him from the autopsy table."

Martin's thoughts suddenly formed a still unclear but nonetheless unpleasant connection between the theft of eyeballs for cornea transplants, the theft of the complete and still-quite-fresh corpse of a healthy man, and the list that he had just put into Gregor's hand.

Gregor read the individual items on the list aloud in a quiet mumble. "Two kidneys, liver, heart, heart valves, lungs, bones, tendons . . ." His face oscillated between doubt and disgust, then his fingers ran down the list and Gregor quickly added the numbers in his head. "Two hundred fifty thousand euros? Wow!"

Martin nodded. "These are only estimates, but since donor organs are scarce, the illegal trade in organs is a thriving business."

"But only in Brazil, India, China . . ." Gregor said.

Martin shrugged. "Can we be so sure?"

Gregor stayed behind in his office while Martin chugged back over to his temporary office in his trash can. Katrin was already waiting for him, her face pale. She jumped up and hugged him.

"The boss wants to see you," she whispered. "Right away."

Martin stood stiff as a board. "What's wrong?"

Katrin whispered in a husky voice: "The third warning . . ."

Martin turned and walked to the boss's office like a robot, checked in with his secretary, had to wait for two minutes as the secretary kept looking at something on her desk, and then he was ushered into the supercooled Supercomputer Center. The atmosphere was icy. In every respect.

"Mr. Gänsewein, I have issued warnings to you on multiple occasions, which have apparently not made any impression on you whatsoever. For reasons of which I'm sure you are aware, I have added a third warning letter to your file. Apparently, in addition to e-mailing publishers, which we have already discussed, you have also been using institute property for personal use. Here, I found these files in the system."

He tossed two pages at Martin with my poems printed on them. Where had he gotten those from? Was that guy scouring through every computer file like a truffle hog in the forest? And what kind of truffles was he hoping to find? In any case, I was not at all happy that Piggy Bank had been pawing through my private poetry here with his manicured fingers. Martin took the pages, folded them unthinkingly together, and stuck them into the back pocket of his trousers.

"They don't belong to you," I yelled, but Martin didn't react.

"I consider the unauthorized utilization of institute property during work hours to be the fraudulent misappropriation of government equipment. I therefore now present you with your notice of termination, effective immediately."

Piggy Bank picked up a sealed envelope that had been lying on his desk and held it carelessly out toward Martin, who had to stretch to reach it.

"Don't you dare stretch out like a chameleon's tongue to catch a fly," I grumbled. "If that asshole wants to pink-slip you, it's not too much to ask him to put a little effort into it himself."

Martin had apparently lost any and all will because he froze midmotion—with his arm stretched forward and butt sticking out in back to keep his balance—then sat back down in his chair without taking the letter.

"Mr. Gänsewein, your termination," Piggy Bank said, waggling the envelope slightly.

Martin stared at Piggy Bank, stunned.

"*Doctor* Gänsewein," I whispered.

"*Doctor* Gänsewein," Martin said.

Piggy Bank turned a rosy color appropriate to his nickname. "I beg your pardon?"

"In Germany the use of an academic title is omitted only among colleagues who hold equivalent degrees," Martin said, dispassionately. "Since you do not hold a doctoral degree, it is expected that you use the appropriate title when addressing someone of superior academic rank."

He sounded like Her Majesty's Marshall of the Diplomatic Corps, slightly blasé and extremely bored, telling a peasant appearing for an audience with the Queen how he should properly address the Mother of Left-Side Drivers.

Piggy Bank stood up, tasseled around his desk, pressed the envelope into Martin's hand, grabbed another sheet of paper that had also been on the desk, pulled a ballpoint pen from his jacket pocket, and held the paper and pen out to Martin.

"And please sign here to acknowledge your receipt of the termination notice."

Martin drew a curlicue on the page, set the expensive pen absentmindedly on the desk, and slunk out.

Katrin tore the envelope out of his hand. "Let's take a look." She read with frantic eyeball movements and grew paler and paler. "You have been 'terminated with immediate effect and are barred from the premises'?" she yelled. "What on earth is going on here?"

Martin shrugged while clearing his personal belongings out of his drawer: five packs of unbleached, unscented facial tissues made of sawmill waste; a bag of organic honey-sage lozenges; a bag of organic chewable vitamins; some organic anticavity chewing gum; and ten minicartons of apple juice from traditionally operated local organic orchards—plus a picture of Birgit that stood on top of his desk.

"You can't just let him do this to you!" Katrin yelled. "Go to the ombudsman, the union, the police, anywhere else. But you can't leave me here all alone!"

She had tears in her eyes.

Martin shrugged. "Take care." And he was gone.

He spluttered home in his 2CV, found a parking spot on the street, and walked past the corner pub on his way to his apartment. Saskia was sitting at a bench and table in front of the pub, noisily slurping a colorful cocktail. She greeted Martin with great enthusiasm in her shrill voice. "Here, have a seat next to me; you look like you could use a break."

Martin sat meekly.

"What are you drinking?"

Martin looked at her colorful drink and pointed his finger. "One of those."

He undoubtedly thought the beverage was a healthful mixture of orange and cherry juices. The drink came, Martin took a long gulp from the straw, and began to cough, choke, and turn red. He coughed once more, quietly, and then took his next sip. That one went down much better. Fifty minutes later Martin was plastered like a Leonardo fresco to the Sistine Chapel. (My editor absolutely put her foot down over my original simile, so I looked up the weirdest reference to plaster I could find on the Internet. If only she would have let you read it, I'm sure you'd have agreed—the dirty one was better.)

When Birgit found him at last, Martin was leaning on Saskia's brand-new bosom with a tipsy smile on his face. Birgit looked aghast, disbelieving, and worried about the scenario laid out before her: Saskia with her head tilted back and mouth open, snoring like a sow, Martin's nose between her breasts and his hand on her stomach. I wished I could explain the situation to Birgit, but there was just no way, unfortunately. All I could do was passively watch the tragedy unfold.

"Martin!" Birgit yelled, shaking his shoulder a bit. Martin's hand slipped lower. Birgit used two fingers to pick his hand up out of Saskia's lap and pulled on it. Martin slid right off the bench, just like that.

The sudden shift in weight briefly roused even Saskia.

"It's not what you think," she told Birgit. "He loves someone else."

Birgit turned her face away to avoid getting buzzed just from Saskia's cocktail breath and nodded.

The sidewalk-sunken Martin was just coming to a little, at least enough to stammer out, "Sweetums?"

Birgit smiled at the nickname, irritated; she had certainly never heard such a silly word out of his mouth before. "Come on, let's go." She shook him, tugged on his arm, went to the bar and came back with a glass of ice water and dumped it over his head. Gasping and moaning loudly, Martin came to.

"This is what's wrong," Martin said, reaching into his pants pocket. He pulled out several crumpled, folded pieces of paper. His termination letter and . . . *Oh my sweet little baby Jesus!*

Birgit was holding my poems about Irina. She read them and first turned pale, then red in rage. Then she started screaming.

"Is this about the whore you went to the museum with on Saturday while I was trying to find us an apartment? Or is it this bimbo here? Or your detective honey? Well, whoever your wildly worshipped Irina is, I couldn't care less." Two tears ran down her cheeks. "I couldn't care less about you, either." Birgit turned up her nose with a loud harrumph. "If you have anything else you'd like to tell me, you know where to find me. Good-bye."

Birgit swept down the street in long strides. I didn't know whether to accompany her or watch over Martin, but ultimately I decided to stay with Martin. He needed me more urgently.

Actually now that he was down on the sidewalk in front of the pub he was doing pretty well. He disappeared under the bench Saskia was snoozing on, rolled up into a ball, and slumbered peacefully on. After about an hour, Gregor appeared on the scene. It was not initially clear to me who had alerted him (Birgit, I later found out), but I was glad someone was finally taking care of him. Gregor pulled him up, threw him over his shoulder, and carried him to his apartment. There he laid Martin down on his bed, took off his shoes, put a bottle of Coke—which he had specially brought for this purpose—and a package of aspirin on the nightstand, and disappeared again. The whole time Martin came to briefly only twice. Both times I caught a short peek into his brain where it looked like a heavy fog was suddenly clearing, but then the next veil of haze would pass over again and his world would disappear into a milky soup. This experience was really spectacular for me, because although I'd known Martin for half a year, I'd never seen him drunk. The effect of the alcohol on his brain was disturbing. Was this what I used to be like too? I preferred not to think about that.

After Martin had shuffled into the bathroom for the second time, downed a pill and half the bottle of Coke, and fallen back asleep, I left him. His sleep was less comatose now, and I was sure he would make it. I looked for Birgit, but I couldn't find her anywhere. She wasn't at her apartment, or at her favorite gelato café, or at her stupid neighbor's—whose mutt she sometimes watched. So instead I started looking for Katrin, who was absentmindedly typing up a report at her desk and gnawing away on her right thumbnail. Wow, she was kind of out of it. Not a pretty sight. So on to find Gregor. Maybe at least one of them would be playing with a full deck.

And he was.

Or maybe not, depending on how you looked at it.

Gregor was sitting with Viktor in an interrogation room at police HQ. There was a voice recorder on the table between them. Jenny was sitting next to Gregor with her pen and notepad at the ready.

It didn't really look that much like a friendly conversation among friends. It looked pretty frigging similar to an official interrogation.

Viktor was a suspect. I couldn't believe it. What would Irina say?

ELEVEN

"But I do not understand what you want from me," Viktor said.

"Nothing more than a few answers, Mr. Kvasterov."

"And for that I must come here? You treat me like a criminal."

"You didn't want to provide us with any information before," Gregor said.

Viktor raised his voice. "How does it look when the police drive up to my workplace and take me away for questioning?"

Given the time of day, by workplace he must have meant the Clinic on the Park, and surely it would not be looked on kindly there for police detectives to be questioning an employee on-site. It somehow didn't fit in with the fart-fancy tit-smith ambience.

"So, getting back to our questions . . ."

"But I have already told you that I know nothing of these things . . ."

Viktor was sweating heavily, continuously wringing his strong hands, scuffing the floor with his feet, and overall giving the impression that he was supernervous. One could interpret that as guilty behavior.

"Let's just go through the questions again from the top." Gregor didn't allow Viktor's objections to upset him one bit. He looked at the piece of paper he had in front of him.

"What were you doing on the night of July eleventh and the early morning hours of July twelfth?"

That was the night before my birthday, when the tattooed dude got nicked from the institute.

Viktor's eyes darted around desperately. "But I have already told you that I spend every evening at home, except Saturday evening when I am at the Russian expat club. And since I started work at the morgue, I am there from eight o'clock at night until six o'clock in the morning."

"Were you already working there as of July eleventh?"

"No."

Stupid question; Gregor knew perfectly well.

"How do you stay awake when you're on the night shift at the morgue?" Gregor asked.

"Tea," Viktor said.

"But you work during the day from nine to four and overnight from eight to six. Can you really get along on so little sleep?"

The huge dark bags under his eyes turned a shade darker when Viktor lied and said yes.

"But if you're always awake and alert, then how do you explain the strange events at the morgue? And why haven't you ever noticed any of them?"

"When the dead man was stolen, I was drugged."

Gregor nodded with a grim face. He looked at the doctor's examination report on Viktor's condition after the theft of the corpse. He had been sedated with sevoflurane, which is a modern anesthetic widely used in hospitals because it lacks the toxicity or side effects of older forms of anesthesia, such as chloroform. Otherwise, Viktor had sustained only a small scrape on his forehead, whereas Jochen had been critically injured.

"Your attackers were thoughtful to be so gentle with you," Gregor muttered. Viktor shrugged unhappily, looking as though he'd have preferred a broken nose after all.

"The other incidents all conveniently occurred outside your working hours," Gregor continued. "I will need precise information about where you were at the time of each incident."

"But I was either at home or at the Russian expat club . . ."

"Who have you given your access card or key to?"

Viktor looked indignant. "No one, naturally."

Gregor jotted something down on the sheet of paper, but his face spoke volumes. He didn't believe a word Viktor said.

"You're not drawing social security, correct?"

"Correct."

"Because your first ten years in Germany you worked illegally, under the table."

Viktor nodded, but he had to speak his answer for the recorder.

"And now you're starting to get worried about how you're going to make ends meet when you retire."

"Yes."

"And so you thought you might sell a couple of body parts now and again."

"No!"

"The cornea is a very resilient organ. You can still remove it two, maybe even three days after death."

"No."

"No? Can't you? Tell me, what is the shelf life of a cornea?"

Viktor ran his hands over his head and then rubbed his giant paws over his forehead. "I don't know anything about that." He shook his head. "I say no because I have not done anything wrong."

"Because you don't consider it wrong to steal a cornea from a dead body?"

Viktor shook his head.

"And the scalpel that was used to slit the Arab's throat? Do you mean to tell me that you didn't steal it from the Institute for Forensic Medicine?"

Shit, the scalpel was pointing at Viktor, too, in addition to all the other evidence!

Viktor's eyes bugged out at that accusation, and then he sunk his head into his hands and sobbed himself dry.

"I think we'll continue this conversation tomorrow; I'll be expecting you here at nine o'clock sharp tomorrow morning. Until then you are barred from setting foot either in the Clinic on the Park or in the Institute for Forensic Medicine. We don't want you to arrange for any further potential evidence to disappear. You should take a leave of absence, Mr. Kvasterov."

Viktor slinked home like a beaten dog and waited for Irina. She was startled to come in the door and see her grandfather slumped down in his rickety kitchen chair. He was staring into space, mindlessly running his right index finger along the embroidered ends of the tablecloth.

Irina carefully closed the door, hung her bag in the closet, and ran to Viktor. "Grandpa, what's wrong?"

Viktor told her in stammers and dramatic sighs what Gregor was investigating him for.

Irina turned pale. "But that's completely absurd. Does he have any evidence?"

Viktor shrugged.

"Tell me!" Irina yelled, shaking Viktor's arm. "What does he have on you?"

Viktor's finger suddenly stopped, and he gave Irina a horrified look. "You do not believe that I have anything to do with this?"

Irina shook her head so vigorously that her ponytail flew to her right and left, past her ears. "That's obviously not what I meant. But he must have come to this idea somehow. What led him to suspect you?"

"A man was murdered with a knife from the institute," Viktor whispered.

Irina looked at him with horror in her eyes, which then narrowed to slits. "Did you take one of these knives?"

Viktor slapped his hand on the table. "Irina! How can you ask that? Of course I did not take a knife. First of all, I do not steal, and secondly, if I had ever wanted to take a knife, then certainly it would not be one they use to cut open dead people."

Irina gave him a reassuring nod and stroked his left hand. "Why does he suspect you, then?"

"I don't know, child."

"Taking that job was a mistake. I knew it from the start."

Viktor was sitting there with slouched shoulders, sounding twice as old as he had yesterday and helpless. I felt sorry for him. But then he looked at Irina with a face I couldn't interpret. Dark, in any case. Shifty? Calculating? I couldn't tell. He looked at Irina that way for quite a while, then away.

Irina seemed not to have noticed anything. She hadn't looked at Viktor's face, instead staring at his hand, which was still fingering the tablecloth. Then she stood with a sigh.

"I have to go away again, but I don't want to leave you here all alone."

"Don't worry," Viktor said, waving her off. It almost seemed as if he were glad she was leaving him all alone. What was he up to?

"I'll probably be back late, so don't wait up for me. Have a good, long night's sleep tonight, Grandpa. That way at least one good thing will come of this terrible misunderstanding."

I watched Irina get ready and change, then I left the apartment with her. Viktor's furrowed eyebrows and the dark look in his eyes still gave me the heebie-jeebies, but I couldn't stay with Viktor and Irina at the same time, so I had to make a decision. And I chose Irina.

She walked about two hundred meters to the bus stop. I looked over the schedule. The next bus was coming in ten minutes. Time to go peek in on Viktor quickly. I couldn't let that weird look on his face go. While Irina rummaged her cell out of her bag, I zoomed back into the kitchen with the embroidered tablecloth.

Viktor was not in the kitchen. He was sitting on the floor in front of Irina's wardrobe, pulling out the shoeboxes that were stacked on the bottom of the wardrobe. He opened the first box, looked in it briefly, and slid it back. Then he turned to the next. What the hell was he up to? What was he looking for? Damn it, I was almost out of time. I had to head back to Irina.

I reached the bus stop still baffled by Viktor and got distracted by a certain purr I hadn't heard in a damned long time: the sound of an approaching Hummer. There it was, on the other side of the street. An H2, which had just pulled out into traffic again. Now *that* was a real car: two meters six centimeters tall, dark metallic black, tinted windows, chrome grille: *a dream!* And most importantly what you couldn't see but only hear: the 6.2-liter V8 engine, 393 horsepower, 574 newton meters of torque. For a moment I felt *alive* again.

So it probably took a few valuable seconds before I realized that Irina wasn't at the bus stop.

I went into panic mode. Had the bus already come? I rocketed in the direction it would be headed, but I didn't see it. On the contrary, when I raced back to the stop, the bus was just taking its time clearing the last turn before the bus stop. But Irina wasn't in the bus stop shelter, she wasn't standing in the doorways of any of the nearby buildings, and she wasn't standing in the shadow that the awning of a pharmacy was casting onto the sidewalk. I checked in every direction, but I knew deep down inside that I had no chance of finding her. There were simply way too many people out and about at this hour. She had disappeared.

I was completely out of sorts. Where now? Back to Viktor? To Gregor? Martin? I decided on Martin because right now I needed someone I could talk to about everything that had happened in the last couple of hours. And I was hoping that Martin wasn't slurring his speech anymore and had started using complete sentences again.

He needed a little coaching to get fully awake again, but in the six months of my new existence I've learned to make myself conspicuous. Finally he opened his eyes.

"Ugh," he managed, closing them again.

"Up and at 'em, into the shower, and have some coffee!"
I ordered.

He pulled the pillow over his head.

"You'll suffocate if you don't take that stupid pillow off,"
I explained. "So get up, chop-chop! Gregor brought Viktor
in for questioning and Irina has disappeared."

The thoughts in Martin's brain were plodding ahead at
snail speed. I was all fidgety and had to really make a huge
effort to keep it together so I wouldn't start screaming at
Martin to hurry. And I really did an exemplary job of exhib-
iting self-control. For three minutes, at least.

"ARE YOU GOING TO GET OUT OF YOUR FUCKING
BED OR WHAT?" I finally bellowed when my patience snapped.

Martin held his temples and whimpered.

"Once more from the top, my dear Martin, so you can
take notes: While you were sleeping like a baby on Saskia's
plastic bosom, Birgit left you, Gregor salvaged you from
under a bench, and Viktor was accused of stealing and fencing organs harvested from corpses. And most important of
all: Irina has disappeared."

He wanted to know more, particularly with regard to
item one on my list, but I refused to say another word until
he'd taken a shower. So Martin got under the shower. Still
in his clothes. So I told him step by step what he needed to
do: Take off your shirt. Take off your pants. Take off your
underpants. (I let him keep his socks on so he wouldn't
slip.) Pick up your curd soap; lather up the whole Martin;
rinse; done. Out of the shower. Dry from the top down.
Remove socks; dry feet; put on robe; go into kitchen;
grind espresso beans; fill stovetop espresso maker; add
water; screw together; turn on stove . . . God, I felt like an

attendant in a group home for the hygienically and caffeinatedly challenged.

"Now tell me what's up with Birgit, already," Martin asked.

I explained the situation to him.

"I have to talk to her right away," he whispered, dialing her cell number. *Caller unavailable.* Landline number: no answer. "I've got to go look for her . . ."

He stormed to the door in his robe and grabbed for his keys.

"Martin, look at your feet," I called.

"You're right. I don't even have shoes on." He squatted down to pull on his black office shoes.

"And what about the rest of you?" I asked.

"The rest of me? What are you talking about?"

He stared at the material of his robe closely, like he wanted to count each loop in the terrycloth individually.

"Just let Birgit cool down for now, and call Gregor instead," I suggested. "Apparently he's learned something that's put him on Viktor's trail. He must be mistaken."

Martin was standing in his front hallway in his fluffy bathrobe with one shoe on, not moving. His shoulders drooped, his wet hair was alternately plastered down and sticking out like crazy on his head, and his keychain was dangling from his index finger.

"Call Gregor," I repeated very clearly.

Martin did so.

"Ah, so you're alive again?" Gregor asked with a grin in his voice. "I'm sitting here with Katrin at the gelato café. Will you join us?"

"Yes," I said.

"Yes," Martin obediently repeated.

"Hang up," I said.

"Hang up," Martin said.

"OK, see you in a few minutes," Gregor said, and he hung up.

———•———

"Gelato? Coffee float? Espresso?" Katrin asked when Martin was finally standing at their table.

Martin shrugged and sat. Katrin ordered him a coffee float.

"So, why Viktor?" I asked.

Martin repeated.

Gregor smiled. "You've gone a bit monosyllabic there, buddy."

Martin listened for me, as if I were going to provide him with a response. My pleasure: "Eastwood isn't a talker, either."

"Eastwood doesn't fall off of his barstool after a fruit smoothie," Gregor teased.

"It was not a fruit smoothie," Martin retorted without my involvement. "OK, then, why Viktor?"

"Who else?" Gregor asked back.

Katrin rolled her eyes. "You're both Eastwoods in my book, boys. So, rule number one at CI is always to look for the perp in the immediate vicinity of a crime. Thus Gregor has been looking for someone at the institute who would have the opportunity, knowledge, and motive to steal parts of and/or whole bodies. And the only person who meets all three criteria is Viktor."

"Opportunity is obvious, right?" Gregor asked. "He has a key and is holed up in the body basement there for ten hours every night. So he could quietly do recon at his leisure and then strike when he was off duty."

"But he's a night watchman and a janitor," Martin said.

"In Germany, yes. But back in Russia he was a butcher. And since he had skilled hands, people who couldn't afford a pricey veterinarian started seeking him out whenever the cow broke its leg or a dog had some nasty bites, so he also ended up working as a veterinarian. Off the books of course, and always for payment in kind. But his buddies at the Russian expat club still remember."

Martin hesitated, but then nodded.

"But the motive?" Martin followed up.

"Money. Viktor has been working a job with social security benefits and health insurance for only six years, and he's been at the Clinic on the Park for only one year. His previous jobs were even worse paid. He has virtually no savings, and if he can't keep working both his jobs anymore, he'll be poor. Germany's low unemployment benefits for resident aliens are probably not how he envisioned his golden years in this country."

"And who did he sell the stolen organs to?" Martin asked. By now he was giving off a fairly good impression of sobriety, slowly sipping the coffee float that a clumsy waiter had set in front of him with a moist clink.

Gregor and Katrin briefly exchanged looks.

"Well," Gregor muttered.

Katrin leaned to Martin. "To his other employer, the Clinic on the Park?"

The conversation didn't get much further than that because then Martin barfed his coffee float back up and

Gregor got dispatched to a murder. Katrin tended to Martin and got him home.

I was once again stuck in limbo, in the truest sense of the word. Martin lay in his bed, unavailable to me for any further nighttime entertainment. Gregor either, and Katrin was watching TV. Birgit wasn't at her apartment, and Irina hadn't turned up again yet. Viktor was sitting at his kitchen table staring into space. Then I suddenly realized: if Viktor was sitting here, that meant no one was watching the morgue drawers. I rocketed over there to see what was going on. The blue-light bucket that had been parked by the entrance since Jochen's assault a few days ago was gone. Two guys from a funeral home had just brought in a new body and were now leaving the premises. The Basement of the Institute for Forensic Medicine was thus devoid of people. Well, of living people. The morgue was filled to the brim with the dead.

I thought maybe I should take guard duty instead. I mean, if anything were to happen tonight, Martin would blame me for it. At least, he'd expect me to be able to tell him precisely what happened and when and who did it, and maybe even why. I was torn. Actually, it was too beautiful a night to be stuck hanging around here in front of the institute, but all the same it was definitely time to shed some light on all the mysterious goings-on.

If I imagine someone stealing the eyeballs out of my own body and a perfect stranger walking around with them right now, well, I would be pretty pissed. I mean, I'd at least like to have a say in approving the donation. Take Birgit for example: I'd totally tear out my corneas for her. Or for

Katrin. For Martin or Gregor, too, and obviously Irina. But aside from those people, I'm not so sure.

While I was immersed in my musings about the sale, rental, and leasing of my dearly departed body parts, a figure had approached the Basement. I was leaning toward saying it was a man, although for a guy his build was pretty slight. He worked at the security door's handle for a bit and—wow—the door swung open. Just like that. That wasn't possible. I whooshed closer to take a look at how he could do that, and I found some kind of film that had been glued over the lock. You almost wouldn't notice it, plus it had to be pretty frigging rip-resistant to keep the deadbolt from sinking to its intended depth in the doorframe whenever someone had last tried to lock it.

The intruder was in the Basement, moving into the morgue drawer area and starting to pull them open, one by one. In the cold light of the ceiling lights, which turn on when a motion detector is activated, I recognized the guy. He worked for one of the funeral homes that had a ton of bodies stored here. *Right!* This was the guy that Jochen had checked in so humorously at the door. Now I understood why he had never once looked Jochen in the face. Even back then, the guy had a guilty conscience!

Apparently he found what he was looking for: the new body. What he would do next, I was betting, would be to take out his big knife, slice the eyeballs and maybe all the other organs, too, right out of the body, and that would prove Viktor's innocence. All I needed to do was make sure the cops didn't pick him up right away. So I had to go see Martin.

This time I was in luck. After puking all over the gelato café, Martin had gone to bed still in rough shape—maybe

Katrin had even put him to bed—but at least the antielec-trosmog netting was open. I woke Martin up with all the energy I could muster. And that was a lot. He went vertical within seconds.

"Someone's in the Basement stealing bodies. Quick, we have to clear Viktor's name. Viktor didn't do anything. And he couldn't have done anything, either, my Irina's grandpa—what bullshit. We can't do that to her. So chop-chop! Aren't you dressed yet? Come on and bring the cops with you."

I raced back to the Basement still in time to watch the guy with the knife whittling away at the body. The murder victim was no longer in the drawer but on the stainless steel table, where the bodies are stored temporarily until their toes have been tagged and someone figures out which drawer is vacant. The dermaphilic thief bent low over his victim, about to peel the skin from the body. I felt sick. I had no idea skin was so tough. The guy was hacking away pretty rabidly at the body without even cutting the skin. It was time for Martin to finally get here.

But the cops came first. Logical, since they drive *cars*. Not trash cans. Two squad cars raced to the scene, blue lights flashing but no sirens, parked on the ramp down to the basement lobby and waited for Martin to open up. God, how dumb could they be? If the door lock were working, the guy wouldn't be inside!

Martin finally arrived, pointed out that based on his information the door was already open, and waited with shaking knees while the uniforms stormed the Basement, overpowered the guy with the knife, puked on the stainless steel table when they saw what was lying there, and called it in to HQ.

"Affirmative, someone is here from the institute who can secure the discovery site immediately. Over," the uniform relayed into his radio.

Martin tugged on the officer's sleeve. "Uh, no, unfortunately I'm no longer, uh . . ."

The man stared at him blankly.

"Please ask Detective Sergeant Gregor Kreidler to come. And if possible he should bring Dr. Zange with him; she can work with CSI to secure the discovery site for forensics."

The cheerful comings and goings in the Basement lasted a few more hours, which I skipped for the most part, however. I kept rocketing back over to Irina and Viktor's apartment, but no one was there. I was starting to get worried about Viktor, now, as well as Irina. Until they were found, there was no way to tell them that Viktor's questioning had been a misunderstanding. The real perp was in custody, and after the cops caught him in flagrante delicto (I heard that in a movie once), the poor bastard collapsed into a blubbering pile of sobs. He would confess, I was certain of that, and then everything would be OK again.

—————

"Did you remove the skin from a body at the Institute for Forensic Medicine on July twelfth?"

"Yes."

"Did you steal a body from the Institute of Forensic Medicine on July twelfth as well?"

"No."

"Did you remove the silicone breast implants from the woman's body that you put into cold storage at the Institute for Forensic Medicine on July twenty-sixth?"

"Yes."

"Did you desecrate a body in Melaten Cemetery on July twenty-eighth?"

"Yes."

"Did you remove and steal the eyeballs of bodies from the Institute for Forensic Medicine?"

"No."

"Did you sell bodies or parts of bodies?"

"No."

Gregor pressed the stop button on his voice recorder.

"It goes on like that for hours," he said.

Martin was chewing on his lower lip as he stood across from Gregor's desk after turning down both coffee and water.

"He admits everything that has to do with the mutilations," Gregor continued. "Incidentally, the police have known about him for a while and he's got several priors. But a court declared his necrophilia to be a mental illness, and instead of landing in the can he spent a couple of months at a psychiatric hospital. He's from southern Germany originally, and he's only been in Cologne since he got out of treatment two months ago. He's picked up a few skills, too: now he always wears gloves, which is why we never got any of his prints off the bodies. The funeral home hired him as an assistant. Clever move on his part. You can't get any closer to bodies than that. Except as a coroner."

Gregor grinned provocatively at Martin.

Martin remained earnest. "Do you believe him?"

"No idea."

They were silent, lost in thought, until Martin suddenly snapped out of his reveries. "Now I'm wondering if it was this guy or Viktor—but either way, there has to be someone else in the wings."

"What do you mean?" Gregor asked.

"Viktor may understand the physical side of organ theft, but I don't think he could pull off the whole thing by himself. Organ trafficking is an international business. You've got to have contacts and know who to sell to and at what price. I don't think Viktor is capable of that."

"You mean someone else is pulling the strings?"

Martin nodded.

They were silent again, thinking, until Gregor finally stood and stretched. "Jenny is handling the questioning of our necrophiliac, and I'm going in with Viktor in a few minutes when he gets here. It'll be ridiculous if we can't convict the guy quickly."

Gregor walked Martin to the door, shook his hand good-bye, and then asked at reception if Mr. Kvasterov had arrived. Not yet. So Gregor left instructions that they should call him the minute Viktor arrived, or put out an APB if he hadn't checked in by eleven o'clock. Then he went back to his office, put his head in his hands, and fell asleep within seconds.

"What are you going to do now?" I asked Martin.

Martin shrugged.

"Did you talk to Birgit yet?" I asked.

Head shaking.

"Why not?"

Shrugging.

There was nothing to read in his brain. Or rather, it was empty. Completely. Cleared out like a fencing storefront after a police raid. I was slowly getting worried.

"Call her and apologize," I said.

"And what then?" Martin asked back. His tone was suddenly aggressive. "What should I tell her? That I do love her but not enough to live with her?"

"Why shouldn't you live with her?" I asked.

"I can't live with any woman as long as you're with me."

"But I . . ."

"No, Pascha. It's a fact. I can't expect any woman to live under the same roof with you."

Ouch! So it was all my fault, yet again. I'd destroyed Martin's happiness with Birgit. And even if another woman found her way into his heart, I would destroy that happiness as well. Forever and ever, I would destroy *any* happiness. Unless I disappeared.

I was pissed, obviously, but then the cruel truth started slowly seeping into my brain. I was responsible for everything that had gone wrong in Martin's life over the past six months. It was my fault that his colleagues thought he was going off his rocker; it was my fault that he'd almost died; it was my fault that he'd lost his job—and now the great love of his life, too. All because of me.

So I made a decision. The most horrible, the most difficult, the most serious decision of my life.

"OK, I'll disappear," I said. In my ears I sounded all choked up. "Farewell, Martin."

I stayed a moment with him, watched him suddenly freeze there, stiff as a board, listening in my direction, but I switched off and he couldn't sense me anymore. Then I slowly flew higher and left Martin with his sagging shoulders and searching eyes alone on the street, secretly wishing him all the best. My heart had never, ever, ever felt so heavy before.

From now on, I was all alone. I felt that the full impact of this terrible decision would only become clear to me later. To prevent a monster wave of despair from suddenly swamping me from behind, I decided to keep myself busy. The best way to keep busy is always a criminal investigation. Investigations really hog every bit of your brain, thereby ousting whatever personal problems you have. Not that it was going to benefit anyone, since if I couldn't tell Martin about what I found out, the whole undertaking was futile, but I couldn't think of a better idea. At least not as long as Irina hadn't turned up again, and she hadn't yet, as my rounds through her apartment, UMC, and the doctor's office confirmed.

What should I do first? Well, anyone who hawks body parts would need to find a buyer for them. A buyer who knew what he was doing. Which meant either reselling the items or reusing them himself. So it had to be a medical facility of some sort, one way or another.

I zoomed over to the Clinic on the Park. Viktor wasn't there. A young woman in a nurse's costume with an irritated expression was carrying pillows for the deck chairs outside while two miraculous mammary masterpieces were waiting impatiently to bask in the sun, which had just risen over the tops of the trees.

The head physician was not out and about at this hour of the morning with his felt-tip, marking up abdominal walls or breast folds, but instead was standing in his face mask and green scrubs over the operating table. Every morning at 9:31, half of the population of Germany can be found stuffing rib fat into their mouths, while the other half is having it vacuumed back out again. Is that what they call a "circular economy"?

I was not particularly thrilled at the thought of peering into bleeding wounds, so I kept watch from the door. Around noon, Dr. Jens Hagenbeck, proprietor and head physician at the Clinic on the Park, exited the operating room, entered his private bathroom, and took a lengthy shower. Around twelve thirty he opened the door to his private office, picked up the receiver to his landline, and ordered two big plates of salad and a half liter of chilled white wine. I wondered if the unorthodox clinic cafeteria offered giant, fat-laden hamburgers as well? That'd be awesome, fattening the people back up again scarcely moments after the fat had been vacuumed out of them. Then the patients could check themselves out and make a new appointment at the same time.

There was a knock at the door, and the apparently expected guest entered the private office of Dr. Hagenbeck along with the salads and wine.

And I couldn't believe my eyes: it was Piggy Bank.

They shook hands, patted shoulders, and addressed each other by first name.

They sat down to eat. Hagenbeck filled his wineglass, which fogged up. Piggy Bank stuck to chilled mineral water. The salad crunched loudly, it was so fresh.

I hovered under the ceiling, speechless. Slowly but surely, understanding took form. Who had found the funeral homes by renting access to the morgue, thereby securing access to a terrific selection of additional bodies? Piggy Bank. Who had connections to an ideal buyer of recycled organs? Him too. Who kept rambling on and on about utilization of resources and optimization of efficiencies and improvement of operating (!) revenue? Piggy Bank.

All the weird events at the institute had started two months ago—practically at the same time that Piggy Bank had come in as its new director.

No one was going to believe me. To say nothing of the fact that there wasn't anyone I could tell about my discovery anymore anyway. I needed proof. Once I had really conclusive proof, I could decide how to get the results of my extra investigating into the hands of the police. But until then it was all up to me. I had to take a much closer look at things, I had to remember everything that I'd learned from Martin and Gregor over the past few months, and I had to keep my eyes and ears everywhere. No more movies, no more TV, no more nocturnal navel-gazing. Starting now I was on duty 24-7.

So far I'd been paying attention mainly to the female patients of the facility—pure male selfishness. But now, if I wanted to seriously jump into the investigation business on my own, I'd have to come off my hormone autopilot and do my own steering . . . so, I tried to find out all the medical details of each patient. There were breast augmentations (7), breast reductions (1), nose jobs (3), face lifts (4), butt lifts (2), liposuctions (9), and one kidney transplant.

The operation list was quite unusual, I thought. You might also say: it stunk like a pile of burning tires. Thousands of tits, and one kidney. The renal customer was the bastard who had driven up a few days ago—I was slowly losing all sense of time—with his entire royal retinue in those stretch limos. He had apparently gone under the knife that morning, because now he was dozing in the intensive-care room under round-the-clock monitoring by a nurse.

Another patient was lying in the next room, which lacked all the intensive-care hoo-ha. He was pale and had tubes coming out of him everywhere, but he still looked good. He reminded me of an actor, but I couldn't think of his name. No matter.

I didn't find any cornea transplants, however. If Hagenbeck was having people nick eyeballs complete with corneas for him, then he was fencing them immediately. He apparently did not handle delicate eye surgeries; he did more of the rough stuff.

I thought about what evidence there was, and I had to admit that it didn't look good. I had no evidence of an organized organ theft ring. Plus, I'd have to verify the route that the bodies in the Basement at the institute were taking to get to the Clinic on the Park. Maybe Martin and Gregor had made some headway. I could probably just check in on them real quiet-like and see if I could get any more pieces to my puzzle there.

"We haven't had a breakthrough yet, but we do finally have an ID," Gregor was yelling through his office. He was alone. *No.* That couldn't be . . . I held my breath. Was he talking to *me?*

"But what was the guy doing in the middle of downtown Cologne?" came Detective Jenny's voice. I followed the direction the voice came from and found Jenny at a copy machine in the hallway. Oh, too bad. I'd hoped many times that maybe Gregor could also . . .

"I don't think he's a unique case."

Jenny came into the office, tossed a couple of sheets of paper onto Gregor's desk, sat down in front of it on his visitor's chair, and studied the copies.

"Haroun Abdelhadi, age forty-four, Moroccan. Application for asylum denied. Court-ordered deportation. Deportation not executed because subject cannot be found. Illegal alien."

Gregor had listened with his eyes closed. "Do you know how many anonymous bodies we're stuck with right now?" he asked.

"We had three," Jenny answered promptly, "and unfortunately we're not actually stuck with all of them because two of three have gone missing. We're lucky Jochen was able to deliver on Abdelhadi's prints *and* that he was already in the system, so that at least knocks our count of anonymous bodies down to two."

"Three dead people who haven't been reported missing," Gregor said. "Statistically speaking, that is suspicious. Or should I say, it stinks to high heaven."

"You think there's a connection?" A realization.

Gregor looked at his watch. "Let's go get something to eat."

Jenny rolled her eyes. "It's not even quite noon yet."

"I'm buying. Chinese."

Gregor and Jenny entered the Palace of Glutamate through the front door, the place that Martin had told them about. Two beat cops were already stationed at the back exit. They ordered a little something, ate it, drank Coke with it, and were happy to accept the jasmine tea on the house. Gregor pulled the photo of the tattoo out of his pocket, the same photo Martin had been in with before. Bedlam broke out in the kitchen immediately. Only this time no one managed to escape through the back door.

"Please tell me who this man is," Gregor urged his eight-person audience after he'd shown them his badge and stated that the man had presumably fallen victim to a major conspiracy.

Nobody said anything; nobody even looked up.

"What we know so far is that this man's name is Yan Yu and that he had an operation. Or was supposed to have an operation. In any case, when he died he had an anesthetic in his blood."

The nice waitress and an older woman quickly stole glances at each other without moving their heads.

Jenny approached the waitress, set her hand on her arm, and quietly said, "It doesn't matter what it is. Just tell us. Please. We're not out to make trouble for anyone. We know that most of you are here illegally. We don't want to see any passports, no papers, nothing. We just need a lead. Several people have died, and we suspect something terrible is going on, but we can't prove anything. Please help us."

Another glance at the older woman, then the waitress slowly looked up. "He couldn't get the operation. He didn't have health insurance."

"Health insurance cards don't have pictures on them," Gregor said. "Maybe he went in with someone else's card . . ."

The young woman shook her head. "No one here has a card."

Jenny looked at the ground, slightly troubled.

"There is one doctor who doesn't ask for an insurance card," the young woman hesitantly said. "But it's not a hospital. No operation."

Gregor hit his forehead. "Where has my head been? You're talking about the Friends of Hippocrates?"

The woman nodded.

"Was your friend sick?"

The young and old women again exchanged glances. The little boy looked at Gregor and shrugged. "Actually he just had a bad shoulder. But he seemed upset after he saw the doctor. He didn't want to tell me anything."

Jenny and Gregor thanked the staff and got back into the car to find the doctor—but on the way they received an urgent call on the radio, ordering them back to HQ: Viktor Kvasterov had turned up.

T W E L V E

Viktor! I screamed his name, even though I knew he couldn't hear me. Or maybe he could, if his soul were still zipping around nearby. If so, maybe he could tell me why he'd strung himself up on that branch in the backmost corner of the clinic park.

But I knew the answer already. Viktor had gotten mixed up in this nasty game. He'd stolen two bodies from the institute because the Clinic on the Park had some interest in them. Were they victims of malpractice? Was the anesthetic that Martin had been investigating in fact related to this case? Did Piggy Bank and the clinic's owner Dr. Hagenbeck hire Viktor to hide the evidence, as well as to remove valuable corneas from the institute's dead bodies? Viktor's suicide was an admission of guilt, clearer than anything else would have been. I felt like I'd slammed into a bridge pier at a hundred eighty. That dear, sweet old Viktor sitting in the basement embroidering tablecloths was actually an organjacker. *A vulture.* How could he do this to his beloved Irina?

"Suicide?" Gregor asked Katrin, who was already at the discovery site and had performed a coroner's inspection of the body.

Katrin nodded. "He climbed up on this wall, fixed the rope to the branch, and jumped off the wall. CSI found his footprints in the planting bed, on the stool, and on the wall.

The knots of the rope are positioned laterally on either side of the neck, which further suggests suicide as opposed to foul play, and his hands don't exhibit any signs that he struggled with someone who might have been hanging him up. It's a textbook suicide."

"And the choice of location . . . ?" Gregor said.

"You are responsible for the interpretation, but I suspect we're thinking along the same lines."

Gregor nodded.

While I observed from above with a hazy feeling in my head, Katrin oversaw the removal of the body, then took off her protective overalls and sat down in one of the deck chairs located outside the police cordon. The patio was empty because the arriving police had banned all patients and clinic personnel from the yard. Except Dr. Hagenbeck, who was now racing across the lawn toward Gregor.

"Are you the lead detective here?" he was yelling from a distance. "This is a personal tragedy—poor Mr. Kvasterov—but it's also quite a terrible experience for us and our patients. I would be grateful if you could deal with this as quickly as possible and—"

"Disappear again?" Gregor said drily. "As soon as we have finished our work, Mr. . . . ."

Hagenbeck was taken aback. "Hagenbeck," he said, offering Gregor his hand. "Dr. Jens Hagenbeck."

"Why do you suppose Mr. Kvasterov chose to hang himself here, of all places?" Gregor asked.

"How should I know?"

Detective Jenny joined the two of them. "But I'm sure you must have a theory?" she said in a sugar-sweet voice.

Hagenbeck was apparently distracted briefly by Jenny's appearance in her tight-fitting blouse and casual linen slacks, but he quickly pulled himself together again. "Mr. Kvasterov loved the park. He was employed here as a janitor and gardener, but I'm sure you know that, and he had a very special relationship with the plants. Perhaps this was the place he truly felt most at home."

"Yes, perhaps," Jenny said with a slight smile.

Hagenbeck did not smile back.

"If we have any other questions, we'd be happy to come up to your office," Gregor said with a curt nod.

Hagenbeck stared with a stupid look on his face until he got that he was supposed to clear out, and then walked back into the building in a huff.

"Does the suicide give us cause to check inside the clinic?" Jenny asked with a furrowed brow.

"Unfortunately not," Gregor said. "We'll have to find the answers somewhere else. Let's meet at my office in two hours."

I was in a dilemma. Should I break my oath and let Martin know that Hagenbeck and Piggy Bank knew each other? Would that give the investigation a leg up? Maybe, but how much of one? But realistically that information wasn't going to help the way things stood, so it'd be a major mistake to contact Martin—and even if I'd decided other-wise at this point in the events, it wouldn't have prevented the impending crisis. At least, I didn't think I would.

At first I went in search of the person who most espe-cially needed support just then, particularly from me: Irina.

I got lucky and found her in her apartment. She was staring at a sheet of paper scribbled full of odd symbols. Russian letters, I thought. But handwritten they looked even trippier than on a vodka label.

"Irina, my beloved, I am so super mega sorry," I whispered into her ear, even though I knew she couldn't hear me.

She looked at the paper, crumpled it, smoothed it out, and crumpled it again. Then, she slammed her hand on the table and screamed something in Russian. I flew back a bit, both in surprise and fear.

Then I understood. It was the suicide note. But Irina's first reaction wasn't sad or despondent—but fucking pissed. It puzzled me at first, but then I got it: a suicide is a cowardly way out, without regard for those left behind. Irina had every reason to be pissed at Viktor. First he was into all those shady dealings, and then he skedaddled off through the back door and left Irina alone to clean up all the mess he'd left behind. How was she going to cope without her grandfather, who had also supported her financially? Who'd been her entire family?

Irina was so trapped in her pain that she never heard the first buzz at her door. She reacted only at the second buzz.

She stood up, turned around again, put Viktor's suicide note into her pants pocket, and went to the door. Two uniforms were waiting outside.

"Irina Yelinova?"

Irina had hardly let him finish saying her last name. "Are you here about my grandfather?" she asked. "Have you found him? I just called the police to file a missing person's report."

The two uniforms looked at each other, their massive frames filling the doorway.

Oh, the poor thing! Here she's moved heaven and earth to find her grandfather before he does something rash—but she's too late.

"May we come inside?"

"Oh, I'm sorry, of course."

They both entered, and Irina showed them into the kitchen, and all three sat at the table covered with the tablecloth Viktor had embroidered.

"You have to file a missing person's report in person," one of the policemen said.

"Yes, they told me that on the phone. I wanted to go right away, but then I thought I should wait a little while longer and see if he turns up."

Nodding. Throat clearing. "I'm very sorry, Ms. Yelinova . . ."

Irina pressed her hand over her mouth.

"Your grandfather has taken his own life."

Irina's beautiful eyes filled with tears.

"He hanged himself in the park near the clinic where he worked."

Irina turned pale as chalk. "In the park . . . ?"

"Can we do anything for you?" one of the men asked. He didn't wait for an answer and instead stood up, stepped over to the sink, took a glass from the dish drainer, filled it with cold water, and placed it on the table in front of Irina. Irina drank mechanically.

"Did he leave a note . . . ?" she whispered tearfully.

Another one? But then I got what Irina meant. If Viktor had publicly admitted his guilt, then she would forever be the granddaughter of the criminal Viktor Kvasterov. To say nothing of the fact that the police would be coming to search through the apartment and inspect every mote of dust under a microscope to prove Irina's involvement. But if there were no suicide note, then the police might leave her in peace.

"No, nothing. I'm sorry."

There were another ten minutes of terse words and many tears, but then Irina straightened her shoulders, dried her eyes with a tissue, and warmly asked the men if they wouldn't mind leaving her alone now. The cops looked both relieved and concerned, but Irina convinced them she wouldn't do anything drastic. They expressed their condolences one more time at the door and then slunk down the stairwell.

Irina sat down at the kitchen table, absentmindedly running her fingers over the embroidery, and did nothing else for ten minutes. I whirled around her, wishing I could console her through my presence.

Suddenly she jolted out of her reverie as if someone had turned her ignition. She stayed seated, grabbed her cell out of her bag on the table, and dialed a number. Who was my angel calling in the hour of her greatest suffering? Who was going to console her? Curious and a little jealous, I got on the phone, literally, between the cell and my angel's ear.

The brash voice that answered the phone with his last name was totally the last name I had expected to hear: "Forch."

What did Irina want from him?

"Hello, Mr. Forch. It's Irina Yelinova."

He reciprocated the greeting.

"Have you heard that my grandfather committed suicide? . . . Yes, that's very kind . . . Mr. Forch, my grandfather left behind a note in which he confessed to some offenses connected with your institute . . . Yes, that's why I'm calling. I would like to speak with you in person about this, but I'd like to avoid having to go through all the commotion my presence at the institute would cause. Could I stop by later after the offices are empty?"

They agreed to meet, unofficially, at seven o'clock in his office, and she asked him if he would mind not mentioning the appointment to anyone so they could decide together at that point how to best deal with the information.

I was surprised. Had Viktor really made a full confession? And did the letter really mention something about Piggy Bank? I cursed Viktor for writing in Russian. His German was good enough that he could have done me that one last favor.

Irina put her cell phone away, went into the bathroom, and took a long shower. Well, everyone deals with their grief differently, so if she wanted to take a shower, why not? I always liked it when Irina took a shower. And this time she spent twice as long under the hot water as usual. She carefully lathered herself from her head to her cute little toes, and she washed her magnificent hair. Then she rubbed lotion into her wonderfully light, smooth, silky, shimmery skin and got dressed. Black-lace panties, a black dress, and black sandals. Black, the color of mourning, looked incredibly good on her. She was hotter than ever.

Irina set her bag on the kitchen table, took out a boxy half-liter glass bottle with a red screw cap that looked like it came from a lab, with a label on it that I couldn't read, filled it with some water, screwed the cap back on, and set it back into her bag. Then she looked around in her bag to make sure she had a vial, the kind with the little dropper in the lid, like you might get with nose drops, and she tucked a regular bottle of vodka in, as well.

I tried to see the rhyme and reason for all the barkeep equipment, but I couldn't think of anything. Nose drops, OK. Maybe even eyedrops, in case of excessive crying? I presumed that all women schlepped around such remedies within the infinite confines of their bags. A bottle of water—fine. Although I'm pretty sure recyclable plastic bottles are more common than glass laboratory bottles, but if Irina wanted to spare the environment from some plastic waste, then we could only give her high praise. But vodka? Did she maybe want to get shamelessly blitzed after her visit to Piggy Bank? Or worse yet: first get blitzed and then go cry it all out on his shoulder? Well, I would pay close attention to her so that she didn't do anything to herself in this time of excruciating pain.

Irina walked, taking majestic strides through the city, her sad eyes hidden from the world and me behind her sunglasses. Her mouth was not as relaxed as usual; one might almost have thought she had a scornful smile on her lips, but I knew that the only thing distorting her otherwise sensual lips was the grief she was suppressing with great effort. The summer breeze played with her hair and with the hem of her lightweight dress, and not a few men turned their heads and whistled as she passed by. She didn't notice any of this; she had receded into her own world and kept walking on, and on, and on. She had estimated the time she'd need well, because it was almost seven when she reached the temporary offices of the Institute for Forensic Medicine.

For the life of me, I still couldn't figure out what she was planning on doing there. If Viktor's suicide note had named Piggy Bank as a co-conspirator, Irina surely knew that he was dangerous. I mean, Piggy Bank would let the conspiracy come out only over his dead body—so she was risking her life with this visit.

The locked door at the main entrance didn't stop Irina. She fumbled out her cell phone, pressed redial, and asked to be let in.

Piggy Bank tasseled downstairs himself and opened the door for her. Forch was a sleazy guy anyway when it came to women, but now he was almost slobbering on his diagonally striped tie. Disgusting, given the grief Irina was in, which he in turn was responsible for. Because who else had driven Viktor to kill himself?

I accompanied them into Piggy Bank's office. Forch offered Irina a seat, she sat down, fumbled around in her bag—and presented him with the bottle of vodka.

"This is how we say good-bye in Russia," she said in a husky voice. She had to suppress her tears, but the effect was just as devastatingly sexy.

Piggy Bank was taken a back for a second, but then took two glasses out of the cabinet in his secretary's office where she kept dishes for visitors, and set them on the desk in front of Irina.

"Do you have any peanuts around, by any chance?" she asked. "Vodka can upset an empty stomach."

Forch was surprised again, but he didn't refuse her request and went back out into his secretary's office.

Meanwhile, Irina poured the water from her laboratory bottle into a glass, set it back on the table in front of her, and hid the bottle back in her bag. Then she took the nose-drop vial out of her bag and squeezed about ten drops into Forch's glass, which she then filled the rest of the way with vodka. She was just setting it down on his side of the desk when he returned with a package of cashews.

Now I was just not following at all. Did she want to get Forch plastered while she kept a clear head? What for? Did she want to get the whole, hideous truth out of him about all of the crimes that had been going on around here as he let things get more and more out of control?

But this was ridiculous. Irina wasn't KGB or something. This wasn't a James Bond movie, where the hottest women have the coolest tricks up their sleeves. This was Cologne, Germany. The Institute for Forensic Medicine, temporary shelter for homeless body scavengers. And my Irina wasn't a Russian agent, just a grieving granddaughter.

"*Za zdorovye*," Irina said, emptying her glass in one gulp.

"Uh . . ." Forch stammered.

"To Viktor," Irina said. "It's only one drink, Mr. Forch. Don't worry, tradition doesn't require you to get drunk."

Piggy Bank nodded unhappily, attempted but failed to smile, and knocked his vodka back. He coughed.

"What can I do for you?" he asked, making a visible effort to steer the conversation back to the sweeter-smelling waters of Cologne.

"Explain what accusations are being made against my grandfather," Irina said, her voice shaking.

Forch cleared his throat. "Well, I'm not sure if there's any sense in that now . . ."

"It has something to do with your institute, doesn't it?"

Forch hesitated. How much did he actually know about the investigation so far? All he knew from Martin were keywords like "anesthetic" and "depression." But how much had he learned about the investigation from the police? From his expression, Forch looked like he was contemplating the same questions.

"Bodies from the institute have disappeared, although they have since arrested one suspect, but he denies several of the allegations." Forch seemed to be slurring his words already.

"Which ones?" Irina asked.

"He confesses to desecrating one body, but not to stealing . . ." Forch nervously wiped a hand across his glistening forehead.

"What did my grandfather have to with that?" Irina's voice was now razor sharp and military cold. She took off her sunglasses. The look on her face was anything other than teary-eyed; in fact, it sent a virtual shiver down my now-defunct spine.

"Your grandfather had access to the institute, and today I heard that he used to be a butcher."

"Have you heard anything else? What did the detectives investigating the case say?"

"I don't feel so good," Forch said, then moaned involuntarily. "You know, when I was a young man I had an infection . . ."

"Yes, Q fever. I know. It permanently damaged your liver, which is why you never drink alcohol."

I was just as gobsmacked as Forch.

"How did you . . ."

"Tell me what the police know."

"I should probably . . ." He grabbed for a bottle of French mineral water that was on his desk, but he missed it by a long shot.

"Drinking water won't counteract what was in your glass," Irina said with a sweet smile. Then she pulled out the bottle with the red screw cap from her bag and put it on the table, with the label facing her. It featured various hazard warnings: a skull and crossbones, a flame, and over that the word "methanol."

Piggy Bank was now in a state of full-on intoxication. He was having trouble focusing, alternating his gaze between the various bottles and Irina, and he was holding his head with both hands. I knew the feeling: like your skull is about to burst open unless you hold it together with your hands. And though I had been in that situation many times, I had never done it sitting across from a woman who was pretty as a picture but who had just turned out to be evil incarnate. Apparently Russian granddaughters do not take it lightly when their gramps are driven first to commit crimes and then suicide.

"What do the police know?" Irina asked again.

Piggy Bank tried to reach for the telephone. Irina unplugged the phone cord in a lightning flash.

"Whad wass in my glass?" Piggy Bank slurred.

"I'll tell you as soon as you've answered my question."

"There're two muuurer victims whose bodies just disappeared."

"And?"

Forch shrugged.

"Has anyone mentioned the term 'organ donation'? Or 'organ theft'?"

Forch shook his head. "Izzad what Viktor did?"

"Viktor?" Irina let out a contemptuous laugh. "Viktor hasn't done anything since he left Russia and settled into that wretched rat hole because he wanted to save his dear, sweet granddaughter from the mafia."

"Mafia?" Forch mouthed.

"Yes, my father is an important man in Russia. And fortunately he has not abandoned me."

Forch wasn't following. Slowly but surely, however, more and more light bulbs were switching on in my seriously confused brain. I recalled Irina's nightly phone calls. Not with a lover as I'd feared—but with her daddy, who was a bigwig in the Russian mob. I felt Siberia-cold.

"Bud your graaafather can tell . . ."

"My grandfather couldn't hurt a fly," Irina said scornfully. "Not even a dead fly."

"And the stolen eyes . . . ?"

"Someone got overzealous," Irina said. "That mistake won't be repeated."

Forch wasn't understanding anything anymore. By contrast, I felt like I was learning something new with each syllable. Things I didn't want to know.

"If Vigdor didn't have aaathing to do with . . ." Forch stammered, all bumfuzzled, "why'd he kill himself?"

"You don't understand," Irina said. "But Viktor's suicide *was* serendipitous. It gave me the idea that you could follow suit . . ."

Forch's eyes opened wide in horror as he defensively raised his trembling hands.

". . . and this way they will hold you both responsible. Very convenient, too, because you connect the Institute for Forensic Medicine with the Clinic on the Park."

"Clinic on the Park . . . ?"

"Your upper-eyelid tightening and your rhinoplasty were a marvelous success." Irina pursed her lips in a mocking smirk. "But as far as the, uh, penis enhancement goes, I have no comment."

Irina sat back, relaxed, and looked at Forch, who had since closed his eyes and rested his head in his hands.

"Whawanmyglaaa?" he asked. I interpreted this as, "What was in my glass?"

Irina put the glass she had drunk from into her bag and stood. "Methanol, or wood alcohol, with a little vincamine. You may not be familiar with that since you're not a doctor. It's an indole alkaloid derived from periwinkle; Germany has banned it in medicinal preparations since 1987. But it remains quite popular in Russia because it's very effective against high blood pressure. It accelerates and enhances the effects of alcohol."

"Woohdaohoe?" Forch sounded dismayed, at least within the bounds of his now very limited options for self-expression.

"Ah, naturally you'd be familiar with that. Then surely you also know that the liver breaks wood alcohol down into formic acid. Especially bad when one already has liver damage. I presume you are then also aware that the only antidote is ethanol, or grain alcohol. Here's a whole bottle of vodka. *Za zdorovye.*" She turned around, put on her sunglasses, and left the office.

I felt flash-frozen for a moment, but one thing was crystal clear: I had to do something fast. But what? Irina had served Forch only from the vodka bottle but claimed he'd had wood alcohol in his glass. And now a whole bottle of vodka sat on his desk; naturally, Forch grabbed for it with trembling fingers and poured himself a glassful. A not inconsiderable quantity ended up on the desk.

I pulled myself together. Whether it was wood alcohol or vodka actually didn't matter: he needed help. Why the hell didn't he plug the phone cord back in? Why didn't he use his cell to dial one-one-two? Was he really so completely out of it that he couldn't think independently anymore? I roared at him to finally call someone so I could stay in pursuit of Irina, but it was no use.

I had to go to Martin as quickly as possible and have him and all auxiliary units I knew sent to Piggy Bank's aid.

Or maybe Martin would be happier if Piggy Bank went belly up? Hmm, that issue was worth some consideration. Piggy Bank had fired him and had pretty much shot to hell the lives and jobs of the colleagues left behind. But no, Martin is one of those people who would save the life of even his greatest enemy—so I had to get a move on. I rocketed at maximum possible speed to Martin's apartment. Empty. God, the minute you need him . . . then it occurred to me that Gregor had asked him to attend an all-hands meeting. Maybe I'd find Martin there? So I Mach-3'ed it to HQ. Gregor's office was the sixth window from the left, if I wasn't mistaken. I flashed right through the window— empty. No frigging way.

I zoomed down the hallway and tried the next office on the left—empty—then the next office on the right.

"Finally!" I roared at full volume.

The only one who winced was Martin. He was sitting between Katrin and Jenny in front of the desk, with Gregor behind it.

"Martin, Forch is in his office dying. You've got save him. Now!"

Martin leaped up as though stung by a scorpion. "Forch?" He called the name out loud in the room.

Jenny, Katrin, and Gregor stared at him.

In staccato I explained the situation to him: "He was poisoned. By Irina. But she's already gone. Put out an APB on Irina, but first get the paramedics to Forch. *¡Ándale, ándale!*"

Martin was holding his head the same way that Forch was, half a galaxy away from here. Then he looked up and into the faces of the others.

"Gregor, dispatch paramedics and the fire department to the institute's temporary offices right away. The director of the institute, Philip Forch, is in his office, uh, dying."

"Dying?" Gregor asked back.

"Yes, indeed." Martin insisted urgently. "He's dying, damn it!"

Gregor and Katrin exchanged quick glances. Jenny stared at Martin, stunned, then her face flitted to Gregor and Katrin—who both looked away as if by command—and back to Martin.

"Is that a message from . . ." Katrin said in a trembling voice.

Gregor glared at her. "But we weren't going to . . ."

Jenny's forehead now looked like the crumple zone of a midsize sedan after a crash test. "Can someone please tell me what . . ."

"No time to get into details; you have to save Forch now!" Martin bellowed with a vocal power I never thought he possessed. I was literally blown away by the sound.

Gregor finally snapped out of it and grabbed his phone, passed on the various instructions, and was about to hang back up when I added, "And Irina!"

Martin reacted promptly: "And Irina!"

Gregor paused, receiver in hand; he rolled his eyes and said, "Wait, one more thing." Then he put his hand over the phone and looked questioningly at Martin.

I fed Martin the line: "APB on Irina Yelinova for the attempted murder of Philip Forch."

Martin interpreted. Then, mentally, he asked me, "Is that everything? What's with the Clinic on the Park?"

I didn't want to say "No clue," so instead I said, "Later."

Gregor ordered the APB, then turned to Martin. "Can we get the long version now?"

"Right now you've got to get to Forch," I told Martin. "I'll explain everything on the way."

Martin told Gregor they had to get moving, so Gregor, Jenny, Katrin, and Martin ran out of police HQ, climbed into Gregor's car, and raced through the city with lights and sirens on. While Gregor executed awesome powerslides around corners, I poured all the information I'd learned from Irina into Martin's brain.

"Forch has liver damage, and I'm worried that the bottle contains wood alcohol," I concluded. "However, Forch believes that he already drank wood alcohol and only the vodka can save him."

Martin shook his head in amazement.

"Irina also gave him some kind of herbal remedy for high blood pressure. A very strong one. Something with periwinkle."

By the time we reached Forch, the situation in his office was completely out of control. Forch was rampaging with such strength that the three firemen and paramedics present could hardly subdue him. One tried to stick him with a syringe, but Forch kept flailing and wouldn't let the needle anywhere near him. He was fending them off with only one arm, however, because the other was busy pressing the bottle of vodka tight to his lips. A second guy was wrestling for the vodka bottle, but Forch clung to it as though his life depended on it. Which he undoubtedly believed. The bottle was half-empty.

Martin stood stiff as a board in the doorway, helplessly observing the chaos in the room. Katrin, Jenny, and Gregor plunged right into the hustle and bustle.

In the end, it took five men to finally tackle Forch.

"God, I've seen my share of boozers in my day, but never one like this," one of the firemen panted.

Martin explained to the EMTs what had happened here, including the chemical derived from periwinkle.

"All right then, let's pump his stomach and administer sodium bicarbonate," panted one of the EMTs, who was perched on Forch's chest.

"If he's on a strong antihypertensive, then we'd do better to skip the sedative," another EMT explained.

With the energetic help of all involved, Forch was strapped onto a stretcher and taken out of the office. Gregor, Jenny, and Katrin stayed behind and straightened their clothes, as did Martin and I.

Gregor was the first to be able to formulate coherent thoughts again. "All right, well, let's get CSI down here."

An uncomfortable silence prevailed as the four of them waited in the hallway for their colleagues to arrive. Martin leaned against the wall like a half-full laundry bag and stared at his feet while Gregor and Katrin made every effort to avoid looking at each other or at Martin. Only Jenny kept looking from one to the other; her face slowly evolved from incomprehension to anger.

"We should agree on an official version," Gregor said after a while.

Jenny gasped. "I'm sorry, a *what?*"

The others ignored her.

"I stopped by because I'd forgotten something in my office, and I found Forch," Martin said.

"You were sitting with Katrin, Jenny, and me in my office, buddy," Gregor said.

"I didn't see him," Katrin quickly said without raising her head.

Gregor shrugged. "Me neither."

Jenny gasped again and folded her arms in front of her chest.

"And you?" Katrin asked her. "Did you see Martin?"

"He was with us at HQ," Jenny said, adamant.

Gregor shook his head in disappointment, and Katrin avoided Jenny's gaze.

"But he left our meeting early because he wanted to stop by here and pick something up, right?" Katrin asked.

Jenny groaned and looked at Gregor, who nodded to her. She nodded hesitantly.

"OK, so that was it," Gregor said, relieved. Then he turned to Martin. "You saw Irina coming out of the building with your own eyes?"

Martin nodded.

"Did she see you?"

"No."

"What was she wearing?"

I helped Martin with the description, omitting the black-lace panties. Duh, he couldn't have seen those.

"And what happened next?"

"I went into my office, I heard strange sounds from Forch's office, and went to check on him. He stammered something about poison and Irina, and I tried to take the bottle away from him, but he became aggressive. So I called the paramedics."

"Why didn't you open the door for the paramedics, and why weren't you here when they arrived?"

"I tried to pursue Irina, and I returned here only as you three were arriving."

"But you've been terminated and you don't have an access card for this building anymore," Gregor objected.

Wow. He was totally on the ball, even in the middle of a lie.

Martin looked at Katrin for help.

"I loaned him my card so he didn't have to stop by during office hours and risk running into Forch," Katrin said.

"And what was it that you'd forgotten?"

Martin pondered a moment. "My coat hangers."

Katrin snorted, Gregor made a wide grin; Jenny was the only one who still seemed upset, now looking back and forth uncomprehendingly from one to the other. Martin was the only person at the Institute for Forensic Medicine who brought his own coat hangers in to work from home to hang his jackets and lab coats on. Still snickering, Katrin ran to her office and returned with two wooden coat hangers. "In actual fact, you did forget these."

"That's what I said."

Gregor spent a moment thinking very hard, which left a really stupid look on his mug. "Now tell me the whole thing one more time," he finally ordered Martin.

Jenny stared at Martin with curiosity.

Martin looked unhappy. "I still haven't quite understood everything completely, myself . . ."

"Sometime in the next two hours I'm going to need a damned good explanation, because I just ordered a manhunt for reasons that remain a complete mystery to me."

Jenny wanted to say something, but Gregor silenced her with a small gesture. She made a face.

Katrin anxiously glanced back and forth between Gregor and Martin.

Martin put the question to me: "So let's hear the explanation . . ."

Ugh, now things were getting dicey. "I'm not entirely one hundred percent . . ."

"Pascha!" Martin said. "We trusted you. Don't mess it up now."

Uh-oh, now he was trying to grab my honor by the balls! Well if that wasn't a cheap psych-out . . .

"Pascha!"

"OK, I'll go slowly. Viktor's suicide really was a suicide."

Martin played megaphone, repeating what I knew.

"Irina wanted Forch's death to look like a suicide, too."

"Why?"

"She's behind everything. She and her father back in Russia, if I understood correctly. I think it's all about illegal organ trafficking. And the Clinic on the Park is involved in it."

Martin nodded. That matched what he had been thinking.

"Where do the organs come from?"

Well, at this point my knowledge had a bunch of holes. A thought flashed quickly through my brain but disappeared before it could really take. I felt like I must know where Irina got the organ donors, but I couldn't quite put my finger—which I no longer possessed anyway—on it.

We waited a few more minutes for the CSI team, and then Gregor gave them his instructions before he drove back to police HQ. On the way, Gregor dispatched two of his colleagues to bring in Dr. Jens Hagenbeck, the director of the Clinic on the Park, for questioning. *Immediately.*

Gregor had already been flagged down by his boss in the hallway. "What were you thinking when you had Dr. Hagenbeck summoned over here?"

Gregor put on his "No idea, except I'm a badass" face. "I'll get you the written justification in two hours. Right now I just have to speak with the gentleman first."

"I want a full report with justification in *one* hour. And the judge who plays golf with Dr. Hagenbeck will also be waiting for this report."

Gregor nodded noncommittally and quickly pushed Martin into his office.

"All right, Mr. Martipants. The two of us have got a problem."

Martin nodded unhappily.

"This is not some movie where a rogue cop can hold a suspect, torture him a bit, and squeeze a confession out of him with impunity. I need . . ."

"That actor!" I interjected.

Martin rubbed his temples.

"Now what?" Gregor asked.

"Please call Birgit," Martin suddenly suggested without my prompting.

"Birgit?"

Martin nodded. "I asked her some time ago to get hold of any current information on the Clinic on the Park. Meaning funding, credit history, sales, profits, things like that. We haven't talked about it again since."

Gregor nodded. "What else?"

I had the answer to that.

"You and I need to go visit someone's sickbed," I told Martin. "*¡Ándale, ándale!*"

———•———

Martin simply strolled right into the Clinic on the Park. No biggie, since he was wearing the white lab coat that he had previously left at the reweaving shop because this tiny hole in the left sleeve did not meet his requirement that his lab coat be in perfect condition. He had picked it up the morning he got fired, and it had never made it out of his car—which came in very handy right now.

I directed Martin to the intensive care unit and to the room where I thought that Latino guy I'd seen was lying exhausted in his bed. And he was still there.

"Who is that?" Martin quietly asked me.

"The first time I saw him was at a doctor's office where Irina works. She told him he had a sick kidney and needed to have surgery to remove it."

Martin turned pale.

"And now he's probably down a kidney, and some fat Russian with a fat wallet is up one."

The young man opened his eyes. "*¿Cuánto tiempo más me tengo que quedar aquí?*"

"What's he saying?" Martin asked me.

"Did I take Latin in school, or did you?"

Martin made a disparaging motion, patted the man's arm, and said, "I'll have you moved to another hospital right away." He gave the man a warm smile and then left the clinic in long strides.

THIRTEEN

After Martin updated Gregor on our suspicions, Gregor had his now-prime, though unfortunately Spanish-speaking, witness moved to University Medical Center, whereupon Gregor received the arrest warrant he'd wanted from no other than Hagenbeck's golf partner—whose loyalty lay closer to the rule of law than to his sports buddy.

I decided to take in the questioning of Dr. Strangelove.

Gregor (quiet): "You have been accused of performing illegal organ transplants."

Hagenbeck (indignant): "This is utter nonsense!"

Gregor (harsh): "Have you performed transplants from living donors?"

Hagenbeck (amused): "Certainly, a great deal."

Gregor (even harsher): "Where did these organs come from?"

Hagenbeck (mocking): "From relatives."

Gregor (incredulous): "From relatives?"

Hagenbeck (arrogant): "Of course. Anything else is prohibited in Germany."

It kept going like this. Hagenbeck confessed everything that was legal and denied ever having done anything illegal or even having had knowledge of it.

"How did you come by your patients?"

"My clinic enjoys an excellent reputation. My patients come to me."

"Isn't it true that your Russian business partner in the mafia sends patients to you?"

"I'm not collaborating with the mafia. A perfectly legal Russian investment company has invested money in my clinic because its fund managers apparently recognized that medicine is a growth market."

"How do you find matching donors? Do you run tests on the whole extended family?"

"No, the tests have usually already been completed by the time patients contact me. Patients call me with the name of the family member who is prepared to make the donation, and they send me all of the medical documentation as well as the donor's signed informed-consent forms. Donors and recipients come into the clinic at the appointed time, a couple of final tests are run, and then the transplant can be performed."

Hagenbeck explained that they provided the best possible medical care to donors for the duration of their stay at the clinic, but the outpatient follow-up care for which Hagenbeck wrote referrals was left to the donors' individual family doctors.

"Have you ever been in contact either by phone or in person with any of these family doctors?"

"No, never."

"Didn't that ever strike you as odd?"

"No."

Of course I couldn't read Gregor's thoughts, but his face spoke volumes. He was watching his airtight case go down the tubes because he couldn't prove Hagenbeck had done anything illegal. And maybe that was the truth, too. Maybe Hagenbeck was just too stupid and had believed everything

Irina had put over on him. The strange "relatives" from distant continents, the fake informed-consent forms from the donors. All of Gregor's hopes were now resting on the Latino guy, but his testimony wouldn't be enough to convict Hagenbeck, only Irina. She was the one who told him his kidney was diseased, and she was the one who presumably had him sign the informed-consent form that she then passed on to Hagenbeck.

"What about a man by the name of Yan Yu?"

"Yan Yu? Hmm . . . was he the one with the lovely dragon tattoo? I remember. That was the young man who backed out at the last minute. He never showed up for his appointment."

"Did he call and cancel?"

"No, he just never showed up."

"What was his relationship to the recipient of the organ?"

"He was his nephew, I believe. But all of that is in the documentation."

Gregor frantically scribbled something in his notepad. I zoomed over and read, "Find body!"

I've always said: that Gregor is a clever one.

Gregor was undoubtedly calculating how he might solidify his case despite a recalcitrant lead physician and a worrying lack of evidence; Katrin was drowning in work without her boss, Martin, or Jochen around; and Birgit was doing overtime at the bank. Martin was the only one who didn't have anything to do. He was sitting forlorn on his sofa, cataloging street names from old city maps.

Should I . . .

No. I pulled myself together. First, I'd already broken my oath to leave him in peace, and second, I hadn't closed this case yet.

So I headed back downtown. This was supposed to be the last hot day, the weathermen had promised, and the streets were clogged with knots of people. I mingled among the boisterous Rhinelanders, enjoying the views of bare midriffs, crop tops, miniskirts, and glistening skin. People were eating ice cream, drinking cold beer, flirting, and even dancing. For one moment, I thought life was wonderful.

But that wasn't true.

Life was shit.

I'd lost the great love of my life: Irina. She was no innocent angel, just a hardened criminal. I hated her for leading me on. For betraying her fat little grandfather and driving him to suicide. For disappearing and laughing into her sleeve along with her criminal father and moving on to some other place and running this same con again. More people would go to a doctor who they were going to think wanted to help them, while Irina sat in the background spinning her web and waiting to find a suitable victim whose kidney she could steal. And that victim would be a lucky one, because at least he could keep on living with only one kidney—as long as some kind of post-op depression didn't drive him to throw himself in front of a train. But if the donor backed out last minute or if Irina's client needed a liver or a heart, then the victim would just vanish into thin air.

I had to find Irina. It wasn't just a question of justice; for me, it was a question of honor.

I already had an idea where to start my search.

My memory may be hole-ridden when it comes to the important things in life, but when it comes to cars, it works like a well-oiled V12. The last time Viktor and Irina saw each other alive, Viktor was at the kitchen table when Irina told him she needed to leave. Then she went to the bus stop, I briefly looked in on Viktor, and when I came back to the bus stop, Irina was gone. However, I'd caught a glimpse of a Hummer driving away. A car perfectly suited to the Russian mafia: huge body, massive weight, almost half a meter of ground clearance, powerful engine. Pure phallic swank as expressed in metal and motor oil. Fortunately, my expert's eye had committed the details to memory: nonstandard tailpipe, stubby roof-mount antenna, and AF Signature 3 chrome wheel rims, each of which runs a couple grand. That was my lead.

I zoomed through the city for almost an hour until I finally found what I needed. A guy with the right cell phone and a wireless headset that he'd attached, like a pompous asshole, to his left ear. The guy was sitting at a street café leaning back casually, his eyes hidden behind some ridiculously large sunglasses. He had an empty cup in front of him that was so small it must have been used as a thimble in a previous century. Next to the cup were the cell phone, his car keys (BMW—I'd have won that bet!), and a bulging wallet. I had to wait for twenty minutes for someone to finally call the gel head.

I wasted no time, immediately butting in after his overly nonchalant hello:

"This is the Criminal Investigations unit of the Cologne police. Please end this conversation and allow us remote use of your cellular device for an important police communication."

There it was again, my voice: a little rusty but clear and direct as ever.

The guy's jaw dropped.

"Bertold Bear?" a no-longer-very-fresh woman's voice called out from the headset. "Did you hear that too?"

"Yes, Mama," Bertold grunted. He looked around suspiciously, probably for one of his smirking buddies or the team with the camera.

"Please end your conversation but do not hang up your cell phone," I said sternly. "This is a matter of national security."

"Bertold!" the mother shrieked. "What kind of trouble are you in?"

"Mama, please hang up. You heard them. The police need me now."

"But—"

"*Now*, Mama. I'll call you back in a little bit."

Mama hung up.

Now it was all or nothing. "Please dial zero-two-two-one..." I rattled off the number I would still know by heart even in ten thousand years. The second most important car fencer in Cologne. My fence, who I'd stolen dozens of cars for.

Bertold dialed.

"Yes?"

It was him. Wow, the number was still in service, and it was clearly Felge's voice.

"Listen, you have to find a Hummer for me." I gave him all the details.

"Who is this?" Felge asked after nearly thirty seconds' silence. "You sound like . . ."

"Pascha?"

"Yeah, man. But he's dead."

"You sure?" I asked. "Did you see the body?"

I could literally hear Felge thinking. Like rocks being crushed into sand, because he always grinds his teeth while he thinks.

I didn't have the time to spare. "Dude. Do it now! Find that Hummer and then send an e-mail to kreidler@kripo-koeln.de."

"Did you switch sides, man?"

He had no idea how right he was! But I didn't tell him that, of course. "Actually, I'm doing you a huge favor," I said. "The guy who drives that ride is the guy who fucked up your business."

I had to grin. Felge means "wheel rim" in German; he swapped out the first letter of his real name, Helge, so people would stop asking him if he'd changed his kitty litter today. I mean, let's face it: even if you don't speak German, you'd ask a guy named "Helge" the same thing, right? But Felge is a pretty straitlaced car fencer, and whenever something goes wrong he always starts talking about some big conspiracy theory. He took the bait without further questions.

"Right on, man. Are we going to see you again sometime?"

"I'll stop by soon," I promised—and I'd keep my word, too.

"Thank you, Bertold," I said after Felge hung up. "I would be greatly indebted to you if you could refrain from mentioning this to anyone. This technology hasn't really been tested yet, you know?"

"Uh, yeah, sure."

"You can now resume normal use of your phone."

"Thanks," he stammered, turned his phone off, and looked around again. Still no smirking buddies, still no hidden camera. Just regular people on a regular summer's day in a regular German city. I almost felt sorry for the guy.

Now the only thing I could do was what I hated most of all in the world: wait. I felt like sugarcoating my wait with some love, reconciliation, and happiness, and I hoped Martin and Birgit could help me with that. Assuming I could find those two, but I already had an idea where to look.

———•———

Martin and Birgit were in fact sitting in front of their favorite gelato café. How original. But while I was still flying closer, Martin suddenly slid off his chair and knelt on the ground in front of Birgit. He took her hand. "The past few weeks I've behaved like a complete idiot. But I would really very, very much like to live with you. I would like to fall asleep each night and awaken each morning beside you. We'll be able to sit on the couch at night, enjoying each other as we read or watch television or play a game."

Birgit beamed at him. I will never understand what attracts a young, vivacious, pretty, funny, and frigging sexy woman to perch on a couch next to Martin and read. Or play games. Because by "play games" he did not mean what I would mean if I said "play games," that was clear.

"I'm going to call every agent in the city and find a nice apartment for us. I'm going to . . ."

Birgit put her finger on his lips. "I've already found the nicest apartment in the city for us."

Martin stared at her, wide-eyed.

"Did you really think I'd give up on you just like that?" Birgit said. "Now, we have to let the agent know our decision by the day after tomorrow. You had until tomorrow morning before I was going to hold a gun to your head."

Only Birgit's athletic reflexes saved her from being pulled to the ground, chair and all, by Martin's clumsy hug.

———•———

I was in Gregor's office early the next morning. He came in around eight and looked like he'd slept like crap, and above all he looked very frustrated. He turned on his computer and sorted papers on his desk while the computer booted up. I waited, curious to see if he'd gotten any e-mail.

He had.

"Anything new?" Jenny asked when she appeared in his doorway with two cups of coffee. After a downpour overnight, the temperature had finally fallen enough that coffee was apparently appealing again.

"N—" Gregor stared at his screen.

I zoomed behind him to read his e-mail, as well.

SUBJECT: HUMMER H2

TEXT: Maastrichter Straße. Two men, one woman. Registered to Medex Corporation, same address. Wipe that bastard out!

Jenny was now behind Gregor's desk, staring at the screen as well.

"What Hummer?" she asked.

"No idea," Gregor mumbled. "I think we should go see what we know about Medex."

He closed the e-mail and opened his browser and went to a German government website to search company registrations for a Medex Corporation. The registration listed the same address as in the e-mail, and the owner of the company was a Russian investment company. *Managing director: Irina Yelinova.*

Gregor turned pale.

"Who the hell sent this e-mail?" Jenny whispered behind him.

"I really don't care," Gregor whispered back. Then he cleared his throat. "OK, we're going to need SWAT. I want action within the next two hours."

Jenny had no experience with special police force deployments, so she only assisted Gregor in his preparations. But even she got flushed cheeks from the excitement and commotion that broke out at HQ.

I zoomed to Medex and checked the situation. The Hummer was parked in the back. The ground floor of the building had an office where Irina was working at a computer. There were cardboard moving boxes everywhere that the two stocky guys from the Russian expat club were filling. Each of them had a gun tucked into the back of his waistband. One of them was quite tall, left-handed, and had a long, fresh diagonal scar over his face and left eye. Was he the overzealous eyeball pincher?

Again I was in a tough spot. The cops were about to show up with a SWAT team, but would they really be prepared for armed resistance? I had to warn Gregor. But to do that, I needed Martin. My oath to leave him in peace kept slamming into fate. In the end my loyalty toward Gregor and his colleagues won out. I had to warn them.

After one more fly-through, where I discovered a well-stocked arms cache in the basement, in addition to the two waistband pistols, I made a beeline to Martin.

"You've got to warn Gregor," I cried.

Martin started, terrified. He'd been sitting on the floor of his apartment studying city maps.

"A SWAT team and Gregor are about to storm the building where Irina is holed up with two Russians. They've got a whole arms cache and arsenal in the basement. Please tell Gregor that."

Without hesitation Martin grabbed the phone and passed on the warning to Gregor. Before he could curse me to eternity, I cleared out again.

The SWAT operation was hard-nosed and successful. They stormed the main entrance, the back door, and the basement door at the same time, seized the arms cache, and had the bad boys and Irina in checkmate within fifty-seven seconds. The only shot fired was by—Irina. It went astray, and now she lay on the floor, her face full of hate as the two cops sitting on her cuffed her hands and ankles and pulled her back up onto her feet.

"Get a move on, girl," the one cop barked at Irina.

She spat squarely into his face.

My heavenly angel had metamorphosed into a sulfur-stinking succubus.

Disappointed and heartbroken, I withdrew and spent the day wandering around random places throughout the city. Despite the thick, low-hanging clouds, everyone in Cologne was reveling in one downpour after another.

I was the only person whose mood was being spoiled by the rain.

Out of sheer habit, and to take my final leave, I spent the late afternoon making my way to Martin's. Once again he was sitting alone on his couch, but he had this stupid-happy grin on his face as he browsed through the IKEA catalog.

"I broke my promise," I told him in the heroic tone I'd heard countless times in action movies. "It won't happen again. I'm taking my leave from now you, and then I'll be gone. Once and for all."

I was having trouble not bawling, but I was resolute in my decision. I was dead; there was just no pussyfooting around that. Of course, it was nice that I had been able to communicate with one living person, but I couldn't keep doing that if it was fucking up his life. This was the hardest decision of my entire life, and I wasn't sure how I was going to keep going. Or whether. Maybe I'd really try to find the light that Marlene had told me about. She'd told me I could come, too, when I was ready.

Sigh. I'm the tragic hero of this story, denied my own heroic ride into the sunset for the sake of others.

I had to give Martin and Birgit a chance. Even if it meant that I had to die again, this time once and for all.

"Farewell," I croaked, cruising for the door.

"Wait," Martin said.

I flashed back to the couch at a hundred times the speed of light.

"You saved Forch's life," Martin said.

"Hmm." I felt like a dog panting and wagging for praise from his master, only to slobber on his hand when it came.

"And you solved several crimes, thereby saving the lives of many more innocent people."

I tried to keep cool. I cleared my throat. "Anyone would have."

"And you found Irina, even though we still don't have any idea how you did that."

"True." I was not planning on burdening him with these details right now.

"And apart from all that, it would really be beyond cruel to kick you out."

"*Yes!*" Now I was bawling uncontrollably. Yes, it *would* be cruel. Inhuman, merciless, a living hell.

"But things cannot continue the way they've been."

"No?" I was panting again.

"The bathroom and bedroom are taboo for you."

"But if I need . . ."

"We will find a technological solution so that you can inform me in case of emergency."

"Technological solution" didn't sound that promising. I mean, everything that is technological and has a power-off button is subject to Martin's whims.

"True," Martin thought. "But that's how we're going to do it, or not at all."

"OK," I was quick to agree. "We'll do it your way." Pant, pant.

"Good." Martin's brain blinked on with the thought of Birgit and their shared apartment. "Do you prefer blue or red curtains? Oh, never mind."

FOURTEEN

ORGAN-THEFT RING HITS COLOGNE

CLINIC HEAD ARRESTED

IMPLICATED IN MULTIPLE MURDERS

Martin folded the newspaper neatly in half and set it back onto the shelf next to the four-seat dining table.

"You're getting so much praise, your boss could hardly do anything but promote you," Martin said to Gregor.

"I already said that," Katrin added with a wide smile. She took Gregor's hand into hers and pretended to tell his fortune, tracing his love line with her index finger and auguring in a terrible accent with a thunderously trilled *r*: "I see the worrrd 'rrraise,' an extended vacation, and of courrrse a sharrred aparrrtment."

Martin and Birgit laughed, and Birgit leaned over to give Martin a kiss on the cheek. Martin beamed at her so happily he was probably literally on the verge of bursting.

"Have they resolved all the outstanding issues now, and secured all the evidence?" he asked.

Gregor shook his head. "Mostly, yeah. It turns out Irina met Hagenbeck at UMC three years ago. At the time, he was still working in transplant surgery there. After an inheritance, he quit the university and opened the Clinic on the Park, but its success left something to be desired. The lesser starlets who wanted to have him blow up their busts couldn't pay him the prices he needed to be taking in, but he couldn't attract a better-heeled clientele, because he just didn't have enough of a name yet. Add the cost of various lawsuits and pricey insurance . . . you get the idea. So his bank started putting pressure on him."

"And then a Russian bought his debt," Birgit said.

"That must have been Irina's father," Gregor added. "Officially it was an investment company that put its funds into health- and medicine-related stocks."

"Did Irina and Hagenbeck work together from the get-go?" I asked. Martin repeated my words.

Gregor shook his head. "Hagenbeck gave a statement that he met Irina at University Medical Center. It was a normal, collegial interaction that ended when he left UMC. We suspect that Irina was tracking how things were going for him. She was likely the person who came up with the suggestion for her father of a business model using illegal organ transplants. The Clinic on the Park was in a lot of debt, and she was able to serve it up to daddy on a silver platter."

"But how did Irina find matching organ 'donors'?" Birgit asked.

"She worked one day a week at a medical clinic for migrants called Friends of Hippocrates."

"What's that?"

"It's a doctor's office where people without health insurance can be treated. Retired doctors or young idealists usually work there, free of charge to boot. Social service charities like Caritas Internationalis or the Order of Malta's Migrant Medicine service finance the work."

"And they found their organ 'donors' there?" Birgit asked.

Gregor nodded. "Irina was very popular at that practice, among other things because she'd brought in an anonymous sponsor who paid for the patients' lab workups."

"Of course," Martin mumbled.

Gregor nodded. "She had access to patient data, which is how she could identify matching donors for the needed organs. It's unbelievable how easy it was. And since these people were in Germany illegally—"

"Their families didn't go to the police when someone disappeared," Martin said, finishing Gregor's sentence with images of Yan Yu and the restaurant flashing in his mind.

They all sat in somber silence for a while.

"Did Yan Yu's body ever surface again?" Martin asked. "Or the body that was stolen from under Jochen's hands?"

"Bingo," Katrin said. "Gregor put out inquiries with the state and federal police as well as Interpol, and they passed the information on to the police in other countries. The bodies turned up downriver along the Dutch part of the Rhine. I had them on my table today. The autopsies confirmed Hagenbeck's statement about the tattooed man. He was slated to donate a kidney and probably got cold feet. But contrary to Hagenbeck's statement, he *was* at the Clinic on the Park. Based on these findings, I imagine it went like this: He was supposed to get undressed and lie down on the operating table, but then he panicked. He wanted to leave, but someone injected him with the anesthetic and restrained his hands and feet until it took effect. We found evidence of this on his wrists and ankles. So then the doctor flipped out, forgot the painkiller and muscle relaxant, slid the guy's pants down and his shirt up, disinfected the abdomen, and started with the scalpel. Since our friend still had the adrenaline in his blood from his first escape attempt, and plus he had a high tolerance level because of copious drug use, the incision made him come to again. He tore the IV out of his arm and the tube from his throat and fled."

"That means what we thought was a stab wound was actually . . ." Martin began.

"A surgical incision that started immediately beneath the rib cage and cut straight down," Katrin said. "If a coroner had seen the corpse the night he was found, we would have homed in on that immediately."

Gregor nodded grimly. "Sometimes everything just goes wrong."

"And the man who was stolen during Jochen's autopsy?"

"The lead physician at Migrant Medicine remembered him. The man had been into their office about a year ago. Achilles tendon rupture. Apparently, Irina took a blood sample from him as well. When she had a customer he was a match for, he had to be secured as a donor. Voluntarily or by force."

"You mean that raid was staged?" Birgit asked.

"No, not staged," Gregor said. "But the point of it was to get hold of the man and cut him up for spare parts, basically."

"But if he's dead, you can't reuse the organs anymore, right?"

Martin shook his head. "That is a common misconception because German law permits the removal of organs only when the donor is brain-dead but his or her heart is still beating. In fact, organs can still be used if properly preserved within an hour or so after cardiac death."

"Exactly," Katrin said. "In the case of this victim, there were clear signs of a struggle. It looks as though they hadn't intended to kill him right away, but then when he came to and started defending himself . . . that interrupted the attackers before they could load the body into their car, and so they had to steal it later on to hide the evidence of what they'd done."

"*My God,*" Birgit whispered.

"And then they stole everything from him that could be sold. Organs, tissues, bones, tendons . . . the corpse that was found in the Netherlands weighed only thirty-five kilograms. That's less than half what a grown man usually weighs."

"Who were the two strong men?" Martin asked.

"Those two were the ones we arrested at Medex," Gregor said. "They belong to Irina's father."

"Did Irina procure the scalpel for them from the institute?" Martin asked.

Katrin grinned. "Negative. Our sets are all accounted for. One of the gorillas had apparently discovered his love of medicine at some point and ordered a full set of that type of scalpels for himself."

"Will Hagenbeck be prosecuted now, or is he talking his way out of it by saying he knew nothing?" Martin asked.

"Hagenbeck made a full confession. He drugged the tattooee against his will, and the anesthesiologist confirmed as much, herself. Hagenbeck had bribed her to keep her from going to the police. Secondly, Hagenbeck was using transplant organs that did not originate from the official European organ donor foundation. And whenever he didn't need them he would sell any extra organs from the so-called donors to Medex himself. He knew exactly what he was doing and will be charged for each offense individually.

"And the stolen eyes?"

"The gorilla with medical aspirations actually stole those himself, for himself. He had learned enough about organ trafficking that he decided he wanted to start up his own little side business. He would stop by on weekend nights and hawk the eyes to an organ broker. He's in trouble with Irina's father, big-time, which is why he's singing like a songbird. He wouldn't live twenty-four hours if we shipped him back to Russia."

"That means that Medex didn't merely supply the clinic's patients with organs but also trafficked in organs?" Birgit gasped.

"Whenever a 'donor' died on the operating table or had to be killed to procure the desired organ, then the rest of the donor's body would be taken and sold off, yes."

"If the railroad body hadn't thrown himself in front of a train, we'd never have gotten a whiff of the crime," Martin said.

"And if Forch had casually complained to his old buddy Hagenbeck about his problems with security at the institute, then Hagenbeck would never have recommended the clinic's janitor to him."

"How did Viktor come by his job as a janitor at the Clinic on the Park, actually?" Martin asked.

Gregor smiled. "That was the only time after Hagenbeck left the university that he and Irina communicated with each other. She phoned him a year ago when the whole con started and asked him to give her grandfather a job. Presumably so that she'd have an insider at the clinic and access to his keys."

"And the second job at the Institute for Forensic Medicine . . ."

"Came as a shock to Irina. The connection between the institute and Viktor and the Clinic on the Park was a potential risk. Especially since she knew that Viktor suffered from dyscalculia, a learning disability involving math skills; she expected that to create some trouble for him when it came to keeping track of numbers and morgue drawers and the like."

"Poor Viktor," Birgit said.

"Yes," Gregor said. "I took the fact that something always happened whenever he had a night off as a sign he was guilty. Combined with his origins and economic situation, on paper he was an ideal offender. I suspected him with undue haste. I feel pretty—"

"Shitty," Martin said, completing his sentence.

This word out of his mouth surprised the other three into silence for a moment. Then they all broke out in a roar of laughter.

"You should probably clean up your language a little for tomorrow morning when you go in to see the boss," Katrin said, grinning.

"What?" Martin said, surprised. "Is Forch back already?"

"No," Katrin said with a wide smile. "Not him."

———•———

Dr. Schweitzer jumped up when Martin squeezed through the crack in his office door and shook the hand Martin extended to him for a solid thirty seconds. "I heard you saved Mr. Forch's life. That's wonderful!"

God, these well-bred academic types are so *weird*. Here were two men, both of which would have ample reason to take pleasure in the premature passing of Piggy Bank, and instead they were making a big fuss over the fact that the bastard was still alive.

"How is he doing?" Martin asked.

"Under the circumstances, well. He'll make a full recovery."

"That's good," Martin said, and he honestly meant it.

"He won't be returning, however," the boss added. "The experiment of appointing someone without a medical background to lead the institute is not considered to have been particularly successful."

Martin forced a smile and said nothing.

"Your disciplinary warning letters and termination have naturally been rescinded and expunged," the boss said. "I hope you can start again, immediately?"

Martin nodded. He had a goofy-ass grin on his face from ear to ear.

"Remember to take your clothes hangers back into the office," I teased, and then I cleared out.

With the case solved and Martin back in good graces, I'd earned myself a couple of days off. I zoomed over to the movies and checked out the new releases. I had some catching up to do.

EPILOGUE

"*Finally*," Martin whispered at me. "Come on."

He quietly opened the door to an auditorium in which about twenty chicks were sitting on wooden folding chairs listing to Katrin go on and on and on about the daily routine of working in the field of forensic medicine. Large-format, disgusting slides bluntly showed what Katrin had described in pretty words. Some of the chicks were suffering from considerable pallor in their faces.

"Pick one," Martin said.

Was poor Martin completely cracking up now?

Martin grinned secretly to himself. "I found a terrific solution for our, uh, little publishing problem."

Finally! I'd been bugging him ever since he'd gotten his job back and could use his computer again. The publisher wanted to make my story a bestseller. Martin was able to sign the contract, but we still needed to find a pseudonym. But Martin kept putting me off and off.

"All these women are crime fiction writers. One of them is going to stand in for you as the author of your book."

"Have you been huffing paint?" I asked. "Let's just pick a pseudonym, and then we're done. I was thinking 'Clint Westwood' . . . or 'Bruce Wilson.' Eh? For all I care we could go with 'DJ Pascha,' too. The main thing is: *cool*. What do these girls here have to do with anything?"

"I've been studying how the publishing industry works," Martin explained, still with unbraked enthusiasm. "If a book is to succeed, then the author has to publicize it. Give interviews, do readings, sign books, things like that. You can't do that yourself, obviously."

Hmm, he was right about that.

"And there's no way I can find the time to handle all that myself."

Would that even work? No, there was just no way that Martin, the über-awkward, megadweeby autops-aholic could ever pull that off. His bedside manner was fine for corpses, but he probably wasn't the best pick for a publicity tour.

"So it has to be someone totally new."

"I have no objection," I said. "But, God, not a *chick*."

"A woman is the only possible solution to our problem."

"There is no way a chick could have written all these hard-hitting facts from the perspective of a supercool *male* hero," I moaned.

"Don't be silly," Martin declared. "Besides, everyone will think the whole thing is just a novel this way."

I had to think about that for a moment. People are supposed to think that some *chick* had merely *invented* my heroic exploits? Nobody would know that I really exist? And if nobody gets that I really exist, then no one will switch their brainwaves to standby in the hopes that they can communicate with me when they drive by the Institute for Forensic Medicine.

"So, which one do you want?" Martin asked.

I studied the pen of hens.

"All the women whose faces are already pale from Katrin's visual aids are out," Martin explained.

Too bad. Because I was going to pick one with a promising—

"The bust size also cannot be a criterion for your decision."

Oh, yeah? Well what then? First he says I should pick one, and then he starts axing all the interesting candidates from the list.

"What about her over there?"

Martin discreetly pointed at a small person in the middle.

"The toilet brush?" I asked.

Martin sent me a question mark.

"No curves down below, a little bristly up on top," I explained. "Plus, not so fresh anymore, right?"

"But she has a sense of humor."

"So?"

Martin rolled his eyes. "It's an issue of believability. A writer who is on track for the Nobel Prize in literature will not want to take responsibility for *your* book in public."

"What do you mean by—"

"Nor do we need someone with an underlying agenda articulating social criticism through the stylistic means of the crime novel."

I was glad Martin saw it that way. An agenda and social criticism and all that psycho shit isn't really my thing, either. I didn't want anything to do with any of that. I considered Toilet Brush thoughtfully. *Great* is not how she looked. But I thought the way she smiled was pretty cool. She didn't seem like someone who'd be constantly bitching.

I conceded defeat. "Ask her," I said. "But *I* get final say on all the pseudonyms that are used in the actual book."

Martin nodded.

At that moment the auditorium surged with applause, Katrin thanked everyone for coming, flipped the overhead off and the light on.

Martin pushed through to Toilet Brush.

"Pardon me. I'm Dr. Gänsewein," Martin said, nodding toward Katrin. "I'm a colleague of Dr. Zange's at the institute. And you are?"

God, how embarrassing. Way to cut right to the chase, Martin.

"Hi," Toilet Brush said, shaking Martin's hand with a big smile. "Jutta Profijt."

ACKNOWLEDGMENTS

As always, my thanks must go to Dr. Frank Glenewinkel, who patiently answers each and every silly question I have about forensic medicine. Unfortunately, I just don't like many of the answers. I accept them—and then avail myself of the right to artistic freedom for my coroner Martin Gänsewein who, according to Dr. Glenewinkel, exhibits "Quincy syndrome": dazzling knowledge not only in his own field but also in toxicology, pharmacology, and comparative theology . . .

I have taken some other liberties, as well. For example, propofol is a completely routine drug used in anesthesia, which I have knowingly defamed in my book. Anesthesia is not as simple as I have portrayed it, nor are organ transplants. The Migrant Medicine program of the Order of Malta in Germany is a blessing and not a curse. And—based on my research—the security situation at the Institute for Forensic Medicine is impeccable.

Additional thanks are due to Michael Heydebreck at the Odysseum Science Adventure Park in Cologne, who explained the cloud chamber and other exciting science exhibits to me. In addition, I would like to make particular mention of the book *Die unglaublichsten Fälle der Rechtsmedizin* (*The Most Incredible Cases in Forensic Medicine*), vol. 1 (Leipzig: Militzke-Verlag, 2004), edited by Professor Markus A. Rothschild, MD, director of the Institute for

Forensic Medicine at the University Medical Center of the University of Cologne. In his chapter "Das Schweigen der Gräber" ("The Silence of the Graves"), Professor Rothschild depicts an unusual case of necrophilia that served as an inspiration for many of the events in my book.

And last but not least, my editor Karoline Adler has once again come along for the ride. She has mentored Pascha and me alike and, of course, is not the same as the fictional editor in this book.

Jutta Profijt

ABOUT THE AUTHOR

Inspired by her visit to a morgue in Cologne, Germany, Jutta Profijt has crafted a spellbinding tale that brings a new layer of depth to the paranormal genre. Nominated for the Friedrich Glauser Prize for best crime novel in 2010, Profijt continues to cast her spell on readers around the world.

ABOUT THE TRANSLATOR

 Erik J. Macki worked as a cherry-orchard tour guide, copy editor, web developer, and German and French teacher before settling into his translation career—probably an inevitable choice, as he has collected foreign-language grammars, dictionaries, and language-learning books since childhood and to this day is not above diagramming sentences when duty so calls. A former resident of Cologne and Münster, Germany, and of Tours, France, he did his graduate work in Germanics and comparative syntax. He now translates books for adults and children as well as nonfiction material from his home in Seattle, where he lives with his family and their black Lab, Zephyr.

Made in the USA
Charleston, SC
17 November 2012